Kissimmee
Ann O'Connel Rust

The Floridians Series Volume III

Amaro Books

Published by
Amaro Books
5673 Pine Avenue
Orange Park, Florida 32073

Copyright © 1990 Ann O'Connell Rust

All rights reserved. No part of this book may be reproduced in any form or by any electronic or mechanical means including information storage and retrieval systems without permission in writing from the publisher, except by a reviewer who may quote brief passages in a review.

First Printing 1990
ISBN No. 0-9620556-2-X (Volume 3)
ISBN No. 0-9620556-4-6 (7 Volume Set)
Library of Congress Catalog Card No. 90-82837
Printed in U.S.A. by Dolphin Press
Cover Artist: Linda Taheri

Books by Ann O'Connell Rust:
Punta Rassa
Palatka
Kissimmee

ACKNOWLEDGMENTS

The author wishes to thank Allen F. Rust, Editor/Copy Editor, and Jim Brown and staff of Empulse, Gt. Barrington, Mass. And a special thanks to the growing number of fans of THE FLORIDIANS.

AUTHOR'S NOTE

The setting of this story is Florida, 1879-1889. The history is as accurate as is needed for the story line, and all the characters are fictional.

FOR MY "BIG SISTER"
MARY BARBARA O'CONNELL SGANGA

CONTENTS

BOOK ONE:	*SOUTH SPRING*	
CHAPTER I	THE RUSTLING	3
CHAPTER II	OLD TOWN	28
BOOK TWO:	*THE TALL TEN RANCH*	
CHAPTER I	TATER HILL BLUFF, FLORIDA	43
CHAPTER II	THOM'S DILEMMA	51
CHAPTER III	CALLIE'S AND TOM'S WEDDING	63
BOOK THREE:	*HARRISON AND CONNER*	
CHAPTER I	FAIRLEA	81
CHAPTER II	RIDGELAND MANOR	91
CHAPTER III	LA PALOMA	110
CHAPTER IV	AVALON MANOR	140
BOOK FOUR:	*THE KISSIMMEE VALLEY*	
CHAPTER I	CALLIE'S AND THOM'S HONEYMOON	165
CHAPTER II	MONIQUE'S	175
CHAPTER III	DELIA ROSE	184
CHAPTER IV	ARCADIA	194

BOOK ONE:

SOUTH SPRING

CHAPTER I
THE RUSTLING

Doodlebug, doodlebug, come out, come out.
A big ole snake's gonna grab yore snout.
This here stick goin' 'round and 'round
Gonna be yore way outa this here ground.

Wes chanted the old Darkie saying over and over as he circled the heavy straw into the mouth of the dry sand mound where the doodlebugs lived at the bottom of the inverted cone. He was underneath Aunt Willa's and Big Dan's front porch flat on his stomach and would spend hours fishing for them. Patiently he waited for one to latch on to the straw. When he caught it, he'd pull it out and place it in the clear jar of sand so he could watch it later.

As much as he liked his twin brother and sister from his Ma's marriage to Layke Williams, he couldn't seem to get used to this new position of not being the baby of the family. He'd always played well by himself, but since the deMoyas, the Cajun family from New Orleans bayou country, had given up their traveling medicine show and moved to South Spring to help out with the ranch, his sister SuSu and Aimee deMoya had become inseparable, and he felt left out for the first time in his eight years.

"Dan, hey Dan, is dat Master Wes Ah heahs unnerneath de house callin' out dose doodlebugs?" Willa called. "Dan, you be dere?" She spent most of her time these days resting on the feather bed that she and Big Dan Roker had shared for over fifty years. Its heavy ticking was stained and patched in more places than she could count, but Willa didn't notice the new tears nor the feathers that had worked their way out of confinement, especially on her husband's side of the bed. Her eyes didn't focus clearly anymore, and her breathing had become especially labored.

She turned on her side and looked for Dan past the only table in the small, square bedroom and toward the kitchen, the only other room in the cabin. The kitchen also served as a parlor with its fireplace and clay and stick chimney. The big, square, scrubbed-clean, pine table and benches and three rockers, made soft by the cotton-filled cushions placed on corn husk seats, were the only furniture in the room. Next to the door was a narrow ladder that led to the loft that their four children had used after they were old enough to leave their cradle.

Their children were grown and gone from South Spring now and had been for some twenty years. It had been over ten years since they'd seen or heard from any of them. Lemuel left for Palatka to work the docks before the War. Louisa followed him and worked as a cook on the steamship *Welaka*, a sidewheeler. Perry and Junie Mae both moved up to Rowland's Bluff, he to work at Jenkins' boat yard and Junie Mae to marry and move up to Lake City, where her husband worked for the railroad, last they heard.

One time after the Conflict, when Miss Berta's first husband Reuben was still living, Dan took the steamboat up to Rowland's Bluff to see Perry and his family in hopes of finding out about the others, but Perry hadn't heard anything about Lemuel or Louisa either. He'd seen Junie Mae only a few times and had promised Dan that they'd try to get together and all come down to South Spring to spend some time with him and Willa, but they never did. So Willa clung closer to Miss Berta's children, especially Wes, who had been so young when Mister Reuben, his pa, had been taken.

It almost broke her heart to see Wes so down, so out of sorts and lonely. He had always been such a happy, open child in temperament, unlike the others except Young Reuben, the oldest child. The twins from Miss Berta's second marriage, Raine and Tucker, seemed to take all their Mama's time and energy now, even with Orlean deMoya's help, and Willa was concerned for Wes.

Willa took the long, gnarled cane that she used to assist her arthritic legs to steady themselves and began pounding the floor so Wes could hear her. He responded by knocking on the underneath side and soon was bursting into the kitchen door past the rockers and into her raised arms. She hugged him to her and brushed his damp hair back from his freckled brow and asked, "How much do ya luv yore Aunt Willa, Master Wes? Hummm? More dan yore pony Fiddlesticks? More dan dark syrup candy? Honey, what's de matter wid ya - don' ya feel good?"

She began rocking back and forth humming an old hymn while stroking his despondent face. She thought, "Somethin' gotta be done 'bout ma chile. Somethin's gotta transpire."

She made up her mind that she'd make the effort to climb the knoll to the main house to speak to the Missus and Mister Layke. Her chile wasn't gonna put up wid no more of dis loneliness. Nosiree!

Wes closed the kitchen door softly as he'd had to since the twins' arrival. His mother was in her and Layke's bedroom rocking Tucker, and when she saw Wes she put her forefinger to her smiling lips. He already knew that he shouldn't say anything. Seemed like every time he came into the house anymore he was told to be quiet, and frankly he was getting tired of it. Every time, he thought as he went back outside and sat on the stoop, cupping his chin in his hands and resting his elbows on his drawn-up knees.

He could hear SuSu's and Aimee's voices coming from the big oaks in the side yard, where the tight rope was strung for their practice, but he knew if he went there that they'd just ignore him. "Boy, that Aimee deMoya really thinks she's something. I don't know why they had to move here. Just because she used to be the tight rope star of their medicine show doesn't mean a thing," he mumbled disgustedly. He looked around for anyone at all but knew that his stepfather Layke, Jonah, his seventeen-year-old brother, and Young Reuben, his oldest brother, who had moved back to South Spring from Perry, were all on the cow hunt up by North Prong. They'd be gone just overnight, Layke had said at breakfast. He guessed Orlean and old Dom deMoya were in their wagon, for he could see that they weren't in the garden and he didn't see Zekiel or Big Dan anywhere. "Guess those two went off fishing and didn't even ask me if I wanted to go. Off they went and didn't even tell me. Shoot!" Slowly he got up off the stoop and decided, "Maybe I'll mosey down to south spring to look at Pokey." Wes's other turtle Slowpoke had just up and died, but Young Reuben had helped him catch Pokey, and he seemed to eat better than Slowpoke, so maybe he'd live longer. He pulled a handful of greens from the garden. Shaking the sand off the hairy roots he said aloud, "Bet ole Pokey'll love these mustard greens," and laughed as he visualized the turtle spitting and spewing those greens out, because the older leaves were hot as fire. But he didn't walk very far. His heart just wasn't into going to the spring or anywhere else he could think of. Throwing the greens on the ground to wither, he returned to the stoop, lonely and bored. He didn't see nor hear Willa as she took her time trudging the sand path toward him.

Leaning against the river oak, her gnarled, shiny black hand clutching the cane, she decided to rest for a spell before climbing on up the hill. "Miss Berta gotta know 'bout mah baby. She gotta know how lonesome he be," and she eased herself down, gasping for every breath. "Think Ah'm gonna jes rest fer a spell." Closing her eyes, she leaned her gray head against the rough bark of the tree.

"Shoot!" Wes exclaimed. "Think I'm gonna go back to Aunt Willas' to ask her if Zekiel and Dan went fishing without me. Boy howdy! I bet she'll be mad at 'em ignorin' me like that." He kicked the sand before him and thought, "I'm sure Ma'll let me follow 'em if they just went to the river." He passed not three feet from Willa, but intent on how he was going to convince Berta to let him follow Zeke and Dan, he didn't see her.

He began calling her even before he got to the front porch. No answer. Wes pounded on the worn door, and when there was still no answer, he opened the door, continuing to call as he went to the bedroom. He saw that her cane was gone and realized that she wasn't there. "Probably went to the outhouse." But as he walked toward it, he could see that the door was ajar. "I bet she's at Zeke's. Maybe he didn't go fishing after all." He brushed past Zeke's bright orange chair and called and knocked. No answer.

Disgusted, Wes sat on the edge of the porch, and swinging his muscled legs out before him he pondered the situation. He knew that Willa couldn't have gone very far - her arthritic legs wouldn't permit it. "Maybe she went to the hen house!" He jumped up and began running, his flushed face perspiring, as he warmed to the task of finding his Aunt Willa.

She was sitting beside the oak when he saw her, and a grin quickly transformed his solemn face. "Aunt Willa, I was getting worried," he called to her as he slowed down. When she didn't hold her thin arms out to him in the familiar gesture, he knew that something was wrong. Hesitant to continue, he stopped.

"Aunt Willa, don't you feel good?" Her mouth was open, and Wes thought that she was going to respond, but as he drew closer he noticed that her eyes were closed.

Frightened, he shouted, "Aunt Willa! Aunt Willa!" He shook the bony shoulders that had once been soft and rounded and had lovingly comforted him from the day he'd been born. But he knew she was gone, and not knowing what else to do, he began patting her softly with his grubby hands. The tears swiftly found their way to his shirt collar, darkening the pale blue as he held her.

He stumbled at first, but then running as fast as he could he passed the girls. "Hey, Wes," SuSu called. "Boy he's sure in a hurry," but without giving him a second thought she continued playing with Aimee.

Past the main house he ran, past the barn, past the garden and orange and lemon trees, past the house-high crimson azaleas that were already in full bloom, and into the piney woods that were thick with the saw-tooth palmettos, low and sharp. He ran until he couldn't run any farther, and finally, gasping for breath, he fell down and curled up on the grassy slope beside North Prong Creek and cried himself to sleep.

"SuSu, call your brother again. He's never late for dinner. I don't know what's come over that child, moping around here day after day," Berta said tiredly - she'd been up before first light, and even before Orlean had arrived she'd nursed the twins and spread the leftover grits in the greased pan for the next day's breakfast. Layke loved it cut into thin slices, dipped in beaten eggs and fried until golden brown in the ham drippings. She laughed as she remembered that that was the only practical dish she could cook when she and Reuben arrived at South Spring. She was so very young, not yet seventeen, and from an affluent family in Macon, Georgia. Sadie, their cook, had given her a quick course in preparing fancy sauces and desserts and everything else impractical for her hard life in the wilderness of west Florida. Without the help of the black families on the place she was sure that she and Reuben would have had to live on fried grits.

Berta pushed the strands of golden hair from her brow, where tiny lines had begun to form in the last few years. She looked out the kitchen window and saw SuSu walking down the sand path toward Willa's and Dan's cabin and could hear her calling Wes. "Where on earth has he run off to?" she exclaimed as she opened the door to her and Layke's bedroom to check on the twins. "Better not be the river or the spring or I declare I'll tan his hide!" She heard SuSu scream.

"Now what!" The scream had not awakened the twins, so she quietly closed the door. She peered out the window and saw Aimee with her arm around SuSu, but before she got off the kitchen stoop Orlean and Dom had alighted from their wagon and begun running toward the girls calling to inquire what all the commotion was about.

"Well, it can't be disastrous," Berta said to herself. "Probably just saw a snake." SuSu was terrified of anything that crawled, but especially snakes, and Wes delighted in teasing her with the little black snakes he kept in jars and even his pants pockets.

As Berta got closer, SuSu's and Aimee's expressions told her that it was something more than a snake...something much more. Before she inquired Aimee spoke and said simply, "It's Willa, Berta." She had to say no more.

"Oh, no - oh, no...Willa!" she called. Aimee shook her head sadly, and Berta realized that her dear friend would not be able to hear her.

"What on earth are we going to do? Where's Dan...and Ezekiel? Have you seen them? Where's Wes? Did that boy go off without telling me?

I'm going to tan his hide, I declare I am...going off..."

Orlean held on to her arm. "Mees Berta. Don't! Don't get all upset. Dom weel find dem. Now you go tend your babes, and we take care of everyteeng."

"Aimee, you take Mees Berta back to de house and your Poppa weel find young Wes, and him and Dan and Zeke weel take care of Weela. Now go Meesy...go to your babes," and Berta relaxed and did her bidding.

Orlean was sure that Dan and Zeke were at the river fishing, and Dom agreed with her. He moved his bantam legs fast over the sand path toward south spring, then headed for the Suwannee about a quarter of a mile farther on.

Orlean knelt beside Willa. She removed her shawl, folded it and laid Willa down, placing the shawl beneath her head. Her eyes were closed. Quickly she calculated. "Meester Layke and de boys weel not return teel de next day near dark. Someone weel have to get word to dem. I have Dom drive de buckboard up to de Swede's to tell hees meesy, and maybe one of her cheeldren can ride out to find dem. Dat's what I do," she decided.

****

When Wes awakened he didn't know where he was. He thought that he might be beside the North Prong Creek that ran from the Swede's ranch into the Suwannee, but he was confused and scared. Again he started to cry. Wiping his face and runny nose with the back of his hand and sniffling, he began to follow the creek, leaving his footprints in the damp sand along its edge. He didn't know which way to go to get home, and shaking his towhead in confusion he allowed himself to think of Aunt Willa and cried all the harder. "I want my Mama...Mama..."

****

"What do you mean Wes wasn't with them? He's gotta be with them!" Berta yelled at Aimee and SuSu. "Did anyone look inside Willa's?" she asked Orlean. "Maybe he's there." But even as she said it, she knew that he wasn't. She began remembering the last time she'd seen him. He'd quietly come inside her room as she was finishing feeding Tucker. Then she finished fixing dinner...Heavens! That had to have been at least two hours ago. Where on earth could he have run off to? "You don't suppose that he found Willa - Oh dear Lord in the morning! You don't suppose that he found her and got so scared that he ran away!" Berta screamed at Orlean.

"Now, Meesy. Why Master Wes do such as dat? Eh? Why? Eef he find Willa he come a runnin' to you, eh?"

SuSu spoke up and told them that the last time she had seen him, he was running so hard that he didn't even answer her when she called to him.

"See, Orlean! See!" Berta shouted. Then reflectively, "Oh, I'm not sure. He's been moping around here lately. Why just yesterday Layke said that he'd never seen him so glum. He said that he needed to sit down and have a talk with him and spend more time with him. But he's been so busy lately, what with the cow hunt beginning. You know how busy he's been. I just don't know."

"Yes", Orlean thought. "We all been beezy. De babes take mos' of der Mama's strength, and Master Wes, he been all alone an' sad."

Aloud she said, "Dom be back soon, Mees Berta, den de men return, an' dey go look for Master Wes. We fin' heem, don' you worry."

What she didn't say was, "I sure hope before de dark come. Poor leetle teeng."

****

Zeke held Dan by the arm, hurrying him along to his house next door so Berta could tend to Willa. But Dan refused to be hurried. "Ah'm not gonna leave. Now, Zeke, let me go. Ah'm not leavin' mah house." "You ain't heppin' Willa none by bein' heah, Dan. Now ya knows dat. Not being nuttin' but bein' unner foot. What ya gonna do? Ya gonna hep Miss Berta dress her? Huh? Is dat what ya gonna do?" Zeke shook his kinky head at the stupidity of Dan. He never did get along with his sister-in-law. They had no kind words to say to each other before or after her sister Myrtice died. But she did fix his meals sometimes and had shown other acts of kindness the last few years. He just chalked them up as bossy. Always calling him a lazy nigger. Well, he wouldn't have to listen to that anymore. But he was sorry that she was dead, mainly because of Dan. Willa had ruled the roost, so guess it'd be up to him to tell Dan when to do every blessed thing, just like she did.

"What we's bes' be doin' is lookin' fer Master Wes. Ah thinks he found Willa and run off scared near 'bout to death. Dat's what Ah thinks. He be hidin' somewheres, and soon be dark, an' how we gonna find him in de dark? Huh?"

Dan didn't answer, and Zeke wasn't sure that he heard him. "Dan, ya knows how much Willa loves dat boy. Why, she loves him better dan any of her own. What'd she be sayin' to us if she 'live, Dan? What? She be sayin' 'you ain't nuttin' but lazy niggers.' Dat's wat she be sayin'."

Dan shook his gray head and knew that Zeke was right. She'd sure 'nuff be giving the two of them a tongue lashing. "Ah knows yer right. Ah knows it. But, Zeke, Ah don' wanna leave her..."

"Now ya listen ta me! Right dis very minute, you listen! Willa ain't gonna be hepped none a-tall by ya bein' here. She done gone off an left ya, Dan. It jes' her old boney body a-lyin' on dat bed with Miss Berta tendin' her. Ya bes' come on wid me an' hep to find her baby...ya bes' come."

Slowly he gave in...

Berta choked back her tears when Zeke told her that he and Dan were going to search for Wes, and that they were sure that they knew just where he was hiding. Not being able to answer, she just nodded her head that she understood and continued bathing Willa with the warm well water.

She had decided to lay out Willa's Sunday dress, the one she loved so. It had large pink roses on a soft green background, and she'd sewn on a big square collar of solid rose and edged it in lace. Her stitches were no longer tiny and uniform, and Berta got a catch in her throat as she could visualize her sitting on the front porch, squinting to see the seams. Toward the end, even in the bright sunlight, she had problems. She'd added big puffed sleeves, that made her skinny arms look that much thinner, and covered the buttons with the same rose fabric as the collar. It hadn't been worn much in the five years since she'd made it - a funeral or a wedding, or once in a while she'd ask Dan to take her to the little Black church in town.

"My, I'll have to send one of the boys into town to tell Leander to spread the word about Willa in the Black community." Not many old timers were left. Most had moved away after the War. "I bet there aren't more than six families left with most all the young ones moving away to larger towns to find work. Oh, and Perry. I'll have to get word to him in Rowland's Bluff - I mean Branford. I wish they'd leave the towns' old names. Every time I turn around, they're changing names. Why, they even changed Rose Head to Perry after Governor Perry. That was an honor, I'm sure, but I just wish..."

"Why is my mind all in a dither? Just can't seem to think straight. I'll ask Perry to contact the other children. I know that Dan doesn't know where they are, 'cause Willa said not long ago that all her children might be dead for all they knew. What a shame! They've been such caring parents and made sure that the children could read and do their figuring. Couldn't do enough for all of them."

She sat down on the bed beside Willa and put her hands over her mouth as she moaned in grief, "Why isn't Layke here? Why is it that I'm always alone when I need my man?"

Berta thought of Reuben's death. She'd almost forgotten that terrible time. She remembered how Willa had taken over so she could have her grieving time. Then she remembered Wes. "Where is he, God? Where is my baby? I haven't given him enough affection lately. Willa knew it. She knew everything that there was to know about Wes. Why, she was closer to him than I. I was so busy trying to run South Spring after Reuben died that Willa actually raised that child. Oh, Willa! Where is he? Where?"

****

Layke had just turned toward Jonah to ask if he had seen the family dog, Old Red, who had insisted on following them even though they should have made him stay at South Spring, when he saw the rider in the distance. "Looks like Pudge, Jonah. Must be something up at North Prong, or Emma wouldn't have let him ride out here."

"Boy, he's hauling it, Layke! You're right! Look at how he's kicking up that sand."

"Better get Swede, Jonah." Jonah headed for the others in a gallop. They'd been scouring the woods for the herd that they thought was southwest of the Swede's place since right after first light and for some strange reason hadn't found hide nor hair of them. Layke and Young Reuben were puzzled, as was Swede. "They just seem to have vanished into thin air," Swede said as he raised his shaggy eyebrow at Layke. "Don't suppose some of those rustlers from Kissimmee got this far north, do ya?" he whispered.

Layke had responded, "Jonah and I'll have a look-see over near Black Bear Run. If the beeves got this far, there should be some sign of 'em over there."

"Hey, hold up Pudge," Layke called to him. Pudge's fat face was red with excitement, and Layke knew that Emma wouldn't have let her baby boy ride out unless she had to. Oh, how she doted on that boy! He was almost as big around as he was tall and the happiest kid in the entire community. Her other big, strapping boys had a ready spark and were more like fat lighter wood just ready to be lit, but Pudge was just a big fat oak log. The other kids didn't try to tease him anymore about being so fat because they couldn't get a rise out of him. He just grinned and asked them if they'd like one of his molasses cookies or piece of candy that he seemed to always have in one of his britches pockets.

Swede said that they had the skinniest hogs in the whole county, 'cause with Pudge at the table the poor things didn't get much slop. But he laughed when he said it 'cause he loved that boy as much as Emma.

As he got closer, Layke could see Pudge's worried expression, but before he could get a word out Pudge yelled, "It's Wes, Layke. He ran off when he found Aunt Willa dead. Miss Berta is having some kinda fit. Old Dom rode over to the house to tell me to fetch you and be quick about it."

He pulled up beside Layke, sweat pouring off his splotched face, and sat there grinning. He'd delivered the message just like his ma had told him to, and with that completed he was turning his horse around when Layke grabbed hold of his reins and asked, "When? When did all that happen? We've only been gone since breakfast."

"Must've happened right after y'all left. We'd just finished up dinner when Karine came a-runnin' for me and told me what Old Dom said and that Ma wanted me to ride out to fetch you. And I said it just like Ma wanted me to. That's all I know, that they can't find Wes and that they found Willa dead, and they figured that he must've found her first and got scared and run away. They've looked everywhere and called and ...oh, heck, I don't know." He was getting flustered and just wanted to ride back home to tell his ma that he'd done exactly what she had told him. Boy, she'd be proud of him, and no doubt he'd get an extra cookie for doing such a good job.

Then he remembered, "And Karine said that Berta is havin' some kinda conniption fit and wants y'all to come home lickty-split. That's all I know," he said breathlessly, and taking the reins from Layke, Pudge put his horse to a gallop and headed back to his ma's good-smelling kitchen.

Pudge had spoken so rapidly that Layke had a hard time understanding him, but he knew from the bits and pieces he could put together that he had to get to Berta. "If something has happened to Wes, I'm not sure she'll be able to handle any more heartache." He didn't allow the thought to enter his muddled mind that he too would have a rough time dealing with it. Heavens! He had just told Berta that he wanted to spend more time with him, that he could see by his quietness that he was lonesome.

Layke understood loneliness. The death of his brothers, Ben and

Walt, who were killed at the Battle of Chattanooga, and of his best friend, Jay Alligood, from the Citadel just about did him in. He remembered death - God, he could still smell it. And his own brush with death when his leg had almost been blown off was forever with him. He still carried a limp as a constant reminder, and when he'd been riding all day that leg would send unwanted messages to his tired brain. He'd see Jay's bloody face or what was left of it, and the tears still came, salty, warm, flowing. Yes, Layke knew death.

His captain, Captain Tucker, had helped him through the rough time in that makeshift hospital in South Carolina and wouldn't allow the doctor to take Layke's leg. Hell, he'd been so grateful to the man that he even asked Berta to name Tucker after him. Recuperating from the wound back home in Tennessee he tried for an entire year to adjust to his new life, but couldn't. All he'd ever wanted to be was an army officer like his pa and grandpa before him. The Williams family was an army family, and he had never considered another life.

He left those smokey hills of Tennessee and wandered down the Appalachian range, settling in the foothills of northwest Florida near the town of Marianna. The spread he'd bought and tried to farm was nothing but lonely. Not a soul around for three miles and no one to talk to. He'd begun to talk to the trees and his chickens just so he could hear a voice, and then a cowdog miraculously showed up on a dark, stormy night and saved his life from a marauding wolf, that was after Layke's last chicken. Layke had given up his gun when he left Tennessee and had bought a cowwhip in Marianna, and with it plus Sergeant, as he named the dog, they put an end to that wolf.

Realizing how much he needed other companionship he began going to town more often. He'd noticed how the cowmen, who came tooting into town on Saturday night, were always laughing and joking. Most had been in the War, but they seemed unaffected by it. So, Layke decided to try his hand at riding the range. Didn't take him long to realize his decision was the right one. He and Sarge wandered from ranch to ranch and made the annual drive to Punta Rassa, south of old Ft. Myers on the Gulf, where they'd load the beeves in the steamships bound for Key West and Cuba and the meat packing plants.

Yes, he knew loneliness. He'd wandered for over eleven years working ranch after ranch. Then he found his Berta.

He had been working the Wilpole spread, Santa Fe, up near Rowland's Bluff, north on the Suwannee, when he took to the trail again. Sarge had died so he knew it was time to move on. He told his new cowdog, Tag, that they were getting no place fast and it was time to think about settling down. When he pulled up rein in Old Town, a small wilderness town on the Suwannee, and met Trudy Stucky, proprietor of the Stucky Hotel, or boarding house as most called it, and the other friendly townspeople, he knew that it was right for him. He rode out to South Spring the very next morning - they'd told him that Berta needed a foreman. The minute he laid eyes on her he knew that he'd found home...and so did she.

As he sat on his cow pony, Bucko, waiting for Jonah and the others to catch up with him, he began remembering when he first met Wes and how they had become friends right off, because Wes didn't remember his own father. He'd been just two when Reuben died suddenly. It turned out that he needed Wes's love and trust as much as Wes needed his, because Jonah, Berta's middle son, resented Layke and tried every way he could think of to keep Layke and his ma apart. He had never accepted his father's death, and when he saw Berta's affection for Layke he vowed to get rid of him any way he could.

Even with the animosity Jonah displayed Layke embraced his new position as foreman of South Spring, and his life took on new meaning and purpose. The past two years' events came rushing to him as he stared into space and wondered as he waited. He wondered what would have happened to his and Berta's love had the feared Skinner gang not shown up in Old Town. Jonah foolishly had tried to capture them by himself but was kidnapped instead. If Layke hadn't rounded up the posse so quickly and ridden after them through the night, Jonah might not be alive today. Jonah returned a subdued and grateful young man and a hero to boot. He had a front row seat at the hanging where R.J. and Joe Bob Skinner dangled from the old oak out behind Miss Trudy's boarding house. From that day he and Layke had been friends, and when he and Berta announced their wedding plans Jonah was as happy about it as were Young Reuben and the rest of the folks around.

Layke wanted to call out to that eight-year-old boy to tell him that he understood, to hang on and to remember his and Berta's love for him, that the affection that he and Jonah now enjoyed was through faith and love and a fight hard fought but won.

The riders galloping toward him ignored the low palmettos as they raced through the sand pines. When they got to the clearing, Layke halted them. "Swede, I know that if they haven't found Wes by the time we get to South Spring Berta will need all the help we can give her. And someone's gotta ride into town to alert Trudy and to tell Leander about

Willa. They've gotta get her coffin ready and get word to Perry up in Branford. We'll all be needed and..."

"Hey, Layke! Take it easy!" Calmly he said, "I told Pudge to ride on back to the house to tell Emma that we'll all be at South Spring. Don't you worry none 'bout him. We'll find that scared little tyke. Don't you worry now, heah?" Swede Heglund's huge frame belied his gentleness. Layke thought, "He's gotta be as good a friend as a body could have. He's good through and through."

He put his hand on Swede's broad shoulder and whispered, "Any sign of the beeves?" Swede shook his head, and Layke could see how concerned he was. "God, that's all we need. Just when I think everything is going fine I get kicked in the teeth again." He sighed and then put the spurs to Bucko.

The men rode southeast toward South Spring, and Pudge rushed toward North Prong with a new message to deliver to his ma. He'd never had such an important day, not in all his years. "Boy howdy! She'll really be proud of me now," and his mind conjured up plates heaped with ginger cookies and shortbread and pecan pralines and mountains of lemon drops and...

****

Berta heard the lusty whistle of the *Suwannee Queen* as it passed by their small landing about a half mile from the main house. No one would be there to wave hello to Captain George or Beau. Reuben had insisted on building the landing the year he died, and it had hardly been used in that six-year period. The boat captains always slowed down and gave their comforting whistle nevertheless. She allowed a smile. Reuben would be pleased, she thought. Layke had said just recently that he and Young Reuben and Jonah needed to get down there to repair the landing. He was afraid one of the children would get injured, for some of the pilings were rotten. He had looked right at Wes when he said it 'cause he knew how much he liked to tag after Zeke and Dan. He also knew that it was their favorite fishing spot, for the bream seemed to like to feed around the pilings.

The family usually went to Old Town to the main landing, where the steamships always stopped and stayed a spell. Wasn't much use in their stopping at South Spring, because Reuben had gone heavily into cattle. The crops were mostly for their own use, so they had nothing to sell. But Reuben liked the idea of having his own landing anyway, and Layke didn't allow anything to go unattended. It wasn't his nature.

Right after the pier was built Berta and the children would walk the sand path through the lush growth toward the river and would spend a lazy afternoon just lolling on the heavy wooden planks, where she'd have spread an old quilt. She'd allow them to take off their shoes, and if the river was high they could dangle their toes in the warm water and wave and yell to the people on board the steamboats. It made them feel less isolated seeing other people around. She decided that after Wes returned that she'd have Orlean or Aimee watch the twins, and she, Wes and SuSu would go to the landing again. Maybe they'd even take a picnic and fish and wave to the passing boats just as they once had.

Orlean had recently mentioned that she'd like to start making meat pastries to sell to the passengers and wondered what Berta thought of the idea. She had thought it a splendid idea. They truly needed more contact with the outside world. Since the twins had arrived she'd just not had time to turn around, even neglecting SuSu's and Wes's lessons. She remembered how much she and her family had enjoyed the pastries when her father took them on the exciting train rides to Savannah. While he conducted his business at the cotton and tobacco warehouses, she and her ma and brother and sister would sit on the waterfront and watch the activity on the wharves and munch on those hot flaky pastries. The ones that the street vendors sold in the Broad Street Park back home in Macon never seemed to taste as good.

The Norwood family spent most Sunday afternoons at the city park. Their servants, Benge, Sadie and Little Woman had Sunday off, so after church Berta's pa would drive the buggy, and the children especially liked that. He was a very impatient man and kept their ma in a dither for fear he'd say words not fit for young ears. Berta grew up believing that no one in the entire town of Macon, Georgia, could handle a buggy worth a tinker's dam and that all the men in Macon were morons and most certainly blind.

"It all seems so long ago...Where are you Wes? Where's my baby? Where's my child? Oh, God..."

She could see that sad, freckled face, his tan hair managing to fall across his forehead despite the cowlick, which he unsuccessfully pushed back out of his curious, blue eyes. Wes had that same lazy curiosity that Reuben's brother Ham had. He looked like Berta but was very methodical like Reuben. When Berta looked at Wes she always saw Reuben as he looked as a child. Strange... they were as unlike as any father and son could be in appearance, but both were easily outgoing and demonstrative.

"But you didn't have a father, my son. Not for six of your eight years. You didn't have the caring and love that I'm sure your father had as a boy." She put her head in her hands and sobbed, "Aunt Willa was more of a mama than I, my baby. Why was I so blind? Why was I so busy with my Boyo and Raine and my Layke that I didn't see your loneliness?"

She implored, "Willa! Give me a sign. Show me where Master Wes is....show me!" She peered into the approaching night toward the heavens...but there was no sign. Exhausted, she wearily found her bed and fell upon it. She dried her eyes and quietly said, "Oh, Lord, please give me another chance. Please..."

****

"She's holding up better than I thought possible," Layke said to Swede as they trudged through the low brush and deep bed of oak leaves while intermittently calling for Wes.

"She had a lot of hardening ever since Reuben died. I guess that once you've experienced deep grief it sort of prepares you," Swede said.

Layke thought of the hundreds of men he'd seen killed and injured in the War and remembered that toward the end that it hadn't affected him as at first. Then Jay was killed. That almost did him in.

"Guess the Swede's right. You just become numb. But I don't think its that way with Berta. I believe she's learned to remove herself from the situation and become immersed in something else, in this case Willa's funeral and burial. And Dan's just the same, but he's put all his energy into finding Wes."

"Wes...oh, Wes. Where are you!" he called and then listened. Nothing but the sound of Bucko's tail swishing and the crunch of the dry leaves. "SuSu said that he was headed toward your place or at least in that direction, Swede. Heck, he might be having a glass of milk and a handful of cookies with your kids this very minute. Do you suppose that we should send one of the boys there?"

"No, I don't think so. I'm sure that Emma would get word to us if he was there. Probably even let Pudge go all the way to South Spring with him."

They continued walking the horses and calling. Just yesterday Layke had gloried in the beauty of the early spring. The wild jasmine's pungent aroma was thick in the pine trees, and the berry bushes were full of bloom. He had commented to Jonah that they'd be having some of his ma's good berry conserve before long if they could get by without another freeze.

No one could out-do Berta when it came to fruit conserve. She added lots of plump pecans and bits of citron for tartness. It was one of the few dishes she learned from Sadie that she could use at South Spring.

February was such a precarious month with sunshine and summer weather one day and the next a freeze. He had seen it drop as much as seventy degrees over night. Layke could see that the light was fast fading. "Once that sun gets over those tall pines we'll have only another hour of light, and it'll get downright cold. I just pray that we find him before then."

"You and me. You and me. There won't be many stars in the sky tonight. Not much more than pitch black with a half moon," he said softly.

"Hold up, Layke! Did ya hear that? Listen. There it goes again. Good Lord, we've stumbled on the beeves. Now how in thunderation did they get way over here? I'm not believing this." But as they stared at them in the half light Layke spoke up, "Swede, those aren't ours." When he drew closer and saw the brand, he exclaimed, "Something's definitely up. These are Charlie's, and there is no way that they would've swum the Suwannee as full as it is to come way over here for a few sprigs of grass. Hell, they've got plenty right on their own side of the river."

"Right you are. Someone had to drive 'em, Layke." He quickly looked around and automatically put his hand on the rifle, drawing it out slowly. "They had to have had a whole bunch of urging, and probably with dogs and whips to boot."

"Can't believe any locals would be involved in this. Must be from somewhere else. We've gotta get word to the other cowmen and telegraph down state to see if anyone knows who it could be," Layke said quickly, his whip already pulled from his saddle horn. Swede could see the leaders in his neck draw up tight with anticipation.

Then he relaxed and said, "But not until we've found Wes. This'll have to wait." Swede noticed that he didn't return the whip to the saddle.

****

"I just don't know what more can happen to Berta and Layke, Luta. First, Jonah being kidnapped and then SuSu almost drowning and now Wes," Trudy Stucky commented as she stood beside the front door of her boarding house. She was directing her concern to Luta Brewster, who was married to Bud the blacksmith and lived in the quarters that were attached to their livery stable across the dirt road from the hotel. "When

Pierre deMoya came a-ridin' up and told me about Aunt Willa and Wes, well, I..." She couldn't continue. The weathered sign, Stuckey's Hotel, creaked above them as they stood on the front porch. Trudy's pa had hung that sign there over thirty years before. He'd had to re-hang it on more than one occasion due to the nor'easters and hurricanes that had visited them. They'd arrived in Old Town from Alabama with all their possessions on that rickety, ox-drawn wagon after the second Seminole uprising in '43` thinking it safe for them, but when the third war broke out in '49 they weren't so sure that their timing had been right.

A number of families were burned out and massacred down in the Ft. Meade area when they weren't able to get to the fort in time, and all their horses and cattle were stolen. The Indians' hit-and-run raids were more toward the interior of the state and along the St. Johns, but you never knew when some of them would show, and Trudy remembered how frightened she and her ma had been.

She remembered the tales the oldsters told on that very porch about when Old Town was called Bowleg's Town and how Andrew Jackson came riding in and chased the Indians away, capturing over a hundred head of stolen cattle. That was even before Florida became a territory in '21 and was nothing but wild. They said that some of the stock on the Old Town ranches were descendants of those very cattle.

"Seems to me, Luta, that for a town where not much happens we sure have had more than our share since Layke showed up...heck, not much more than two years ago. Can you believe it?" Luta just shook her head and was about to comment when Trudy started up again. She drew up the rocker, and Luta knew she was in for some of Trudy's front porch philosophy. And she was.

"Do you know that ever since the state of Florida began it's been doing some kinda warring, what with their flitting back and forth between Spain and England. Heck, even the French got their licks in up in Ft. Caroline near Jacksonville. Didn't get to fly their flag though. Then the Indians fighting all over the whole state. Soon as we thought we had 'em settled in the Everglades and Oklahoma, doggoned if the secession didn't up and get us going again."

"Here comes Bud, and I know he'll agree with me. I'd vow that Florida has gotta be the dagblasted, fightin'est state this country ever saw. Bud said that very thing the other night sitting right in that chair there. He said that Layke told him that we got us another kind of war on our hands with this cattle rustling business. Did he tell you 'bout it, Luta?"

"Tell me? Well, I just can't believe it. I'll declare I can't. Did he tell you everything what Layke read in the *Tallahassee Floridian* that came in on the *Lucky Lady?*" she said with great theatrics. "Why, I never in all my borned days heard of such lowdown folks as we've got in this state."

She pulled her chair up real close and continued talking secretively to the attentive Trudy. "Over in those yellow sand hills just south of Chipley right outside of Marianna some cowmen caught a gang of 'em changing the cattle brands..." She let that sink in and rushed in for the finish. "In the broad daylight, mind you, and they up and hung 'em right on the spot. Imagine!"

She rolled her large brown eyes toward the heavens and continued, "Makes a person wanta just up and move away, it does," and waited for Trudy's response that she was sure would be just as emphatic.

"Well there's not any other state I'd wanta move to, Luta. I'd feel like I was letting the lowdown skunks best me, and a Stucky doesn't run from anyone - not Indians, not Yankees, and sure as shootin' not rustlers. Not a Stucky!"

"Oh, I was just spouting off, Trudy. Don't let on to Bud what I said. I didn't mean it. Why, this is home and it always will be. Come bear, wolves, rattlers or, even like you said, rustlers." She sighed and said sad-like, "At least I don't have a lost little boy who is probably scared half to death and... Look, the sun's going down, and I guess no sign of him yet."

"Hello, honey," she said to Bud as he stepped up on the worn, wooden porch. "Me and Trudy was just chatting about all the terrible things that's been happening right before our eyes, weren't we, Trudy?" Bud pulled up the other rocker and said, "Guess no word 'bout Wes is there?" They shook their heads. "Poor little feller. Bet he's mighty cold about now."

"Where are Palmer and Davis?" he continued. "Not like them to be at the store when something's going on. You don't suppose Palmer's cold got worse?" he rattled on and on just making small talk while they all three kept their eyes steady on the road from South Spring.

Trudy looked toward McCoy's Dry Goods Store where the two brothers and their wives, Erma and Martha, lived in the rear. "I sure hope not. You remember that bad spell he had last year? Whew! I thought he was a goner for sure. You know it took that to get Martha to open her mouth. She actually said *thank you* when I took him a pot of my rich chicken soup. I told Palmer that he'd hafta get sick more often so's Martha would talk." She laughed along with the others but occupied her mind with some of the funny things that had happened ever since Palmer brought his bride back to Old Town, and her not a hundred pounds and not much more than a child...about sixteen or so.

Now Palmer McCoy was a slow going man and not very much of a talker, but Martha truly never opened her mouth. She was a good cook and took good care of him but had the meanest younguns Trudy had ever seen. Homer, the youngest boy, had moved up to Jacksonville and surprised the entire town by getting a good job in a bank. He seemed to shuck his meanness off, and the other two boys had gone on to Rose Head and had good jobs.

Trudy began to chuckle. "What're you amused at, Trudy?" Luta asked.

"I was just thinking about Martha. She is comical even if she doesn't know it. You know how she is always in her rocker with that grin on her face so's you can't tell what on earth she's thinking or if she's thinking anything at all?"

They both nodded yes.

"Well, I got her to get as riled up as I've ever seen her when I hauled that Homer in by the ear and told her what that youngun had done to my rooster."

"I was standing at the kitchen door looking out toward the chicken coop when I saw Homer inside my coop. So I watched to see what he was up to. Sure 'nuff he had a heavy string tied in a noose and lying on the ground with a row of corn scattered out from the noose and had hung the string over the fence post and was calling my red rooster. I thought I knew what he was going to do, but before I could get out the door that rooster took the bait, and Homer had yanked the string, and that rooster was hangin' upside down with every feather on his entire body stuck straight out and squawking his head clean off, and that Homer was laughing to beat the band."

"Well, that did it! I grabbed my bresh broom and went for him. He saw me coming and dropped the string, and the poor old rooster fell on its head and started running around in circles drunk as could be with Homer trying to out-distance my broom. But I gave him a good one right on his bottom, and when he stumbled I grabbed his ear."

Trudy was bent double with laughter. "Go on, Trudy. What did you do next?" Luta asked. The fact that she'd heard the story a good dozen times didn't make a bit of difference. She knew that Trudy was just trying to keep their minds off of Wes.

"That's when I marched him into her back room, and sure 'nuff Martha was in her rocker going at it and grinning. When I told her what that mean Homer had done, she stopped rockin' and stopped smiling. Well, she didn't say a word, and when I realized that was as riled up as she could get and I saw Homer's expression and realized that he knew it, too, I got out of there. I could hear him hollering all the way back to the house. I went out back to check on the rooster, and that poor thing was still just as drunk as a skunk, and all his lady friends were surrounding him, and if a chicken can laugh, well, they were laughing. I got so amused that I joined in with them."

Luta and Bud laughed right along with Trudy.

"Bugs are getting bad. Think I'll go on in." Trudy looked around the town and commented, "Have you ever seen an earlier spring? My camellia is still in full bloom, and right beside it the azaleas are loaded with blossoms a good three weeks early. Just hope we don't get another cold spell." She pulled her shawl closer around her plump shoulders and said goodnight.

"Trudy won't be getting much sleep tonight, Honey," Luta said getting up from her chair and walking over to Bud. She squeezed his protective shoulder. His arm circled her waist as he rose and pulled her to him, not saying what he thought. But she knew what he was thinking. "We won't, either," he'd be thinking as he thanked the dear Lord that his Bethy and Frankie were safe in their quarters and not lost in the woods.

****

"Well, lookee heah, Bose. Would ya just. Now ya don't suppose this little boy saw what we was a doin', now do ya?"

The man nudged Wes with his dirty boot, and Wes quickly pulled down the shirt that he'd pulled over his head to keep any mosquitoes from biting him more, not that there were many around in late February, and sleepily asked, "Who're you?"

"Well, he can talk jes lak folks, now can't he Bose? Jes lak a youngun's supposed ta...except he didn't add the *Sir* lak he done been taught."

Wes rubbed his eyes but could see little more than a shadow lumbering over him. But, boy howdy, he could smell him..lordy how he could smell him. Smelled worse than the time Old Red tangled with that skunk and his ma made him and Jonah take him to the river to wash him with the soda powder. Whew!

The man turned and walked a few paces away from him, and he and the other man began mumbling, but Wes couldn't make out what they said. There were two of them. "They've gotta be from somewhere else 'cause I don't know them," and while he was thinking that, he strained even more trying to hear.

"Now, Lou, don' go gettin' frisky wid this youngun. He probably lives right around here and his pa is close by. Ain't that right, boy?" he questioned loudly because he could see how Wes was straining to hear them.

Not liking the way they were talking, Wes decided that he'd better be real polite. "My Pa's dead, but my new Pa is called Layke. He's probably looking for me right this minute."

"Don't he know where you are, boy?" asked Lou, the skinny, dark-haired one with the bushy beard.

"I ran away on account of Aunt Willa died...and I got scared, I guess," Wes said trying to not cry.

Lou looked at Bose, grinned and said, "How long you reckon you been runnin' and which way did you come from?"

"I don't know. I'm lost but I come from South Spring."

"I happen to know just about where that is. Bet you wanna go home right now, don ya?" Lou said, his face not more than a foot from Wes's. Wes saw the red scar that ran clear down the side of the man's face right into his tobacco stained beard and cleared the catch in his throat before answering, "Yes sir, I sure do. I know my Ma's worried about me 'cause it's near 'bout dark..."

"So you think yore ma's worried, do ya? Well...well.."

"Oh, yes sir. I know she's mighty worried, 'cause I never ran away before."

Lou excitedly grabbed hold of Bose and pulled him away from Wes and whispered so Wes couldn't hear him.

"Now, Lou, I'm not thinking that that's such a good idea. I went along with changing the brands but holdin' a youngun for ransom - well..."

"God damn it, Bose! By the time we drive those beeves all the way down to Charlotte Harbor or Tampa and get our money, hell, it'll be near a month," he said through clenched teeth angrily. He saw that Bose was backing down. Could always tell by the way he shuffled his feet nervously. He knew that he was getting to him, so he whispered sweetly, "And with this little lost boy, well, hell, we could be rich in a matter of days and over at Sadie's poking some ripe little tart and not hafta fool with these stupid cows."

But shaking his long greasy hair and planting his feet firmly, Bose said, "Now, Lou, I did the stealin' right along with you, but I ain't gonna get strung up for no kidnappin' a youngun. Folks is funnier 'bout their younguns than they is about some old cows. Now you rightly know that."

"You ain't got one God-damned ounce of adventure in yore fat ass.

Not one ounce. Where'd ya be without me doing the thinking for both of us, huh? Where in the hell'd you be?"

His voice was getting louder and louder, and Wes could see the short one back up real slowly, and when he turned around toward him, Wes could see by the man's scared eyes that they were in for a lot of trouble. Wes turned his back to them and, making circles with the toe of his shoe in the wet creek sand, tried to decide whether he should run for it. They both had rifles slung through the cinches on their saddles and had big guns in their holsters, so he decided that maybe he'd better go along with them for a spell. Maybe by then Layke or Young Reuben or Jonah would find him. Maybe.

****

Would you look at this, Jonah! Good grief! No wonder we couldn't find the cattle. Must be at least fifty of 'em. And Lordy, you can see that the brands are fresh. Turned the SS into 88 big as you please...And look at these North Prong brands? Put a tail on the P and made it NR - No wonder..."

Young Reuben turned back to Jonah and exclaimed, "Wait 'til Layke and Swede see these...we'd better ride out..."

Jonah quickly spoke up, "We got a more important job on our hands, Young Reuben. Finding Wes is a helluva lot more important than catching some no-good rustlers." Jonah had been very protective of his little brother, even before their pa had died.

Young Reuben, excited by their find, acted like he hadn't even heard him, gave his leg a hard slap, pulled his sweat rimmed hat off and continued, "Bet they're the same ones who struck over in Kissimmee couple weeks ago or maybe even part of the gang from up Chipley way. I'd bet Cloud on it. You'd better get your rifle ready," he said looking around expecting one of them to jump out of the shadows any minute. "They can't be too far from here," he said barely above a whisper. "Maybe they pulled up by North Prong Creek and are gettin' their fire ready for the night. Should we wait for them to bed down and jump 'em?"

Jonah could see him salivating just like he did when they went hunting. "Now, Young Reuben, I already told you that we're not gonna give up on finding Wes just 'cause we stumbled onto this." He was getting really exasperated with his older brother but, he, too, was very nervous just sitting on his horse without any cover to speak of. Sitting ducks they were.

"Oh, I know that, but we'll hafta be on ready now that we know they're here. No more calling for him as before."

Jonah realized that what he said was true. "What do you think we oughta do? Maybe one of us should try for the Swede's to alert them just in case one of his boys went home."

"That wouldn't be such a bad idea, but I sure don't like the idea of leaving this," he gestured toward the herd. Young Reuben's mind was going lickety-split, Jonah could tell, and he started in with the *what ifs*. "What if they decide to come back before pitch black to guard 'em, and what if there're more of them than us? Can you tell how many there were?" he asked Jonah as he scanned the ground. But it was just too dark to see any tracks. Young Reuben continued, "I sure as hell wanta be here in the morning when they come back, and I'd like to have some help. Why don't you ride into Old Town on the river road? Moon's 'bout half full, so there should be enough light. You can get up a posse to look for Wes and help get these thieving skunks at the same time. And have someone get word to the other cowmen. Hell, they'll swarm over here from every section of the state just like the locusts in the Bible."

All Jonah could think of was Wes being out in the dark, scared to death, with no protection and wolves and cats thick all around him. He oughta know, because he'd hunted them in these woods many a time.

Young Reuben interrupted his thoughts, "Maybe Wes found the road and is already in town. What do you think? Did you hear what I said, Jonah? Listen, do you want to stay here and for me to go?"

"I'll go, but you best not have a fire, and you sure as heck hafta stay awake..."

"Jonah - hey Jonah. You're talking to Young Reuben. Hell, I've been taking care of myself since I was fifteen years old, remember?"

He patted his younger brother on the back to reassure him and said, "But one thing I've never had to do was string up rustlers."

Jonah was remembering when he watched the Skinner brothers hang from the big spreading oak out behind Stucky's Boarding House. "Its not a pretty sight, Young Reuben. Not pretty at all, even if they do deserve it." He turned around in the saddle and said with more conviction than he felt, "I'll be back before first light with a posse. Be careful."

"No need to worry 'bout me. Careful I'll be," but as he said it all he could think of was how he was going to catch those stinking bastards. He was a cowman just like his pa before him, and the very idea of someone changing their brands got him to licking his dry lips and rubbing his sweaty palms together.

"Now you be quiet, you hear," he said sweet talking the cow, not more than a yearling, as he stroked it. The rustlers had bedded them down about fifty feet inside some sparse piney woods, and Young Reuben knew that the North Prong Creek was only about a quarter of a mile from them. He figured that they'd take turns guarding them once they'd had their supper. They were probably having their coffee on the creek bank laughing and joking and feeling mighty good about their thievery.

"Bet they're planning on running them down to Punta Rassa or Charlotte Harbor so they can sell them to Cuba. Probably tell Sr. Gato or Yankee that they're from Georgia or Alabama. Hell, those two wouldn't know the difference."

He listened - no sounds but an occasional screech owl warning her mate. His mind was racing. He got on Cloud and thought, "Guess I'll go on over to the creek to see what gives. Shoot! They think they've out smarted us and probably don't even have a lookout. If I knew where Wes was, I'd stampede those cattle, and that'd give 'em something to keep 'em busy 'til morning, and by then Jonah'll be back with half the state of Florida."

He thought on it as he pushed the low limbs from the scrub oak to the side nuzzling his head low on Cloud's mane. "Maybe I'd better find out how many there are before I get too carried away."

CHAPTER II
OLD TOWN

Trudy heard Jonah's horse whinny, and being a light sleeper when there was trouble brewing, she grumbled, "Who in the world can that be this time of night?" She removed her night cap, pulled her robe off the iron bed post and put it on while reaching for the lamp on the dresser. "Hold up, I'm a-coming," she called down the stairs. She lit the lamp and, as she became more fully awake, remembered Wes. Down the stairs her plump feet went. Hurriedly she rounded the newel, the parlor table and reached for the front door.

He was standing with head bowed, hat in hand, and before he could say a word she spoke, "Oh, Jonah. I guess there's no word, huh? Poor little tyke. Poor little thing. Come on in here this minute and get yourself something to eat." He reluctantly followed her to the kitchen. Trudy always had a remedy for any problem, and it was more often than not getting food in a body. The fact that she had delivered almost every baby in and around Old Town for the past thirty some years gave her a special status in the community, and it wasn't often anyone refused her.

But Jonah persevered. Out of breath he continued. "I was hoping that Wes had found his way here, but I see that he didn't. Now, Miss Trudy, I've gotta get Bud and the McCoys. Young Reuben and me ran into some rustled cattle. They changed the brands of ours and the Swede's and Reuben's out there waiting for me to round up a posse. I've gotta get hold of Bud...don't have time for any supper."

She sat down hard on the kitchen rocker and began, "Lord, have mercy! When in the world did all this happen? Me and Luta and Bud was just talking about rustlers this very night."

"Miss Trudy, begging your pardon, ma'am, but I've gotta get hold of Bud. We gotta let the other cowmen know, and Young Reuben's out there all by himself, and we don't know where Layke and the others are, and..."

"Don't you tarry, son. You get over to Brewsters'. Won't take me but a minute to crisp up this slab and get the coffee going, and look here, I've even got some pone left over from supper."

"I've gotta get back to Young Reuben 'fore first light," he called back to her. "I'll eat later," and with that he was gone.

"Saints alive! Rustlers right here in Old Town. Well I never! Jonah, wait up, son, I'll get the lantern. Won't take me but a minute to light it," but he hadn't heard her. "Well, I'll light it anyway. They'll have need of it."

Jonah made his way along the dirt road to Brewster's stable and, dark as it was, managed to avoid the trough out front. He felt along the boards on the wall until he found the door latch. Knocking loudly, he called. Bud had been getting ready for bed but hadn't heard him 'til Frankie yelled out.

"Pa, who's at the door?" Rubbing the sleep out of his eyes, he waited for his pa to answer him before opening it. "Son, might be news of Wes. Here, let me get that," and when he opened the door, they stared at a frightened Jonah McCrea.

Didn't take them long to pull on their pants, get their jackets and rifles and swiftly walk to McCoys'. "Sure hope Erma and Martha aren't awake. Don't much think Palmer will be up to helping us out, Jonah. He's got a deuce of a cold."

"Maybe we can go get Leander and the other colored men from their quarters, Bud. They've got a stake in this too, you know." The colored people ran their few cows along with the local ranchers' cows. It saved driving them to nearby lumber camps or railheads, and they could be assured of getting top dollar from the Cuban markets.

Davis was leaning against the store window looking out toward Trudy's. The yellowed muslin curtains, thin with years of washing, were pulled back with the ribbon that Erma had put there long ago. When he saw Trudy's lamplight he knew something was up. He could barely see Jonah as he walked to Brewster's until Bud opened the door. "There's gotta be news of Wes." He had already called to his brother, and when Bud knocked, he was there waiting for them. "Palmer isn't up to helping out," is all he said. Bud could see the light shining from underneath Palmer's and Martha's door. He would have liked to check on him but knew that Jonah was anxious to get to the task of finding Wes and rounding up the rustlers. They hadn't even rounded the corner of the store when Trudy came with her lantern. "She's not going to give up on you, Jonah," Bud laughed. "Better go ahead and accept some rations or we'll never get this posse grouped." He and Davis headed for Leander's, about a quarter of a mile nearer the river, while Frankie and Trudy sat around Trudy's long pine table watching Jonah eat greedily. Bud and Davis talked as they followed the lantern light. "Maybe six men not counting Young Reuben won't be enough. Hell, Davis, we don't even know how many there are. No time to ride down to Charlie's. Best we see how many Leander can round up and then go back to Trudy's to make our plans."

"Yep. Good idea," Davis said. Bud thought, "Those McCoy brothers are men of few words. Man alive! Here we've got a runaway and a rustling and he talks with no more expression than if he was asking me how much coffee or flour Luta needs. The Lord sure made some peculiar folks, but they're the salt of the earth, they are. They're fine men, and we're lucky to have them in Old Town."

"Well, what did Leander say? Did they get the coffin finished? Does he know that Frankie couldn't wait for an answer from the telegram to Perry on account of Luta wanting him home from Ft. Fannin before dark?" Trudy was nervous and wouldn't give Bud or Davis a chance to answer.

"Good grief! Trudy. Take a breath."

Bud patted her hand as he said it and was afraid she was going to give in to her concern, but she pulled herself up short, took a deep breath and calmly said, "I know that Berta's got Aunt Willa all laid out for her folks to visit...little lost boy or not. Don't you think so, Davis?"

"For sure, Trudy. She knows her duty."

"Well, did the boys get the coffin finished, or not?" Bud answered, "Leander said that they'd leave Jefferson behind so he could put the finishing touches on it. You know how particular those two are."

"Yes, I surely do. They do fine work. Jefferson just told me that he and Cleda's girl Dollie were going to get married and stay right here in Old Town. That's good news, isn't it? Leander was afraid that he'd move away just like his other children did."

Trudy began clearing the table, and Bud and Davis decided to go out on the porch for a quick smoke while Frankie and Jonah discussed the rustling over in Kissimmee just a few weeks ago. They finalized their plans and waited for Leander and the rest to arrive.

"We know we'll have eight men. Wish we had time to ride down to Beattie's so's Charlie and his boys could help."

Frankie spoke up, "Heck, Pa, Jonah and me can leave right now and get there and back with them and be at North Prong 'fore first light. Can't we, Jonah? Heck, maybe even get a little rest in between the river road and the creek, huh? Then we can meet y'all there and go in together, and it'll give us four more. That for sure would give us enough."

Bud looked at his slow-talking son and thought, "He might talk slow, but he sure thinks fast," and proudly put his arm around his sturdy shoulders. "Good thinking, Frank. Good thinking." He was trying to call him Frank as Luta had requested. "He's almost a man grown, Hon. Time we started callin' him by his given name." She was right, he knew. He was already as tall as Bud and had filled out real good - baby fat turned into muscle almost overnight - and now he was thinking like a man.

Trudy was standing at the porch door when she heard them. Her emotions got the better of her as she looked at the two of them, and, sniffling, she left the room in a hurry. Heck, she'd brought both of 'em into this old world, and when she thought that, she thought of poor little Wes.

"Oh, poor Berta...poor thing." She called through her tears to Jonah and told him to go on up to the front bedroom when he got back to town, so's to catch a few winks. "Probably take the sheriff a day or two to get down here for the hanging." No one said a word. Boy, she's sure everything will go smoothly, they all thought. Never occurred to Miss Trudy that they'd not accomplish their mission. "And, Frankie, you and your pa and Davis come right on over here for your breakfast, too. No need in Luta havin' to get up that early..." They looked at each other and smiled. Miss Trudy sure loved to run things. Did a good job of it too, they all thought. She was second mama to most all of 'em.

****

"If I surprise them, then should be no trouble at all capturing 'em," Young Reuben thought as he stroked Cloud. He could see the glow of the campfire in the distance. He got off Cloud and tied him to a low branch. "Jonah and the posse can't possibly get back here before first light, and heck by then they might be on the trail with our beeves. Hell, I'm just not about to let that happen. Not this year or the next!" he exclaimed under his breath. "But I'd better make sure how many there are before making my move...surprise or not." He could now hear them talking back and forth and knew that there were at least two of them. He strained to hear what they were saying and tried to distinguish the voices but couldn't. "Some of 'em could have gone back to guard the beeves, but I didn't see a sign or hear 'em. Think I'll wait a while...they might be taking turns." He got to about twenty-five feet of them. He saw two real good, but it looked like there was a third one all bundled up on the other side of the fire. "Damn! If I knew that there weren't more of them with the beeves, it'd be a cinch," he said fingering his rope while his gun hand was on ready. About then Wes stood up and told the dark-haired, fat one that he had to go pee. Young Reuben got so excited when he saw him that he had to quickly stifle his outburst.

"Bose, ya better go wid that boy. Don't want no cat to gobble up our meal ticket, now do we?" And he laughed real hard when he said it.

"Now, Lou, I done told ya that we ain't gonna kidnap this youngun. Now get off it!" But he didn't say it with much conviction, and Young Reuben could see Wes's eyes get big in his white face; every tan freckle stuck out like a copper penny in the firelight, giving him an eerie expression.

"What the hell are they talking about...KIDNAP! My God! He must be scared to death...KIDNAP!" He heard the rustle of the dry brush not twenty feet behind him and couldn't figure out why the rustlers hadn't heard it too. "Probably their replacements. Good, now I'll see how many I've got to get rid of. Yep, that's who they are, walking right up to them..." When he heard, "Hello there," he recognized Layke's deep bass voice and saw the rustler beside the fire go for his gun. Rapidly Young Reuben fired, getting him in his gun arm, and when Swede jumped out in front of Layke, gun drawn, Layke hit the brush, and Young Reuben yelled, "Layke, there's another one, and he has Wes!" But before Layke could use his whip, the one called Bose came out of the shadows, Wes in front of him, shielding him.

"I don't want to hurt this boy..."

"You touch one hair on his head, and you're a dead man. I'll blow you to kingdom come, Mister!" Young Reuben said as he stepped from behind the pine and into the light. "Swede, get a bead on the one writhing on the ground. These two rustled our cattle and changed the brands."

"Did Charlie's, too. Me and Layke found them."

"I said I'd go for your head, mister!"

Bose tried to scrunch down behind a squirming, kicking and yelling Wes but realized that he didn't have a chance in hell of getting away with it, so he let Wes go as he dropped his gun and raised his arms in surrender. Wes ran to Layke and was in his strong arms by the time Swede and Young Reuben got to the men. Swede said, "We saw just the one, so thought the others were guarding the beeves. Whew! I'm sure glad you were here. Think I'd have got him though."

Young Reuben was busy getting the two tied up. "How does this big old scruffy rope feel, boys? Its gonna feel real bad around your no-good necks, but we'll have to wait for the posse comin' in from Old

Town before we take you in. Gonna be hard, Swede. I'm just itching to send these two to Mister Satan, so he can have himself a nice hot supper, aren't you?"

"Hell, Reuben, he'd spit 'em out. Ain't even fit for the devil himself." He wrapped Lou's bloody arm with his handkerchief and said, "Sure don't want you to die before the hanging, Mister."

They decided that Young Reuben should take the prisoners on into Old Town. He'd probably get there before the posse even left. Swede would stay and guard the cattle, and Layke with Wes holding on tightly rode Bucko back to South Spring and Berta. "Just wait 'til your mama sees who I've got on Bucko. Boy will she be one happy mama," and he squeezed Wes's arms as they sped home on the river road.

****

Old Town had another hanging on the oak tree back of Trudy's. Hadn't been but a year and a half since R.J. and Joe Bob Skinner had twirled round and round on that very same tree.

Trudy said, "First we bury Aunt Willa respectful like, because she was a good woman and will be mightily missed. Then we've gotta hang these no-good varmints."

And as on the day that the Skinners were hanged there came up a ferocious storm, unusual for an early March day. It was more like the dog days of summer, when it was so hot that the first few drops that hit the ground turned into hissing steam. The wind blew in gusting waves increasing with every gust, and through the stinging white sheets of rain, Trudy called back to Berta while trying to shield her face with her drenched hat, "You don't argue with the Lord. Nosiree. He's gonna have his say and his way, just like he did before. I think he's talking to us right now, Berta." They sought the safety of Trudy's warm kitchen. "I'll get the fire stoked for the men's coffee, Berta, and you, young lady, get yourself up to your room and get changed into something pretty and girl-like before that handsome husband of yours gets here. And, Berta, SuSu and I'll take care of the twins, so you and Layke can do some socializing. Luta and Bud want just the two of you to eat supper with them. Now don't you protest. I've made up my mind."

Berta turned back from the narrow stairs. Hugging her friend to her said, "You are a perceptive woman, Trudy Stucky. How could you tell that Layke and I needed time alone?"

"I had a love once, my dear. He was the love of my life, just like

Layke is yours. The same fire...the same passion for life. But he was killed at the battle of Ocean Pond or Olustee, as some folks call it, and for the life of me I can't forget. Oh...I can tell when two people need time alone. I can tell." She brushed away the tears that managed to slip out.

"I love you, Trudy. And so does Layke."

****

"Berta, I'm proud of you. Very proud." Layke was turned away from her putting his hat on the mahogany dresser that had come from Alabama with the Stuckys on their ox-cart.

She went to him, turned him around and looking up got a catch in her throat before asking, "What do you mean, Hon?" Shaking her blond head in confusion.

"You've just been through a terrible time, what with Wes and Willa, and yet you had the compassion to allow Wes to return to South Spring so he could spend the night with Dan. Now, that, my love, told me that my wife has as much heart as..."

"What are you doing, Layke Williams!" she exclaimed as he swiftly lifted her and carried her right to the bed.

He continued loudly, "As much heart as PASSION."

"Shush! For heavens sake everyone in the boarding house will hear you," she said giggling. "I think Bud gave you too much shine," and she rolled over and went to the other side of the bed. She wanted to say, "Bet you can't catch me, Layke Williams," but knew that would be as silly as any school girl. But she wanted to, anyway, and Layke knew it.

He lunged across the bed for her. Jumping back she hit the wall between their room and Trudy's with a thud, and, stifling a giggle, she reached for her playful husband, breathlessly exclaiming, "Trudy better be a hard sleeper or she's going to be in here to see if we're all right."

"Oh, my darling girl, we're just fine, and she knows it. After all she's the one who arranged this rendezvous. Come here. I can't wait any longer. And, my sweet, the first thing we're going to do when we get back to South Spring is move the twins out of our room and in with SuSu. Now, don't protest. Wes has agreed to move up to the loft with Jonah. He's a big boy now."

"My, my. Haven't you been a busy feller, though. Busy, busy, busy!"

"Not another word, my sweet. Shush. Not another word."

"Oh, Layke. I need you so...." She hurriedly unbuttoned her pale grey jacket.

****

"Look, Ma, I gotta bite!" Wes called excitedly back to Berta, who was lounging beside Layke on their river landing.

She rose and went toward him, "Well, for heaven's sake, pull it up." Turning back to Layke with a smile she said, "Now you'd think that he just learned how to fish, wouldn't you?" She ruffled his blond head as she teased him. "Throw it back, honey. It's too small to keep. Not that way. Here let me help you." Wes relinquished the squirming perch, and Berta said, "Push the hook through gently so you won't tear its mouth...see, like this." The fish splashed loudly and swam happily off toward the middle of the dark red river. "Now it can eat a lot and get big enough to become a keeper."

Layke spoke up, "I bet it's telling its mama about what an exciting adventure it just had, Wes, and about how a beautiful blond princess saved its life, huh?" He pulled Berta to him and kissed her soundly.

Layke had decided to not accompany the other cowmen on the annual drive to Punta Rassa as he had been doing for the last thirteen years. When he told Berta of his decision, she was delighted. Having him gone for those five or six weeks was more than she wanted to handle. She had been so run-down since the twins' birth almost a year ago that the very thought of his being away made her more nervous than ever.

Since Wes's near kidnapping, they had made it a point to spend more time with him. SuSu and Aimee had been given the job of watching over the active twins. Berta had started them on table food earlier than she had the other babies, and her strength was finally coming back. SuSu loved the responsibility, but Berta saw to it that she had her free time for the other things she loved. She and Aimee still practiced on the tight rope, not that Aimee planned to ever return to the act, but just because they enjoyed it. SuSu continued to do beautiful handwork, just like her ma, and amazed Berta and Layke with her skill.

"She should have dance lessons, Layke. I've never seen anyone move with such grace, have you? She seems to glide when she walks, doesn't she?"

"Where could we take her for lessons way out here, Honey? You've given her piano lessons, and I think she does very well with her recitations, even though she's shy and doesn't project as the others do."

"But, Honey, she's thirteen years old and fast becoming a lady. Oh, I was just dreaming, I guess. I want so much for our children to have some polish, don't you?"

"You know I do," he answered while holding the ecru yarn as she rewound it. They were sitting on the front porch of their small house, that had been built by Reuben's Uncle Elon many years ago. It was a typical, heart pine, four-room house with a sleep loft like most in the area. The front porch ran the length of the house and the steeply pitched, cedar shake roof extended over the back stoop. "I also want to add onto the house. Think I'll ask Leander and Jefferson to help as soon as the men get back from the drive."

Berta was beside herself with excitement. "Honey, you know how much I want it. Maybe two rooms, huh? And a wrap-around porch like Mary and Pierce have. Oh, Layke, thank you. But can we afford it? I know we did very well last year with the beeves, but, Honey, with Young Reuben back home and the expense of the deMoyas...well, it seems to me that..."

"Hey, lady of mine, would I suggest it if we couldn't afford it? You know me better than that."

"I'm sorry. I'm so used to worrying about the next meal that I forgot what a smart man I captured for myself, Sir." She got up from her rocker, sat on his lap and kissed the top of his dark brown hair.

"Is that all I can expect from such a generous offer, young lady, a kiss on my head?"

"Well, sir, in the middle of the day and with a half dozen people wandering around, I believe that is all you'll get." She jumped off his lap and ran inside laughing as Layke rapidly followed.

When he saw Orlean at the stove, he winked at her and said, "Orlean, the honeymoon is over."

"Layke, for heavens sake, can't we have any secrets? Gracious!" But she too winked at the smiling Orlean and took the knife from her and began chopping the onions.

Layke had not confided all his secrets to his wife. He had been considering running for the state senate. He hadn't fully made up his mind but had to before the year's end. Senator Stiles' term would be up, and he knew - at least that's what the papers stated - that he was not going to seek another term. He still loved being a cowman but felt that with Young Reuben and Jonah back home, plus the deMoya brothers, everything would run smoothly and that they would be able to handle the financial responsibilities. He, too, wanted their children to have more opportunities than Old Town afforded them. It was a wonderful place for the young, but Wes was going on nine, and, as Berta said, SuSu was a young lady. They could accompany him to Tallahassee when the senate was in session and attend a private school. SuSu could have her lessons and Wes...and on he planned. It never occurred to him that he might lose the election.

Berta and Layke and the younger children were in town for the day. The deMoyas had remained at South Spring to handle the stock and prepare the meals for Dan and Zeke. Berta and Orlean had taken over that job - they were sure that they'd not eat properly since Willa's death. Leander's daughter, Annie, had been doing the laundry, so Berta had more free time to go to town with Wes and SuSu on their school days. They attended three days a week, and Etienne deMoya taught them French when he could be spared from chores. Since Layke had not gone on the drive, he accompanied them as well. They especially enjoyed Wednesdays in town, for that was the day the *Suwannee Queen* arrived with the mail. Berta was hoping for another letter from Mary Garvin, whom she and Layke had visited while on their honeymoon at her and Pierce's Bullseye Ranch outside of Crescent City.

The loud whistle sounded over the tree tops and up the high bluff toward town. Every kid around seemed to pop out of nowhere and run toward it.

"Wes, you be careful! SuSu watch your little brother!" She turned toward Layke and saw his expression. "Well, you know how rambunctious he is. He'll be all over that boat, probably swinging from the lookout." She had become so protective of him since he ran away that she was having difficulty letting go. She and Layke had discussed it numerous times, but she'd react before she could catch herself. SuSu's long brown skirt prevented her from keeping up with Wes as they ran toward the porch. She had been elected to give out the mail by Beau Sawyer, Captain George's youngest son, who anyone with eyes could tell was sweet on her. Wes was upset that he hadn't been chosen 'cause he could read just as well as his sister, and he let everyone gathered on Trudy's porch know it, too.

"Now, son," Layke began...

"She always gets to give it out! Just because that dumb old Beau Sawyer thinks she's pretty..."

"Wes, that's enough." Layke interrupted. "Now look here, young man," he said holding Wes's arm as he tried to grab the mail from his sister.

"I said that is enough."

He turned to see Berta taking her letter upstairs to Trudy's room and wondered who it was from. "SuSu, who did your mama hear from? Mary Garvin?" She didn't know, she said. He was curious, but not enough to follow her. She seemed so far away when she heard from Mary. He followed Trudy into the kitchen and sat sipping the hot, strong coffee she had poured for him.

She could see that something was bothering him, so she said, "Berta is so anxious to find out if Callie Meade and Mary's boy, Thom, are going to wed at the end of the drive that she couldn't wait to read that letter."

"We all need our privacy, Trudy. All of us." What he didn't say was, "But I don't like Berta keeping things from me. She hasn't even mentioned Thom's and Callie's wedding, or if there's going to be one, in I don't know how long."

He was so quiet that Trudy felt she'd better not interfere. Layke Williams was a deep man, not a bit like Reuben. Him she could read, but not Layke. She left him to his coffee with, "I'll be on the porch, Layke. Help yourself to the coffee."

Berta ripped the letter open even before she got to the door. "I wonder if she and the girls went up to Jacksonville and Savannah on the *Robert E. Lee*, and if she saw...them."

March, 27, 1880

My Dear Friend,

I am sorry it has taken me so long to answer your very interesting letters, but time has not permitted it. As I wrote before, on February 14, the girls, Lucinda and Sarah and I had planned a trip, at your suggestion, I might add, on the beautiful steamship, Robert E. Lee, but to our dismay we were unable to secure passage and instead were able to board the Savannah on January the 20th. Berta, I cannot thank you enough for telling me about what a glorious trip it would be. We found the shops in Jacksonville, Savannah and Palatka to be as delightful as you described, and the meals were excellent. The girls and I met such interesting people from every part of the country who were planning on relocating in our beautiful state. They seemed interested in everything we said and made us feel so important.

Shortly after we arrived home we had a visit from that Greer family, the big ranchers from up near Palatka. That daughter of theirs, Marthanne, has been after Thom, seems like forever, and no matter how many times he tells her that he's betrothed to Callie Meade, that girl just won't give up.

Well I finally got the courage to tell that little trouble maker to get off of Bullseye and to not come back. Can you believe I could have done such a thing? I think that our boat trip put some extra starch in my spine.

Berta lowered the page. "She's keeping something from me. More went on than she's telling. Thom's a very handsome young man, and after all, Callie is way down state. She's worried, I can tell. Oh, well." She resumed reading, eager yet apprehensive of what the letter held.
So, dear one, if nothing prevents, there shall be a wedding in Tater Hill Bluff at the end of the drive, and I do so hope that you and your family will be there to celebrate the union of our children. And, yes, before I forget, we did see and talk to the girl you mentioned, Juanita, and saw the man she'd taken up with, the gambler, so handsome my dear...

The letter quickly found its way to the floor. She was afraid to read further. "What has come over me? I can't believe I'd let a chance meeting with *that gambler* get me so flustered...so curious. Heavens...I didn't even recognize him at first. I wonder how he knew me after all those years. What would Layke think if he knew what a ninny he'd married?" Her hands were shaking uncontrollably.

BOOK TWO:

THE TALL TEN RANCH

CHAPTER I
TATER HILL BLUFF, FLORIDA

Callie paced back and forth on the porch of Jeeters' Dry Goods store. She just couldn't seem to get a handle on the new way of acting now that she was a betrothed lady.

"Why can't Clay and me be just like we've always been?" and she glared at old Gus Jeeters. "He gives me the willies every time I look at him. Why, it's barely more than a year that he couldn't do enough for me after Thom and me found some of the doubloons that the Skinner Gang buried. Boy howdy! He couldn't say enough sweet, gushy old things to me then. And now...well, he glares at me with those old bug eyes, just daring me to give even one little smile at Clay. He ought to know that Clay Willett and me have always been best friends, and if Thom were here, the three of us would be sitting around talking, and no one would have a thing to say about it. I'm sick of it! I'm sick of the whole blessed mess!"

Callie was in Tater Hill Bluff and it was week's end. The Meades spent Saturday night in town at Thom's Aunt Beulah's and Uncle George's hotel and would return to their ranch, Tall Ten, after church on Sunday. Since her betrothal she had to be accompanied by her folks to all the shindigs, and the restraint had taken its toll. Tomboy Callie had always been free.

As she looked at Clay stock the canned goods on the shelf behind the counter, she was aware that he knew she was watching. He'd glance her way once in a while, smile, then resume his work. He wasn't ignoring her, and he wasn't shy, but he'd been warned by his Uncle Gus and Aunt Ione that he had to know his place with Callie now that she was spoken for, and he felt that out of respect he should abide by the custom. But the more he felt her watching him the more he wanted to drop everything and head for the porch.

She looked so pretty in the soft, gold, polished cotton dress. The color made the lights in her rich brown hair spark fire red. He remembered when Mrs. Meade had purchased the fabric and was glad that she had decided on the beige lace instead of the white, that she had sewn around the deep bertha collar and leg-o-mutton sleeves. Callie was so soft and feminine looking. He could even smell her jasmine perfume, that he knew was a gift from Thom. He'd given it to her before the last drive to Punta Rassa, and she was especially fond of it.

Clay was taller than Thom by a couple of inches, slender but not skinny, with intelligent, gray eyes and thick, wavy, reddish-brown hair above a strong, square face. His hands were manly but somehow pretty; they'd never worked a whip nor rustled a calf to the ground and were more at home holding a pen or pencil. He wore a plain blue work shirt and overalls and was neat and clean.

He seemed to have always been a lot older than Callie. If anyone needed to know anything, they'd ask Clay, or if they needed advice, he'd be asked - even by the oldsters. But when it came to Callie Anders Meade, he was jelly. She was truth, honesty, strength and beauty, and he had worshiped her from the minute she kicked wet sand onto his new overalls her first day at school. She was but six and he an aging nine.

Somehow he knew he'd never have Callie, not that he felt unworthy - Clay knew his worth - but, for whatever reason, he felt that if he pursued her, he'd be interfering with a master plan.

His Uncle Gus went to the back storage room. "If I walk out onto the porch now...Why am I analyzing this? Why can't I act spontaneously? Must I always evaluate everything?" He became mellow. "Callie is sun - she's light - she's energy - she's all the things I'm not but would like to be. Why can't I just walk out there and say very nonchalantly, 'Hi Callie, I'm going to walk down to Big Spring. Wanta join me?' Why can't I say that?" But he couldn't.

Gus and Ione Jeeters were not Clay's blood relatives. They had taken him and his mother into their home after Clay's father died of the fever. Clay was not yet two, and his mother taught piano and helped out at the school as Miss Taylor's assistant in order to supplement their income. Having no children of their own, the Jeeters treated Clay as theirs, and Callie got plumb put out with them. They bossed him around just like he was their own son, and it burned her up that they thought just because she was spoken for that she and Clay had to stay apart.

The whole town was proud of Clay but no more than Callie. His ma kept a scrapbook jammed full of his articles that had appeared in the *Tampa Tribune* and showed them to everyone who'd take time to look. The article he did on Callie's brother Jay, about when he took his stuffed animals and birds and pen and ink drawings to the state fair in Gainesville, was Callie's favorite. She kept a clipping of it on her dresser, and every time she saw *"by Clay W. Willett"* in the headline, she got such a knot in her throat she could hardly swallow.

When Gus returned to the front of the store, Clay was still stacking the cans, and Callie, disgusted and bored, had decided to give up and had gone back to the hotel.

"Guess I'm supposed to twiddle my thumbs 'til supper time," she said aloud as she plopped down on the quilt covered bed. "Maybe I'll go to Maida's and Marta's room for a visit," then decided that she'd rather look out the bedroom window at the people passing by than to have to listen to Thom's cousins' girl talk. "Wish I'd brought my pants. I'd ride BeeBee to Big Spring and fish," but she knew her ma'd have a fit if she got her dress dirty. She was supposed to be real careful so she could wear it to church the next morning.

There weren't a lot of rules in the Meade household, but one was that when they went to town on Saturday, she and Jay were to remain in town and keep their clothes clean for church on Sunday. Kate did not think that was too much to ask of her children, especially since Callie was supposed to have put aside her tomboy ways.

They'd arrive about noon, have their big meal with Beulah and George Young, their girls and the other boarders, take their afternoon naps, visit their friends and shop for the week's supplies. There was always a new shipment that had come in on the steamboats that came up the Peace River from Charlotte Harbor. After supper they'd gather in the front parlor to sing old hymns or George's favorites while Beulah played the piano, and Parker and Jay would duck out to join the other men for a game of checkers or the telling of the tales on the Barnes brothers' porch next door to the hotel.

Callie and the other young ladies would go upstairs to the girls' room to giggle and gossip, look at magazines, or Maida would read aloud. She was real talented that way, and Callie would be bored near 'bout to death. She'd much rather have been with her pa and Jay on Barnes' porch or, better yet, back at Tall Ten, like she used to be allowed, watching Jam and Slick play cards and get high as a kite on shine. They were so comical when they told their stories. Boy howdy, they told some real knee slappers. But no...she was now promised to Thom Garvin, and her life had become just one long nothing...day in and day out while she waited for their wedding to be held right after the spring drive to Punta Rassa.

As she sat staring out the bedroom window, she saw her brother Jay and Sap, their colored housekeeper Mattie's boy, walk past Mae's Boarding House. Mattie had allowed Sap to come to town with them, but he was staying at his sister Zinnia's cabin, 'cause he wasn't allowed to stay in the hotel.

Callie brightened up. "Bet they're headed for the spring. I can't stand it in this old hotel another minute. I'll be real careful and just sit on the cleanest log I can find." She was out that door in a flash, her long, muscled legs flying down the stairs. She looked neither right nor left and headed for the wooden sidewalk, where she caught up with them.

"Hey, Jay, y'all goin' to Big Spring?" she asked quietly for fear her folks might be around somewhere.

Jay rolled his eyes at Sap and replied, "Why you wanta know, Callie? You know you can't go with us. Might get your under drawers dirty," and he laughed as he hit Sap, who was his best friend in the whole world, on the shoulder. "Can't be traipsing all over now that you're promised, now can you?"

That did it! They weren't going to poke fun at her. Not that brat brother and Sap. "Not on your best day, James Parker Meade. Not on your best one." she declared to herself. She decided a smile would mask her true feelings. She smiled sweetly, "Oh, I was just wondering where you were going so I could tell Ma. She and Aunt Beulah are over at Mrs. Pritchard's working on the church quilt, and I was sure she'd be concerned of your whereabouts."

Jay couldn't get over how prissy his sister had become. Boy, she talked fancier than Marta or Maida Young, just the snootiest girls in all of Tater Hill, she did. "Well, if you really want to know, Sap and I are going to mosey over to Will Jones' place to take a look at that big cat he shot over near Nocatee. And since you aren't interested in seeing an old dead cat, you needn't ask to tag along."

"Why is he being so mean? He knows I'm bored 'bout to death, and it wouldn't hurt one bit if I went along. I'd be willin' to make book that those two are sneakin' off and going fishing and don't want me to know it." Callie wasn't going to give them a bit of satisfaction, so she said, "You're right. Looking at an old shot-up cat is certainly not my idea of how to spend an afternoon," and she drew up her five and a half feet and held her head high in her most queen-like pose.

Abruptly she turned and began to walk away from them but changed her mind. She simply had to get in the last word. She planted her hands firmly on her hips and bent from the waist, her face not a foot from Jay's, and yelled real loud, hoping that everyone passing by would hear, "If you come back smellin' of stinking old fish, Jay Meade, I'm sure Pa will have a bunch of words to say to you, Mister...Smarty Pants" she added under her breath. Sure enough, heads turned and with her mission accomplished she triumphantly marched back to the hotel knowing that Jay was so mad at her that he was about to pop.

When Callie got inside she realized that she was alone. Not even Rube, Beulah's hired hand, was around. She had about three hours before supper and knew that she'd simply die if she had to spend all that time listening to the girls.

"I'll not. I absolutely will not!" she said. She turned and walked rapidly to Jeeters' store and Clay, the only person she wanted to be with in the entire town. Heavens, Thom wouldn't care. He knew she loved him and only him. It was just such long times between visits. She hadn't seen him since the state fair way last August, five long months ago.

Before changing her mind, she said, "Good afternoon, Mr. Jeeters." She didn't see Clay anywhere but knew that he'd have to be in the back. Saturday was their busiest day of the week, so he'd be needed to help out. She gulped hard and continued, "Is Clay around? I'd like to speak to him if I may," she added very lady-like.

Gus looked at her suspiciously. "Why does she want him? She best not be causing him any trouble. She's up to something!"

Aloud, he said, "Well, Miss Callie, I believe he stepped into the back room. I'll call him."

"Gus," Mrs. Winthrop called, "Tell Clay that Orry wants a pouch of tobacco, too."

"Will do, Ida."

He called to Clay as he pushed the blue floral curtains aside. They came out together, Clay with the tobacco and sacks of flour and meal. He looked quizzically at Callie. Gus Jeeters took it all in, even while Ida Winthrop was bending his ear about the weevils she'd found in the last sack of flour she'd bought. He tried his darndest to overhear Callie as she spoke to Clay but couldn't make out a word for Ida's chatter.

Callie swallowed hard. "I've come this far," she thought, "So there's no backing down."

"Clay, there'll be singing in the parlor at the hotel after supper. Why don't you plan on dropping by? Everyone'll be there, and gracious, I haven't talked with you, seems like forever."

"That would be nice, Callie," he responded quickly. "I'll drop by soon as I finish up here." He actually blushed. So did Callie, she was so excited, and Gus didn't have to hear their words.

"She's struck pay dirt!" he grunted. "We're in for trouble."

"What'd you say, Gus?" Ida turned and asked.

"Oh, nothing, Ida. Tell Orry I hope he starts to feeling better, heah?"

"I'll do that. G'day to ya and I'll see Ione at Sunday school first thing in the mornin'."

Callie left in a hurry, her legs feeling rubbery. Not like when Thom kissed her - gracious no - nothing in the entire world could feel like that. "Gracious me, my whole, entire body is tingling just thinking of Thom's kisses." Oh, but she was excited. "Now I can stand the next three hours," she thought as she sought the dark of her room.

****

Beulah and Kate cleared away the empty plates while Callie and Marta scraped the scraps into mama cat's bowl, as George's hound Mike sat patiently outside the screen door waiting for his share. Maida put the bits of corn bread, biscuits and cold grits in a pan and set it aside for the chickens the next morning.

The mantel clock chimed seven o'clock, and Callie anxiously checked it to make sure she had heard it correctly. Then it chimed 7:30, and Callie couldn't figure out why Beulah hadn't begun playing the piano. There they sat, she, Kate and Louise Pritchard around the parlor table sewing the binding onto the church quilt and taking their own sweet time, Callie thought. When Kate told her that there wouldn't be any singing because they simply had to finish the quilt that very night for it to be completed in time for the church raffle, Callie almost had a fit.

"Good grief! Clay'll come over expecting some of the men to be here and will find a parlor full of women just a- sewing and chatting. Not even Uncle George around," she mumbled under her breath as she ran for the porch to head Clay off.

The door handle was wrenched out of her hand as Clay opened it. She noticed that he had changed his clothes, putting on his very best waistcoat. His dark hair was slicked down and smelling of fresh pine. Quickly looking around she realized no one was about. She tugged at Clay's shirt sleeve pulling him back onto the porch and quietly closed the door.

"Oh Clay, I'm so glad you came over." She couldn't see his face clearly in the half-light, but she knew just what his expression would be. She had studied his handsome face enough times, goodness knows.

Rushing to continue before he could reply she said, "There's just a bunch of women in the parlor working on the church quilt. I thought there'd be a sing, as usual, but Ma said they had to finish it tonight, so the men headed for the livery stable. I'm sorry."

"It doesn't matter, Callie." The clock chimed eight o'clock.

"Let's sit over here a while and visit," she said, gesturing toward the rockers that were away from the light. "Mosquitoes aren't bad since we've had so little rain."

They sat quietly then both began speaking at the same time. Laughing, they relaxed and Clay started talking just like he used to. Oh, she could listen to him forever - he was so intelligent and interesting and had such a beautiful way with words.

"I'm never bored when I'm with him. I wonder if I'll be bored with Thom after we're wed?" She laughed to herself. "We don't talk much except about the ranch and...what do we talk about?" She couldn't think of much more than the cattle drives and ranching in general. They never seemed to talk about the same things that she and Clay discussed. But when she thought of Thom something happened to her entire body - she burned all over. "We'll think of something, I'm sure," she thought.

"Oh, I'm sorry, Clay. My mind was wandering, I guess. Please continue." He told her about when General Zachary Taylor led his men clear down to the Big Lake, Okeechobee, while chasing the Seminoles into the Everglades; and about how Dr. Lykes gave up his doctoring to build the sailing ships, so he could have a way to take the beeves to Cuba and Key West; and how way up in Tallahassee they had just voted to sell all the land from Kissimmee all the way past Lake Okeechobee and on to the Gulf, so a man named Disston could drain the Kissimmee basin and more settlers could move there.

She listened and asked questions and thought, "I don't know if I can stand not listening to Clay talk for the rest of my life. I don't think I can stand it."

Callie wasn't conscious of his holding her hand - neither was he. It was so natural being close. She didn't see nor hear the door open behind her and was startled when Marta said, "Why, there you are, Callie. We were all wondering where you'd run off to." She cleared her throat before asking suspiciously, "Oh, is that you, Clay? What on earth are you two doing out here in the pitch black anyway?" and the way she said it made them know that it'd be all over town before church the next day, and they'd both be in for a tongue lashing. Clay stood up dropping Callie's hand, the gesture not going undetected by Marta, and calmly said, "Hello, Marta. Callie and I were discussing the new business transaction that the state entered into with Hamilton Disston concerning the purchase of the Kissimmee Basin."

She looked from one to the other, and they could both read her mind. "Sure you were, Clay. I'll just bet that's what was going on. Wait 'til cousin Thom hears about this, Miss two-timing Callie Meade. Just you wait!" she thought.

Aloud she said, "And what did this Mr. Disston do, Clay?" He started to respond but Callie quickly spoke up, "Clay thought that I should know about all the land he is buying, Marta. He thinks that it will affect Thom's and my life...after we're married, that is, and he thought I should know about it. You know me. I seldom read a paper. Gracious, the whole world could go topsy turvy, and I'd not even know it." She laughed a small laugh, while not taking her eyes off of Marta.

Taking Clay's hand, squeezing it slightly to thank him, she continued, "Thanks, Clay. I know Thom will appreciate it when I write him about the news. I'm going up to my room this very minute before I forget just how you explained it. If Thom were here, I know he'd be grateful too." Lightly she said, "See ya," and turned toward Marta.

"Marta, are you coming back in?" She took her by the arm and in a secretive voice so Clay couldn't hear said, "I think Clay Willett is just about the nicest young man in all of Tater Hill. I can't for the life of me believe that you and Maida haven't given him some consideration."

Marta pursed her lips tight together and thought, "You're not gonna get out of this one, Miss Smartie Callie Meade. Everyone in this entire town knows that Clay's been sweet on you for almost forever and has never even looked at another girl. I just think I'd best get a letter off to Cousin Thom tonight, too."

She turned to Callie and removed her arm. "Why, Callie, how you do carry on," and she left Callie standing at the bottom of the stairs as she raced upstairs to start her letter...she was salivating.

CHAPTER II
THOM'S DILEMMA

"I don't believe who's riding up here! I just don't believe it," Mary Garvin said to Risa, who was finishing up the dinner dishes. Removing her apron and straightening her house dress, faded into light blue from its many washings, she pushed the strands of dark hair that had loosened from her bun back from her forehead before going out to meet her guests. She turned back to Risa and said, "Go get the Mister and tell him that the Greers are here. I'll declare to you here and now if he knew that they were coming for a visit and forgot to tell me, I'll...I'll...oh, I don't know what I'll do to him." As she put her welcome smile on for the Greers, she said under her breath, "But I'll think of something, Pierce Garvin."

Here I am in this old wash dress, barely presentable, and..."Well, well, just look who's come for a visit! I just sent Risa down to the barn to summon Pierce." She addressed her next remark to Madge Greer, who was climbing slowly out of the buggy. "Why didn't you let me know you were coming to Crescent City, Madge? Why, I'd have had Risa bake something special for you."

Madge and Jacob Greer, both tall and bone-thin and as homely as two people could possibly be, and who were much too old to be trying to raise a rambunctious, headstrong daughter like Marthanne, met Mary on the sand path that led up to the wrap-around front porch. Out of the back of the buggy rose Marthanne, who had obviously been sleeping. With a scowl on her perturbed face she muttered about what a mess she must look, what with her hair all askew, and Mary wanted to say, "What difference could it possibly make, 'cause my Thom is taken, young lady."

She noticed that Marthanne had put on quite a bit of weight since she had last seen her at the state fair. "If I didn't know better, I'd think she was with child," but then quickly dismissed the thought.

Madge and Jacob had inherited their ranch, Deep Spring, west of Palatka, from Madge's father Ben. They raised two orphaned boys and thought that they'd never have children of their own when lo and behold, when Madge was almost forty-two and Jacob forty-eight years old, Marthanne made her appearance. She was beautiful from the day she was born with spun gold ringlets and saucer-sized, deep blue eyes, and as she grew older she became tall and slender with an hourglass figure. It was difficult for anyone, including the Greers themselves, to believe that they could have had such a beautiful child.

Anything Marthanne ever wanted, her doting parents gave her, money being no object. Her expensive clothes were purchased in New York City when Madge accompanied her there twice a year, and they stayed at the fanciest hotels and dined at the most expensive restaurants. When they returned to Deep Spring, Madge would invite her few Palatka friends for tea and entertainingly tell about their exploits in the exciting city.

The Greers wanted Marthanne to attend Miss Bolivar's Girls School in Savannah, but Marthanne had set her cap for one Thomas Pierce Garvin of the Bullseye Ranch outside of Crescent City when she was but fifteen and didn't want so much distance between them. So her parents allowed her to remain at Deep Spring and had a tutor come several times a week for her lessons. They weren't too disappointed about her decision. As Madge often said, "My Marthanne is all I live for," and everyone knew that the same could be said for Jacob.

Marthanne talked her parents into inviting the Garvins to Deep Spring for visits several times a year, but Mary had managed to beg off with some excuse or another. So Jacob, at Marthanne's insistence, began coming to Bullseye under the pretext of purchasing some of Pierce's stock. They did have distant cousins in Crescent City, and Madge always said that she and Marthanne came along so they could visit them, but Mary knew that they stayed at Mary Edward's Boarding House and hardly even visited them at all.

On these visits, Thom had a difficult time escaping Marthanne. If he was hunting down a bunch quitter, she'd be there pretending she was out for a ride. If he was in the corral or in the barn or at the groves, she'd think up some excuse to be there. Everywhere he went Marthanne miraculously appeared. He had to admit that she was some looker, and boy, was she ever put together. Around him she was sugar sweet, hanging onto his every word and praising every little thing he did. Thom didn't exactly see through her act, but he did feel uneasy around her, not like when he was around Callie.

When his pa told him that the Greers had arrived, he and his brother Thurmond headed for the barn. They knew she'd soon find them, but Thom was determined to make it difficult for her. "Hell, Thom," Thurmond whispered, "that girl even thinks your farts smell like honeysuckle," and he hit him a good one. Thom had noticed that Thurmond had given her the once over on more than one occasion and retaliated, "Bet you wish yours were as sweet as mine. I saw your eyes bulge out as you checked out her tits. Now don't go denying it! Oh, man, were you ever licking your chops - couldn't get your eyes past 'em."

"Well its hard to when they're 'bout to pop every button on her blouse and come tumblin' out. Hell, there ain't a hand around here that doesn't have a bulge in his pants when she prisses past 'em."

Thurmond and Thom were only a year and a half apart and were very close. Thurmond took after Mary's side of the family. He was not quite five feet nine with a good set of shoulders and his grandpa Johnson's barrel chest, strong as an ox and the undisputed joker of the family, whereas Thom was tall, well built and by far the handsomest of the Garvin children. He was personality plus, never knew a stranger, having the ability to put them at ease, and had mastered difficult rope and riding tricks to entertain and delight his family and friends. Everything came so easily to Thom.

Sure enough, Marthanne found them with little effort. They were outside the barn laughing and joking, and she tried to hear what they were saying but couldn't. They hadn't acknowledged her presence, and that perturbed her. She knew they knew she was there by the way they were acting, and she was used to being made over, but they continued to ignore her.

"I'll have you in this very barn before I leave Bullseye, Mister Thomas Garvin. You just wait, Mister. If that Monti Fiske thinks he's gonna have me, he can think again!" She whirled around and walked back toward the main house. "I'll wait 'til near dark, when you return to the barn, Mr. Garvin, and I'll make sure you're alone." She laughed confidently.

Mary had felt obliged to invite the Greers for supper and was in the summer kitchen giving her Bahama Island cook instructions. "Nothing fancy, Risa, just some chicken salad, and slice the ham real thin and roll it around the tiniest sweet pickles you can find. You'll have to make an extra pan of biscuits, and I think the remaining pound cake will be enough with the spiced peaches and pears. I'll send Lucinda in to help you. Just put everything on the sideboard, and we'll set the table on the side porch. I'll declare I'm really put out with these people!" she said tiredly.

Mary had looked so worn out since she had returned from the state fair in Gainesville last August that when she mentioned a trip on the St. Johns River on one of the large steamships, Pierce thought that it was a wonderful idea. He suggested that she take the two oldest daughters and that they stay for an entire week, going all the way to Savannah and then back to Jacksonville and Palatka. He did ask that they make their journey before the cow hunt began in March, so they did.

Risa was as perturbed as her mistress. Not that she minded the cooking - she didn't, but she was concerned about her mistress. "Ma'am Mary, you go get yourself some rest. Me and Lucinda take care of everything. Don't you fret, Ma'am." Her concern was apparent to Mary. "Oh, I'm fine. Its just so demanding having to be nice to these people. As my mother would have said, 'they've got no more manners than a billy goat at a clothesline,' and she'd have been right. They could have easily wired town, and Hank Jones would have sent someone out to tell us...but no...they just show up unannounced."

She sighed. "Its more than that, Risa. I guess it's that Marthanne most of all. She's still making a play for Thom, just like he's not spoken for, and he's been acting so peculiar of late ever since those letters arrived from Tater Hill. He said everything was fine, but he does have a worried look about him. Haven't you noticed?"

Risa had. She'd noticed that he'd even been picking at his food of late - he was usually a big eater. He seemed to be far away and worried just like Ma'am Mary suspected, but she didn't want to let on to her mistress.

"Ma'am Mary, you worry too much about your brood. He be fine, Ma'am, just fine," but she didn't believe a word she uttered.

"I just want everything to work out for him and Callie. They're so right for each other," Mary added.

Mary removed the wedding ring quilt and folded it gently. She and Pierce had got it as a wedding present from the church guild almost twenty-three years before. She only put it on for show anymore - one more washing might be its last, she felt. She could see the tops of the dogwood and flowering plum outside her bedroom windows and sighed. Closing her eyes, she drifted into half-sleep.

"What a wonderful trip it was," she thought, as she remembered feeding the seabirds from the polished mahogany deck while she and the girls giggled and tried to hold onto their new, wide-brim hats, the sea breeze tugging at them. That was when we saw them leaning on the rail and looking just like they stepped out of a magazine, she so smartly dressed and him in his white linen suit, so dapper.

"I must remember to write Berta to tell her all about it," she thought drowsily." Just as soon as these people leave, I shall."

****

"You son of a bitch! Get your hands off of me. Now! Do you hear? Right now!"

"Would ya listen to Miss Marthanne...would you just! Now that ain't no way for a lady to talk, now is it? Don't you dare, little lady. Your pa'll not like to see his top hand all scratched up so he has to send for Doc Bolun. Bet you'd like Thom Garvin to be holding you like this, huh? I just bet you'd open up your pretty lace drawers for him. But that long-legged colt Callie Meade grabbed him away from you, now didn't she?" He wrenched her head around and pulled off some of the hay that had found its way onto her golden hair. "I said, didn't she?" He held her hands tightly behind her back, his face not six inches from hers.

There was no way she could have scratched him or anything else, he was so strong, but she could spit in his face, and that's exactly what she did.

He howled...deep and guttural, his dark head leaned back against the rough wooden beam with delight, just like he liked it. "You think you can flit those hips at me and every hand around here and we won't do anything about it, huh? Well, little lady..."

"Don't call me that!" she said through clenched teeth. "Take your stinkin' arms off me, Monti Fiske. Take 'em off!" She squirmed away trying to break his hold, all the time aware of Jester's labored breathing on the other side of the stall. Marthanne wasn't scared of any of the cowmen around Deep Spring. She knew that they feared her and her pa. But Monti Fiske didn't seem to care a bit what her pa thought or would do. He'd been working at Deep Spring for over three years, and Jacob Greer said he was the best hand he'd ever had and had elevated him to the number one spot six months after he came riding in from Monticello, his hometown.

She didn't like anything about him. The way he looked at her made her feel like a common cowgirl. No respect at all for his boss's daughter. It infuriated her. She'd decided a long time ago that she'd do everything she could think of to tantalize him. She'd put that low life in his place. Just who did he think he was looking at her that way, practically drooling down his dirty, sweaty shirt with his mouth hanging open, licking his wet lips. She had to admit that he was good looking, in a sort of unrefined way. And even after she had fallen in love with Thom and had decided that she'd have him, she still played her teasing games with Monti just to break the monotony.

After the War Monti had decided to not return to his folks' farm in Monticello. He went back to South Carolina, where they had originally lived and still had relatives. He soon realized that a person can't go back - nothing was the same - so he returned to Monticello and worked his father's farm along with his other brothers. But Monti was an adventurer and couldn't seem to settle down for very long at a time, not long enough to take a wife as did his brothers and not long enough to feel permanent. He didn't want that kind of responsibility. So he took to the trail.

He was a man's man, who had ridden with Capt. J.J. Dickison, the Confederate Swamp Fox, and had found a home in the army. He missed the army. Being a cowman was as close as he could come to that kind of life, and he took to it. Men naturally followed him...he was a born leader, and Jacob Greer recognized his talent. What he didn't recognize was Monti's lusting after his wild daughter, but then Jacob saw just what he wanted to see when it came to Marthanne. Monti was well aware of that, so he played his hand accordingly.

They, he and Marthanne, did have one love in common, their love of her horse, Jester. Monti had assisted at his birthing, had broken him, trained him and loved him. He'd never worked a more intelligent horse, and he respected him more than most men he knew. He'd get almost teary eyed when he'd see Marthanne stroke him, as gentle as could be, and if she had any softness in her - he wondered if she had - it had to be for Jester. He was as upset about Jester's condition as she.

He let the struggling Marthanne go. He was sure she'd turn to lambast him for a final time, but she didn't. That was out of character. Normally she'd have insisted on the last word.

He called to her, "If you want what I think you want, you'll be back here after dark. I'll be waiting."

That did it. She whirled around and shouted for the entire world to hear, "Then you'll wait 'til the cows come home, Mister Fiske. Your head'll be white down to your knees by the time I come to you. Do you hear?"

She looked around Jester's stall and realized no one would be coming into the stable 'til later. They'd all be taking it easy in the bunkhouse after supper. He saw her evaluating the situation and laughed. "You're so hungry you're slobbering, little lady. Your ache is as strong as mine, if you'd just admit it. But you won't, will you?. Guess I'll hafta take charge..."

"Let me go! Let go of me you..." but his mouth hard on hers silenced her. He could feel her struggle - then go limp and suddenly she responded, her nails digging into his taut back.

"Gawd almighty, I knew you were hungry, little lady, but, Jesus Christ...you're starved!" Heaving, out of breath, he watched her roll away from him and begin buttoning and straightening her blouse, like she'd just gotten up from the tea table. Monti watched her quitely, her every move heightened his need of her, then not being able to control his desire, reached for her, pulling her toward him, but she pushed him away with a scowl. "You've had all you're gonna get from me, Mister. Do not think that this will ever happen again, 'cause it won't."

He laughed. "Why, little lady, I've got your ticket. You need it just as much as I do, and if I insisted, I'd get a dose of you right this minute. Don't play this high and mighty bitch with me, little lady."

He let that sink in and, breathing hard, said, "I'll expect you right here in Jester's stall every night after your folks are abed. If you don't show, then I'll just hafta march right into your room for you."

"You wouldn't dare! You wouldn't dare! Why my daddy would have your head on a platter just like John the Baptist. If you even attempted to come into my room ...he'd..."

"He'd do what? Just what would he do? Why every hand around here knows..."

"Knows what? What on earth are you talking about?"

"They know that you're ripe, and so does Jacob, and that's why he's trying to get you married off to that Thom Garvin. But you don't stand a chance with him, do ya? Why that long-legged filly from Tater Hill's already got his cock in her sock and..."

"Shut up! What do you know about it, anyway? You don't know beans. That Callie Meade is more man than woman, and when Thom finds it out this finger of mine will be sporting a ring, Mister Smartie Pants!" She held up her left hand and wriggled it in his face.

He grabbed her arm, took her hand and kissed it, and as she tried to pull it away he bit it. She was so shocked that she yelped and swung at him but he easily pinned her arms behind her with one hand and held her head with his other. Looking her right in the eye, he said, "I'll be expecting you tonight, little lady. You best be here, do ya hear?" She whirled around and defiantly walked away from him.

He laughed out loud. Leaning against the barn door, he watched her walk the path to the main house. He watched until he could see her no more. He turned with a knowing smile on his face and said, "I'll get to her through Jester." He mellowed. "We have him in common." He wouldn't admit even to himself that he loved Marthanne, spoiled, headstrong, beautiful.

He swaggered into the barn and said to himself, "Hell, she'll be back. She's hungry...so am I. All along I thought it was that kid, Thom Garvin. If I'd had any brains I'd have known it was Jester. I'll have her through

Jester."

"Best not let Miss Marthanne in here, Charlie. You know how she feels about him." Monti was holding Jester down. Charlie Bivens, Jacob's horse trainer, was in the barn with Monti.

"I think he got into that loco weed over near Crazy Creek. Buz said there was some over there and that we'd best be careful of it, but I don't know if anyone warned Miss Marthanne 'bout it, do you, Monti? I never saw anyone so crazy 'bout a horse, and I know full well she'd never have ridden him out there if she'd known."

"I think Marthanne thinks more of Jester than she does of us, Jacob. I'll declare I do. Why she spends more time with that horse now than she did when she was training him for the events at the fair. Have you noticed?"

Jacob had noticed and thought that after Jester had recovered from that bout of loco weed fever, Marthanne would spend less time in the stable. He'd also noticed how relaxed she'd become around the hands lately. He knew she taunted them with her swishy hips, but it seemed to him that recently she'd calmed down. He was relieved. He'd been very concerned. He knew how headstrong she was and had always been but couldn't help but be disappointed that she hadn't won Thom Garvin's heart.

Marthanne couldn't stand failure. Not that he'd let on to Madge, so he responded, "Oh, she just needs something to care for at this time of her life, Hon. What with no other girls her age around here and her getting to the marrying age, her needs are different than they used to be. I think that you should insist on going into town more often. Get her interested in the festivities your friends are engaged in with their daughters. Madge, there are plenty of young men just as eligible as Thom Garvin, you know."

"I know, dear, and I've tried...really I have, but she just refuses to even discuss it and hangs around the stable and Jester when she's not out riding him." She looked softly at Jacob and continued trying to assure him. "But I'll ask her again. She's bored, Jacob. Have you noticed? She's eating just like a field hand. Had seconds on the rice and gravy, and I bet she ate three biscuits for dinner."

Madge shook her head in dismay and continued, "Did you hear what she said to me when I mentioned it? She jumped down my throat and said, 'nothing else to do around this old place but eat, so don't take that away from me, too!' and threw down her napkin and ran up to her room."

"Now what on earth is she talking about? I've never taken a thing away from her, Jacob. You've got to talk to her. She's got me so upset...I declare, I don't know what I'm gonna do."

"Honey, calm down. I think she's just upset about Thom getting himself betrothed. At least I guess that's what it's all about. Now..now.." he patted her, "Don't do that, Hon. Here, dry your eyes. You know how headstrong she is. She didn't mean it."

Marthanne stood staring at her naked form in the tall, oval mirror. Her plans suddenly changed. "That son of a bitch! He said I was safe! What's he know, anyway? No wonder I could eat a horse. God, what'll I do?" she patted her slightly rounded belly, and before she even got the words out, she knew exactly what she'd do. She'd make Thom Garvin marry her...she'd force him to.

Monti hadn't said he loved her, and she knew he probably didn't. She was glad - she sure didn't love him. Every time he touched her she'd pretend that it was Thom. And Monti was right - she hadn't missed slipping out to the stable a single night or meeting him down by Crazy Creek after breakfast when she could.

She wondered if he had said anything to the other hands. They seemed to treat her differently. "Oh, well, who cares anyway. What they think about me doesn't matter, but I'll fix all of 'em. If that Monti Fiske thinks for one minute that I'll be his, he is very much mistaken!" She laughed. "Mr. Fiske, you played right into my hands and paved the way for me to get Thom. If you only knew!" and she continued to laugh as she threw herself across the rose satin coverlet on her high bed and planned her next move.

The main house at Bullseye was a good distance from the barn but in Marthanne's view as she sat talking to Lucinda. When she saw Thom head for it, she excused herself and said that she thought she'd take a little walk. "I have some thinking to do, Lucinda, and if you don't mind I'd like to be alone. I know you understand," she said sweetly. Lucinda understood alright. She'd seen Thom head for the barn, also.

Marthanne knew that her ma was with Mary Garvin in the kitchen and that her pa had ridden with Pierce and his other sons to the orange groves. Perfect timing, she thought.

Lucinda left the front steps and joined her ma and Madge Greer in the summer kitchen. When Mary asked her where Marthanne was, and she told her, Mary became suspicious.

"Madge, you come with me this instant. Why, you're bushed from such a long journey. Now, I want you to take a little rest before Jacob returns and you have to drive all the way to Crescent City." Madge began to protest, but Mary took her by the arm and led her upstairs to the guest room. "I insist, Madge. I really do, dear. I'll not let you rest too long." She did feel worn out and appreciated Mary's thoughtfulness.

"If that little twit thinks she's going to get Thom alone, she had better think again!" She slipped out the side door and headed for the barn.

At first she heard nothing, then she slipped inside into the shadows and waited. She heard Thom. He was speaking low at first but then became louder.

"Marthanne, you shouldn't be doing that..."

"Why, Thom, whatever are you talking about? Doing what? You mean ...this?"

"You know full well that's what I mean - grief! A fellow can take just so much, you know."

"Oh, Thom, who says you have to take it? Why don't you just relax and..."

"Relax! How can I relax with you doing that? What if your folks came in and caught us and..."

"What if the sun and moon don't rise? Oh, Thom, you know how I feel about you..you have to..Does this feel good, Thom? Don't pull away, silly. No one's gonna know. Oh, that's better..here I'll help you, these old buttons are hard to unbutton.."

"Marthanne, don't! Now I think we'd best stop before we go to..."

"Don't you pull away from me, Thom Garvin," she teased. "You know you want to as much as I do."

What he didn't say, but he sure wanted to, was that he wanted to save himself for Callie even after he read Cousin Marta's letter telling him about Clay Willett. And then the letter came from Callie saying that they were just good friends, and he believed her. He really did, but there was that little seed of doubt that kept cropping up.

Finally, he had had enough. "Marthanne, I think you'd better make yourself presentable. This has gone far enough." He disengaged her determined arms, turned and quickly made his way through the shadowed barn toward the twilight that was descending on Bullseye. He didn't bother to look back to see if she was following. He just wanted to get away.

"Thata boy, Thom," Mary thought, holding her hand tightly over her mouth. "Put the little tramp in her place." Relieved, she leaned against the rough boards and waited for Marthanne to make her move. It didn't take her long. She rushed out from the dark of the barn into the light that was streaming diagonally inside the opening, challenging the shadows. Mary saw her petulant smile change into fierce determination as she ripped her blouse and called to Thom to stop.

"Stop right this minute, Thom Garvin. You're not gonna do this to me and get away with it!"

She moved swiftly from her hiding place and rushed toward Marthanne. She swung her around, and Marthanne was caught by surprise. Thom had reached the sanctuary of the house and did not hear what ensued.

"Do what to you, Marthanne? Just what did Thom do to you, young lady?"

Marthanne stammered, "You..you were spying on me...you were..."

"Yes, I was spying on you. Not on Thom, but on you. There was no doing on Thom's part - only on yours, and if you think for one minute you're gonna force him into marrying you when it's obvious to me that someone else got in the hen house first, you're very much mistaken."

Mary heaved a sigh of relief, and before Marthanne could compose herself to deny the accusation, she continued, "Thom and Callie will be married as planned and I'd suggest that you make other arrangements for your future."

"Don't you have relatives up north that you can stay with for an extended visit? Like seven or eight months?" she added sarcastically. "Or maybe you can force the father of the child to marry you. But hear me right now. If you cause Thom any more trouble, it'll be me you'll have to reckon with."

Marthanne, ready to protest all that Mary had said, thought better of it, and shrugging her shoulders said, "Whatever do you mean, Mrs Garvin? What baby..what baby indeed? I don't have the slightest idea what you're talking about."

"We both know what I mean, Marthanne. You might be able to fool your folks and wrap them around your little fingers, and you might be able to hoodwink Thom, but I've been onto you for a long time - and so has Callie."

"Now make yourself presentable, and I'll tell your folks goodbye."

She turned back to Marthanne, who stood dead in her tracks trying to think of a retort, and said, "Oh, and don't bother talking your folks into a return visit to Bullseye. You'll not be welcome." She turned and went into the house slamming the door hard.

Mary picked up the Palatka paper, the *Eastern Herald*, and sighed. "So that was who it was." *The parents of Marthanne Susan Greer of Deep Spring, Palatka, are pleased to announce her marriage to Aaron (Monti) Fiske formerly of Monticello, Florida, and more recently of Deep Spring, on March 10, 1880.*

After an extended honeymoon trip touring the northern states the Fiskes will make their home at Deep Spring, where Mr. Fiske is engaged as foreman of the ranch..."

"Well, that's that. At least I hope so. That girl is not one to embrace defeat. I'll have to keep my vigilance. When does a mother cease to worry about her chicks, I wonder. I'm beginning to weary of it. I truly am."

CHAPTER III
CALLIE'S AND THOM'S WEDDING

"But Callie, your wedding dress should be special. I don't know why on earth you want to wear the same dress that you wore to your first dance. I don't care what Thom says."

"Mama, don't, please. What difference does it make anyway?"

"Beulah said she'd help me make it, and Jeeters' got in the prettiest pale pink satin I ever saw, so soft."

"Mama, now Thom and me don't..."

"That's Thom and I..."

Callie continued ignoring Kate's correction of her grammar, a sore subject for both of them. "We don't want all this fuss. If we had our way, we'd just get on Goldie and BeeBee and ride down to Ft. Myers and get hitched right there and spend our time on the Gulf fishing - that's what we'd do"

"I just bet you would! I just bet... and deprive your pa and me of seeing our only daughter properly wed, and him building you and Thom a house at Ole Piney Creek, just where you wanted it and everything."

Kate turned toward Callie to lambast her one more time. "You're selfish, Callie Anders Meade. You're selfish through and through!"

She bit off the thread and shoved her mending back into her bag and straight as you please walked back into the house grumbling all the way about how she had tried so hard to bring her up right in this wilderness and how she refused to cooperate and.... Callie shook her rich brown curls and decided that she'd let her cool off for a spell. Then she'd better follow to talk some sense into her.

She was grateful that Thom had decided to move down to Tall Ten to join her pa on the ranch. Goodness knows, Jay never would. He couldn't be around horses because they gave him asthma, so naturally he wouldn't be any help at all. But then he already had his life's work planned out. There wasn't a living creature that he couldn't draw, and he had already received recognition from as far away as Washington, D.C. Why, Miss Taylor, the school teacher, said that he had as much talent as that Audubon fellow, whose pictures hung in the big museums in New York City and the likes.

Thom's brothers were old enough to help his pa up at Bullseye, and it just made sense that Thom would move to Tater Hill. When Callie's pa asked them where they wanted their house built, Thom and Callie rode all around. She knew the very spot, but she wanted Thom to have a choice too. When they rode the mile and a half from the big house to Ole Piney Creek, Thom said even before she had a chance to ask, "Right here, Callie. I want it right here." She couldn't believe that he'd pick the very place that she wanted.

"Are you sure, Thom? We've gotta be absolutely sure." That was where Callie and her best friend Pet, Mattie's daughter, who had moved back to Bartow to live, used to camp out and fish, and Callie's most favorite place in the world.

"Did Ma tell you that this is where I wanted it? Did she? I just bet she did, and now she's spoiled everything!"

"Hey, Honey, now don't go get bent all out of shape. Your ma didn't give anything away. I just remembered that you told me about when you and Pet used to come here, and whenever you told me about those times you got all drifty- eyed and such. I knew that this was the very place."

"Oh, Thom, you're so smart. I should've known that you'd know." She reached up and kissed his cheek, his all- color eyes danced with mischief.

"So's all I get is just a old peck on the cheek? Now I think I deserve more than that, Missy." He took a giggling Callie into his arms.

"Honey, it's getting downright difficult for me to wait for the wedding night. Whew!"

Callie continued to sit on the front porch. Her ma's ferns in the tall stands were hanging almost to the floor, and the rocking chairs, the same ones that had been there for all of Callie's life, were lined up the length of the porch, their caned seats and backs covered with faded rose and green flowered cushions that Kate had made, goodness knows, how long ago.

Callie sighed. "I think I'd just up and die if anything happened to Tall Ten or Ma or Pa, or grief, even Jay. And now I can add Thom." She leaned back and began rocking and thinking about when she first fell in love with him, not even two years ago. She couldn't believe that she hadn't even liked him before then. He was such a show-off on his gelding, Goldie, and everyone made over him and liked him, and that Ruby Thomas, Yankee's and Hannah's niece, made such a to-do over him at their boarding house on the Gulf at Punta Rassa.

She rocked and reminisced. "Grief! If it hadn't been for Thom she'd probably never have worn a dress." She laughed as she thought of it.

Her ma had been trying forever to get her to go to the town socials, and she'd very cleverly, she thought, avoided them with the pretext of having whatever incurable disease she could conjure up. Callie had been a tomboy all her life and had never felt close to the girls in town, just Pet. She was the only girl Callie could talk to, so going to girls' functions sure didn't appeal to her.

It was comical now, but it hadn't been when Thom had asked her to go to the social right after the drive to Punta Rassa, when they found the stolen doubloons that the Skinner gang had absconded with. She was scared to death about going to an old dance but accepted his invitation mostly because he had asked her in front of the ranch hands, and Callie thought of it as a dare. Her ma had to teach her in a hurry how to follow the caller, 'cause Callie had refused to learn the dance steps before then.

Her dress was the most beautiful dress she'd ever seen, and Thom thought so, too, so why should it matter that her wedding dress was that rich blue-green color of the Gulf at daybreak, so clear and shiny instead of pale this or pale that, and why did it have to be a new one?

She continued to rock, and when she thought of Big Cypress Swamp and the hammock where she and Thom had made camp to await the robber whose buried doubloons they had found, she realized that was when she had fallen in love with him. They had felt sure that the robber would come back to the hammock for his stash after dark, and he did. She'd never been so scared in her entire life. Thom shot the robber, but he escaped into Big Cypress never to be seen again. The only sign of him was his old black hat at the edge of the swamp. Nothing nor no one wounded ever came out of Big Cypress...no one.

If her pa had known that she was riding with the posse, he'd have skinned her alive, so she and Thom didn't tell the others about having found the doubloons for fear one of them would tell her pa that she was there. Off the posse rode all the way over to the Ten Thousand Islands in the Gulf, in the belief that there was where the gang had gone, and she and Thom stayed and waited for the robber. She felt so protected with him there.

Her pa hadn't found out that she had ridden with the posse until they all got back to Punta Rassa, and she and Thom had brought back the doubloons. He had been upset with her and had said that he'd never have forgiven himself if anything had happened to her. That was one of the few times Callie had ever seen him cry. But a few tears managed to roll down his cheek before he turned away from her. She'd never felt closer to him.

"Yep, that was the very time I fell in love. I was shaking so hard after Thom shot that robber, that he wrapped Pa's old army blanket around me and said real soft-like, 'It's alright, Callie, it's alright...'"

Callie went to the kitchen, patted Kate's back lightly and said, "Mama, now did I say that we weren't gonna let you and Pa give us a fancy wedding? Now did I? No, I said that Thom wants me to wear the dress I wore the night he fell in love with me. It's a beautiful dress, and I love it just as much as he does. What's wrong with that, Mama?"

"Oh, honey, its just that I want everything to be so special, and somehow wearing an old dress just doesn't seem quite right."

"Who says! It's our wedding. Why should everyone in the whole country try to tell us what I should wear?" and her voice got louder and higher.

Parker came walking into the kitchen and asked, "What's all this hollerin' about, anyway? Have you lost your senses, young lady?"

Callie pursed her lips and slammed the kitchen door as she raced outside and headed for the stable to get BeeBee, so she could ride away from all the fuss. She had to go to Ole Piney Creek and just sit and clear her muddled mind.

"Grief! You'd think I was the Queen of Sheba the way they're carrying on. Grief!"

****

May 1880

It was a beautiful, clear and cool day in May. The cattle drive to Punta Rassa was completed, and half of the cowmen in the state of Florida had remained in Tater Hill Bluff for Thom's and Callie's wedding. Mary Garvin and Thom's three sisters and youngest brother had made the arduous journey from Crescent City, first taking the steamship on the St. Johns River to Mellonville on Lake Monroe, then the mail stage to a landing south of Bartow. The Peace River was too low for the paddle wheeler to get as far north as Bartow. Her sister, Beulah Young, met them at the Tater Hill Bluff ferry landing. Pierce and sons Thurmond and Lanier had remained in town with Thom and stayed in Beulah's and George's Hotel.

Berta was so disappointed that she couldn't attend, but the twins were just a year old, and though she had partially weaned them, she felt that it would be too hard on her. She was truly upset at the situation, Layke could tell, so he tried to talk her into going and having Aimee deMoya accompany them, but she wouldn't hear of it.

"Now, Layke, don't make such a fuss about it. I'll get to hear all about it from Jonah and Young Reuben and especially Etienne - he's so observant and will even notice what the ladies wear. There'll be other weddings and festivities we'll be able to attend. The world won't come to an end simply because I missed this one."

If she'd been honest with herself, she'd have admitted why she was so upset...but she wasn't. She was so anxious to speak to Mary about her trip to Savannah and Jacksonville and to inquire about Juanita and the gambler, Conner O'Farrell. Mary had seen them on board the *Savannah* and had said that she had spoken to them, but Berta was curious as to whether she had found out what their relationship was.

The fact that Juanita had left the deMoya's medicine show and gone to Palatka in search of Conner was very puzzling to Berta. Juanita was wild but practical. She had confided in Aimee about her obvious obsession with the gambler, but, according to Orlean, she had seen him but twice, when they performed in Palatka and she had fallen, miscarrying R.J.'s baby, and again about a week later when the gambler had returned to Palatka on the *Savannah*. It had been obvious that they were drawn to each other, and when Etienne, who could not contain his jealousy, insisted that they leave, Juanita protested loudly. There had been no correspondence between them, Orlean was sure. It would appear that Juanita was as she told Aimee - obsessed.

Berta knew that Juanita was self-centered, but this move seemed out of character. She had appeared to be more of a planner to Berta, never allowing chance a part in her schemes. "Am I jealous of her? How could I be? Heavens, I have Layke, and I hadn't seen Conner O'Farrell since I was a girl in Macon, until my honeymoon, and then didn't recognize him or realize who he was until Layke and I returned to South Spring. I hardly realized he was around when I lived in Macon...why now? Those haunting pale eyes should have warned me...but they didn't. Why is he in my thoughts so much now?"

She wondered if Juanita was his mistress, or if he had actually married her. She was such a wild girl! Anyone who would run away with a gang like the Skinners, bank robbers, rapists, and goodness knows what all, had to be wild. The fact that she hadn't encouraged Etienne's obvious love did indicate to Berta that she was not all bad, but why should Berta care so much about the boyo, as his sister Maeve had called Conner in their Mum's millinery shop in Macon?

Was it the way he had looked at her, brazenly, knowing that she was on her honeymoon, and yet with the same intensity and caring that Layke did? For the entire trip aboard the *Robert E. Lee* he seemed to be following her...on both decks, in the grand salon. Everywhere she turned he'd be there dressed in his starched white linen suit and always smoking his black cheroot. It was obvious that he recognized her, so why didn't he identify himself? She found the adventure exciting but was wise enough to not mention it to Layke. So many questions with so few answers!

When she and Layke disembarked in Jacksonville, she turned back toward the *Robert E. Lee* to bid it farewell and saw Conner standing beside the black porter. Why did he smile so forlornly at her, pleading with those opaque eyes, as if to say, "I'll always love you...don't leave me." Her heart ached when she'd not been able to erase that sad picture. Not then...not now. He had looked as if he'd been ill with dark circles under his eyes. Goodness knows, she had tried to forget. Berta was a practical woman, not a silly romantic who did what was expected of her. Was that why Juanita's actions disturbed her? That Juanita was allowed such a carefree life without responsibility, and Berta's burdens were always with her, heavy...never lifting.

Berta didn't realize who Conner was until a year after the honeymoon, when the twins were born. When Tucker first opened his eyes that sunny May morning, she finally realized who the gambler was and said aloud, "Boyo!" Layke had asked her what she meant. She casually told him that Tucker's eyes reminded her of a young Irish boy's she had known as a girl in Macon, that same pale blue, and that his sister had said that boyo meant boy in Irish. Layke was very firm when he said that he didn't want Tucker to have a nickname, that his name was a proud one, and he wanted it used. Berta had agreed but had secretly called him *boyo* ever since.

Was the *mick* the Devil himself, as her father had said? Or did he love her? Had he loved her from afar all those years?

There...she finally allowed the possibility to penetrate. She shivered. "Why am I behaving like this and loving the romance of it? I'm as silly as that Juanita!"

****

Kate had ceased showing her disapproval of Callie's choice of gown and busied herself with the reception at the Young Hotel, while Callie was busy supervising the construction of her and Thom's new home. It was a small house locally referred to as a dog trot house: front porch and central hall with two rooms off the hall on each side, one the parlor with the kitchen behind it and two bedrooms on the opposite side. The back porch overlooked Ole Piney Creek. It was built about three feet off the ground to allow the air to cool it and to keep the high water from coming in during the rainy season.

Callie's pa had had the cypress and heart pine brought in from the big sawmill, and the cedar shingles came all the way from Otter Creek by barge, first to Cedar Key, then to Port Charlotte. The only other building was the outhouse, but she and Thom planned to build their barn before they took their honeymoon. They would delay it until the following February before the cow hunt season began. They would travel to Crescent City to visit Bullseye and then take a long boat trip all the way to Charleston. Thom wanted to return by way of Kissimmee to check out Hamilton Disston's operation, that was just getting under way.

****

"You bes take dese thimble biscuits on dis here tray, Miss Kate. Ah can anchor dis tea towel over em wid dese clothes pins to keep 'em from bouncing all over de buckboard. An, here, let me hep ya wid dat...gracious me! You all thumbs," Mattie chuckled at Kate, who was indeed all thumbs.

Beulah and Mary had been cooking for two solid days, she knew, and what with all the fancy lemon tarts and coconut balls and tiny thimble biscuits to hold the chicken salad that she and Mattie had made there should be enough food. She knew those cowmen's appetites, so Beulah had had Rube boil and parch enough peanuts for an army, Parker had reassured her.

Parker and George Young, Pierce and Thom along with Jordan Northrup had been put in charge of barbecuing the wild hogs, an entire beef, plus chickens, and they'd been tending the hickory fires all night long underneath the tarp that had been strung up over the cook fires out back of the hotel. Rube's wife, Pearlie, was in charge of the chicken perlo, chicken and dumplings and swamp cabbage and had been standing over the big black pots since before first light. The aroma had drawn every dog and cowman from miles around, and the town's children had gathered too close to the fires and were having tussling matches, kicking up sand and carrying on something awful.

"Pearlie, you best not let these rambunctious younguns dip into those pots. Lord have mercy! Get out of there, William. For heavens sake! Didn't Janie teach you any manners? Next thing we know you'll be head long in one of the boiling pots with chicken wings hanging on your ears. Now git!" Beulah said shooshing them away, fussing over the preparations.

Pearlie had been eyeing the fattest hens in her hen house all week long and had assured Beulah that they were full of eggs for the rich egg gravy that they all liked. No one could out-do Pearlie when it came to chicken. "Miss Beulah, Ah done found a whole mess of wild onions out back of Samuel's cabin for de swamp cabbage and de pigs, and Ah's cut de salt pork into tiny pieces so it'll cook to nothin' and season up dis cabbage jes right."

"Well, you best cook enough for an army. Parker told me that he'd counted over a hundred and fifty people, and he was sure that he'd missed some. Imagine! I bet Kate'll die on the spot when she gets to town and sees all these people."

And she almost did. "A hundred and fifty people! Parker Meade, that little church won't hold anywhere near that many. Now you know it! What on earth are we going to do?" and she sat down hard on Beulah's parlor chair.

Kate, Callie, Mattie and Jay had arrived in two buckboards loaded down with food and their wedding clothes before nine o'clock that morning and had gone directly to the hotel. Jay had hopped down and dashed inside to warn Thom that the bride was there so that he wouldn't see her. "Don't want any more bad luck to befall my sister. Marrying Thom is bad luck enough," he had said jokingly to Maida and Marta as they rushed downstairs to help Kate and Callie with their finery.

Parker could tell that Kate was a nervous wreck and took both her hands in his and said real tenderly, "Honey, you know most of those cowmen haven't ever been in a church. They'll just be here for the..." he almost said drinking and eating, then thought better of it, "ah, the festivities."

He wasn't fooling Kate. "You'd better make sure that they leave their drinking and horsing around for after the wedding, Parker. I don't think I could stand it if they ruined Callie's wedding. I don't think I could stand..."

"Now, Honey, don't start the tears yet. You hafta save some for the actual ceremony. Here, dry those eyes. You don't want Callie to see you like that, now do you?"

He assured Kate that there would be no drunks interrupting the ceremony, but as he said it, he wasn't sure how he was going to keep his promise. He'd speak to them, but what good it would do..."I think Callie was right. Maybe she and Thom should have ridden to Ft. Myers instead of creating all this fuss."

Parker and Jay were to change into their frock coats in Thom's and Pierce's room, so Jay checked that room first. But no Thom. "Bet he's out back with all the others watching those pigs roast." Sure enough, he and about a dozen hands, who said that they were needed to help with the cooking, were surrounding the pits. Rube had asked them to turn the spit every once in a while just to give them something to do, and the aroma from the wild onions and whole oranges that Rube had stuffed the pigs with had every one of 'em licking his chops. Rube or Pearlie would douse them with the hot pepper sauce mixed with wild honey every once in a while. You could smell that sizzling meat all over town, and every few minutes a few more men would join the others. The skin was getting golden brown and crunchy, just as the hands liked it.

Parker told Rube that they might need the sheriff to guard them while everyone was in church, and although he laughed when he said it, Rube decided that he'd not take a chance and positioned himself right there to stay 'til Mister George told him to move. Parker knew that the men had a jug, and he warned them, as Kate had asked, about getting high and messing up the wedding. They assured him that they'd just take a few snorts for the time being, but no one would give him his assurance that after the wedding and the dancing began, that they'd abstain.

He wasn't too concerned about afterwards, because he knew that they'd save their shennanigans for the street and not mess up Beulah's parlor. That was one thing about George Young. He wasn't a big or forceful man except when it came to Beulah. Boy howdy! He'd take on anyone if he tried to disrupt any of Beulah's shindigs. There'd never been a fist fight nor a gun drawn inside the hotel. It was an unwritten law that any disruption was saved for outside on the street, and so far it had been abided by for over twenty years.

The women from Kate's church circle had prepared covered dishes. There would be bowls of tender spring greens and freshly picked green beans cooked with new red potatoes, baby limas, summer squash, creamed onions and pickles of every description, large bowls of potato salad and cole slaw and platters of sliced tomatoes, fig and guava preserves and gallons of fresh fruit punch to wash down the orange marmalade and burnt sugar cakes. The pans of biscuits and corn bread covered Beulah's kitchen table two pans deep.

Beulah and Mary had baked the wedding cake the day before, and it had turned out perfect, three tiers high with lemon filling and divinity icing. Mary had surrounded it with a delicate, pale coral vine that ran up the cabbage palm beside Beulah's back door and had intertwined the vines with the maiden hair fern that Kate had brought all the way from Ocala as a bride and planted in her mother's fern baskets on her front porch. She centered the cake on the lace-covered tables, three tables long, in Beulah's front parlor.

They stood back and admired it. "Oh, Beulah," Kate exclaimed, "this has got to be the most important day of my entire life! Where're Mary and the girls? She said they wanted to help me make Callie's gardenia crown. I've got it started and it won't take but a minute to finish. Would you be a dear and look for her?"

There would be no church service that Sunday. The Reverend Mr. Lincoln would begin the ceremony at eleven o'clock sharp, he had told Thom the night before as they visited on the hotel porch. When he cautioned him that he did not like to start late, he winked at Jam and Slick, Parker's hired hands, who could see how nervous Thom was getting. But Thom took everything in his stride. Their teasing was to be expected, and, being of an affable nature, he went along with their sport of him.

Gus Jeeters was taking it all in and wondering how Clay was doing in Tampa. He'd left two weeks before the wedding, stating that he wanted to get settled in at the boarding house before his job with the *Tribune* began, but there wasn't a person in all of Tater Hill who believed it. He just couldn't stand being there, and Callie understood. She was so happy for him...happy that he had a wonderful job and knew that he'd make everyone in DeSoto County proud of him. But she missed him so. "I don't think this town will ever be the same without Clay," she'd said to her ma right after he left. "I know I'll never be the same," she thought but couldn't say.

Callie's dark curls sprang up all around the crown of gardenias that Kate had secured with hair pins. She didn't try to smooth them down as she usually did. She was going through the motions, in a daze, when

Parker rapped on the door for the second time. He was patiently waiting, leaning against the wall with a soft smile on his face when he heard the music.

"Kate, Constance has the piano warmed up. When are you two coming out? I thought we were gonna have us a wedding."

You could hear the music all over town. One thing you could say about Constance's playing...she sure didn't have a light touch.

It was Jay's job to tell Thom and his dad when they were to go into the back of the little, white, frame church, and then he was to run back to the hotel to fetch Parker, Kate and Callie. They heard him yelling at the foot of the stairs that Thom was in the church, and Callie, fidgeting with her full skirt, was just bursting to get it all over with.

Parker shook his head at Kate, who was already brushing away her tears and trying to keep up with Callie as she raced down the stairs. "Now, Kate, don't you get started yet. Heavens, we aren't even in the church!"

"Come on, Ma - he's already there!"

Kate took Parker's arm, and he called after Callie, "Your mother's gonna fall down these stairs and break her neck, young lady. Hold up, he's waited this long."

Kate was panting for breath by the time they had raced the two blocks to the church, holding her bright blue dress up so it wouldn't snag on the rough wooden sidewalk. Positioning her new straw bonnet, she took Jay's arm. Constance saw her, and right in the middle of the hymn she was playing she changed the tune.

"Grief, Constance. That sounds like a funeral dirge," Kate thought and shook her head at Constance's serious face to let her know it. She wanted everything light and lively to match Callie's personality.

Thom and Pierce entered with the Reverend Mr. Lincoln. Thom did look so handsome in his brown frock coat with his beige brocade waist coat. Kate got a catch in her throat when she remembered how simple her and Parker's wedding had been.

Constance's splotchy hands ran up and down the length of the keyboard several times, she was so carried away. Then she began the wedding music. Every head there turned as they stood. They were smiling from ear to ear, and Kate forgot all about crying when she saw Callie practically pulling her pa down the aisle so she could get to her Thom, who was also grinning and so excited that he forgot to stay beside Pierce and almost ran toward her. Everyone laughed.

The Reverend Mr. Lincoln began the ceremony. When he asked

Thom if he'd take Callie for his wedded wife, Thom said real loud, "I sure will," and the laughter rose. Then Callie said real loud, "I sure do," and everyone clapped, and the cowmen hooted and hollered so loudly that no one even heard the preacher pronounce them man and wife, and those rowdy cowmen were up and out of the church even before Callie and Thom could walk down the aisle.

"I told you so, Parker Meade. I told you they'd spoil everything," but when Kate looked at Parker standing there grinning, her perturbed expression was quickly replaced. She thanked the women who grabbed onto her and exclaimed over Callie's dress, just like they hadn't seen it two years earlier, and gushed over how handsome Thom looked and said all the proper things that ladies were supposed to say at a wedding.

She responded with "Oh, thank you, Eunice, and you're sweet to say that, Agnes Mae; and Gladys, would you be a dear and tell Beulah that she can have Rube and Pearlie start setting the food out."

The dancing was over, and Kate and Parker tiredly climbed up the stairs to their room, but Parker couldn't let go of their day. "Well, this town hasn't ever had a day quite like this one, Katie - not ever. Rube said those cowmen didn't leave enough meat on those carcasses for even the buzzards, and I know for a fact that there's not a full jug in all of Tater Hill, not even half-full, probably."

He turned to her, kissed the top of her head and exclaimed, "You did yourself proud this day, Kate Meade, and you did me proud too."

She hugged him to her and wondered how Callie and Thom were doing. She worried about her. "I should have had a good talk with her, honey. I just couldn't somehow, but I should have. I know I should have."

"Honey, don't you worry. Callie's quick to learn, and Thom is a good lad. He'll be gentle with her, and before you know it we'll be helping 'em out with our first grand-son, Parker, III."

"So you've already named it, have you now. Well, maybe, Mr. Smarty Pants, it'll be little Kate or Katie. What do you think of that?'

****

"Already got your slippers off, have you Callie Meade? Oh, I mean Callie Anders Meade Garvin." She was rubbing her swollen feet and laughing as Thom kept Goldie in a steady trot.

"Can you believe it, Thom? Can you? Whew! I didn't think that year and a half would ever pass, did you?"

"Your Pa was right, honey. You just hafta be sure when it comes to anything as important as marriage." He patted her hand that had found its way to his thigh and continued, "You remember Casey at Barnaby's in Punta Rassa?"

She shook her head no.

"You remember, the tall red-headed man 'bout thirty some years, spends most of his time fishing and the rest of it at Barnaby's. Well, anyway, he was telling me that he'd had a wife once. Real nice girl from a good family and everything. She was from up north somewheres - Ohio, I think. Well, Casey said he'd known her going on a year when they decided to wed. Everything was going along fine, and one day when he came home from work she wasn't there. She'd just up and left him a note telling him that she was going away and for him to not try to find her. Imagine that? That's when he came down to Florida. Said he'd thought about getting married since then 'cause he'd like to have some kids but that he already got a wife, so he can't by law take another."

"That's awful. Why can't he go after her or at least find out if she's alive? She might've got the fever or something and be long dead, so's he could marry again. Did you ask him that?"

"Well, no, I figured he'd be smart enough to know that, and then again, I think he was just talkin'. He doesn't strike me as the steady type wanting him a wife to beget him some younguns."

Callie was quiet. Finally she said, "Thom, you do want me to beget you some babies, don't you?

"Why, Callie Meade, you know darned good and well I want you to. Why, the idea of not having a son near scares me to death. Why, who would carry on Tall Ten? Huh? Who?"

"Maybe I can't beget you a son - then what? Maybe your daughter would hafta marry a cowman so's he could carry on Tall Ten just like I did. Wouldn't that be all right?"

He squeezed her hand hard. "Anything you do is all right with me, Callie. You couldn't do anything that wasn't all right."

But wasn't an hour gone by before he was so put out with her while she was sniffling and facing the wall in their beautiful new bedroom, and Thom was standing looking out the window at the moon doing flip-flops behind the silver lined clouds. He didn't know how to handle his dilemma, but he knew he had to do something. He'd hafta figure it out all by himself, 'cause he sure as heck couldn't ask anybody. Here she was acting silly like a little school girl. How in the world did she expect to beget him a youngun when he hadn't even planted his seed?

Callie could hardly wait to put on her pale pink nightie with wee little rosebuds all over, except the lace-edged, sheer pink yoke. It had short, puffed sleeves of the pink and a wide, leaf-green, satin sash to cinch in her slender waist. Heck, it was pretty enough to wear to church, Mattie had said.

Didn't take her long to undo her waist length hair and hop under the new sheets that her ma had deeply hemmed and picot edged. The women of the church had made them a beautiful quilt with wedding ring pattern done in aqua, gold and rose on an ecru background. It was just about the prettiest thing that Callie had ever seen. And Thom's Aunt Beulah and Uncle George had given them the pretty, deep rose and aqua oil lamp for their birdseye maple dresser, that had been Thom's grandmother Pierce's and with the bed to match.

She had lit the lamp, and a soft glow, almost as pretty as firelight, lit the square room. Thom had undressed in the other bedroom, and when he came in Callie almost burst out laughing. Here she was in her pretty gown and all he had on was funny looking BVD's, but she could see his tanned skin shining in the lamp glow, and before he blew out the lamp Callie got such a lump in her throat that she was afraid that she was gonna choke right there on her wedding night.

Thom cleared his throat, seemed like forever. "He must have a lump in his throat, too," she thought. She could feel the heat of him, and next thing she knew, she was in his arms and the smell of gardenias from her hair softly invaded the room.

"Oh, Callie, I love you so. This has gotta be the most important thing that's ever happened to me."

But she couldn't respond, her head was swimming so. All she could think of was what Pet Morgan had told her about six or seven years ago right out back beside Ole Piney Creek. They had been fishing and had decided to spend the night. She could hear her so plain, just like it was yesterday. She was telling her all about begetting. Callie knew she was foolin' her, but my how she was carrying on. She said that her sister Camellia wouldn't be tellin' her no untruths. But Callie told her that that was the biggest bunch of hog-wash she had ever heard. About how a man's tool looked like a big old wrinkled grubworm, but that when he was ready to plant his seed, it blew up just like a blow fish so it could plant a whole bunch of seeds in her furrow, so that for sure one of 'em would take hold.

Thom was getting all hot and sweaty and Callie was having so much trouble trying not to think of what Pet had told her, that when Callie felt Thom next to her, and it started blowing up just like Pet had told her, she started laughing so hard that she couldn't stop. Thom got so put out with her, 'cause she couldn't tell him why she was laughing, that he called her a silly child and took to the window and just got quiet and stared and stared.

Callie couldn't help but cry a little, she was so upset about the whole thing, but she was especially put out with the Lord. Seemed to her that was some kinda dumb way for him to have a man plant a seed, and she lay on her side facing the wall trying to figure out a better way to do it. She couldn't, and the next thing she knew Thom was back under the cover, and she flipped over so fast and was in his hungry arms and was kissing him all over, and he was kissing her all over the place, and wasn't very long afterwards that Callie couldn't breathe, and a kind of numb but tingling feeling came all over her, and she felt like a million needles were pricking her skin but not hurting her a bit.

As Callie lay gasping for breath, she decided that she guessed that the Lord knew what he was doing, so she wouldn't argue with him anymore about this business of begetting.

BOOK THREE:

HARRISON AND CONNER

CHAPTER I
FAIRLEA

April, 1879 Palatka

Conner put his arm protectively around Juanita, or as he preferred to call her, Cherie. She had been billed as *Cherie the Golden Girl* in the deMoyas' traveling medicine show, where he had first met her. All the way from the St. Johns Hotel to the *Savannah* he held her in that fashion, the mule drawn trolley taking its time gliding down the dirt street toward the docks. People turned toward them and smiled, vicariously enjoying the young lovers, he so dapper in his white suit and she beautiful in the sky-blue, twill dress that she had purchased from the exclusive shop on the waterfront, Monique's.

When they walked up the *Savannah's* gangplank, they were met by a nice looking, middle-aged Negro man dressed in a neat, dark blue uniform. Conner introduced Juanita to his friend Harrison. "The *Savannah* doesn't operate without his expert assistance," he stated proudly. What he added under his breath was, "And yours truly doesn't, either."

"Now what is he up to?" Harrison wondered, as he watched the two of them walk toward the men's saloon. "That's all I need, him bringing that wench on board and getting us in a jam we can't get out of. What's she doing here anyway? I haven't heard of the medicine show being in town and surely thought we'd seen the last of her last September. I knew she was bad luck the minute I heard about how he had helped that doctor set her arm when she fell from the high rope. That's not like Conner O'Farrell."

"She's the kind trouble follows, or why would she have shown up at the same time that that hurricane did? Trouble just seems to follow some people." He thought again, "But maybe with this little trick around he'll stay sober until we can build up our stash. Unfortunately, she looks so ignorant, no matter how fancy she's dressed, that she'll probably get us into more trouble than she did during the hurricane, and Maeve will have to come to our rescue again."

He reluctantly put Juanita's bags, including the one containing the stolen doubloons that R.J. had given her the night before they had been captured, in Conner's cabin. "God, what's she got in here anyway, gold?" and went below deck, his mind reaching a solution as to how to get Juanita off the *Savannah*, so he and Conner could resume their daily card games, Conner playing and Harrison signaling his partner. He hit on an idea that might work, if only Conner's sister Maeve would cooperate.

Frightened! Yes, frightened! Juanita had at last realized fear. Not the cold-all-over fear she'd felt when she first saw the black, devil-eyes of R.J. Skinner, when he and his gang camped on the banks of the Caloosahatchee near her home only a year ago, or the fear of being shot when the posse surrounded them outside of Perry, but a new, unexpected, even more exciting fear, the fear of loving a man as awesomely complex as Conner O'Farrell. R.J., she could read, and Etienne deMoya, so sweet and loving, she had easily controlled without any effort. But Conner!

Her vision blurred. Not truly comprehending her situation nor her newly felt emotions, she was hesitant to act. Doubt invaded her stout reserve that still day, and as she lay motionless in the soundless half-light of Conner's magnificently appointed cabin, she systematically took stock of her situation.

She was not the same Juanita Jane Graves who had run away with the Skinner Gang a year ago, an almost seventeen- year-old, ignorant girl. The time she shared with the deMoyas' traveling show had given her confidence, and Etienne, who loved her beyond all reason, had taught her so much. Each day as they traveled the back roads between the small towns, where she performed on the high rope, he gave her French lessons and read with her the great books. *Jane Eyre* and *Wuthering Heights* were her favorites. She had also earned money for the first time in her eighteen years, and that plus the stolen doubloons from R.J. gave her more money than she had ever imagined having.

Conner was everything she had ever dreamed of even in her wildest imaginings. He was well educated, spoke beautifully with his delightful Irish brogue, not at all like R.J. or the country boys she had grown up with in LaBelle, and he dressed stylishly and had the manners of a gentleman. She was overwhelmed by his intensity, his animal strength, and his gambling intrigued her. But she doubted. She knew that she was not his counterpart.

"I have just gotta get up from here," she tried to convince herself. But Juanita Jane Graves was not convinced. So again she said louder and in an affected voice, "Cherie, you must take hold of your situation," thinking that if she said it in a more polished fashion she'd pay heed to the declaration. But she did not nor could not move from her reverie. Slowly she was released, released to the quiet slumber of his warm, airless cabin, where her demanding inquiries went ignored as she floated into nonawareness.

The cabin door shook with heavy pounding. Again and again he knocked as he tried to turn the black iron latch on Conner's cabin door. Harrison's black, furrowed brow was beaded with perspiration. His obvious concern distorted his otherwise amiable features as he again pounded on the heavy oak door. She stirred and stretched lazily toward the low, paneled ceiling. Not quite awake, she was startled by the incessant pounding. As she became more fully conscious, she realized where she was but was hesitant to respond to the persistent knocking. She saw her valise containing the doubloons and her earnings from the show and was relieved. It appeared that no one had disturbed it. Tying her soft muslin, sea-green wrapper more securely around her tiny waist, Juanita leaned against the door and answered haltingly. "Yes - yes, what could I be helping you with? I mean, may I help you?"

So it was the girl. He should have realized. A very relieved Harrison answered her. "Oh! It's you, Miss Cherie. It's Harrison. I'm sorry to disturb you, but I thought Conner was there, and I wanted to waken him." He neglected to add that he had made it a habit of awakening Conner every afternoon so he could have a light supper before the games began, and that for the past year it had become harder and harder to arouse his friend. The emptied whiskey bottles had multiplied steadily, and he was concerned for his friend's welfare. It was a self-imposed labor of love on his part. Conner O'Farrell did not want nor would he tolerate any show of concern from him, and yet theirs was the only close bond either had ever experienced. Not since their youth in the black bowels of New Orleans had they been separated. Not even during the War.

Fairlea Plantation

"Talmai Harrison, you come back heah dis instant, ya heah? Ah nevah saw sech a rambunctious youngun in all mah days." Silvey grabbed one sandy leg, holding on for all her worth, as her three-year-old son flailed his arms, determined to escape the clutches of his mammy.

"Don ya talk back to me - now don ya! Talmai! Ah declare dat boy will be de death of me yet," she said looking at her mama, who was her only witness. They were the house people. All the field hands had been in the cotton since first light, her husband Luther being one of them.

Talmai scrambled toward the quarters and his granny, Ma Sarie, who stood beside the weathered building as she watched her daughter and grandson.

"Marse Samuel gonna take his whip to ya boy if'n ya don mind ya mammy. Come heah to ya granny, an let me bresh ya off. My..my..already dirty an not even breafus time yet." Talmai relaxed and hugged her as far as his small arms could reach around her grey skirt, that was brightly patched and smelling of pine scent, clean and fresh. She brushed the sand off. "Clean sand ain't evah hurt nobody..nobody."

Silvey closed the door to the summer kitchen, opened it again and shooshed out a pesky fly, then resumed frying the smoked fat meat Marse Samuel liked every morning early right after the hands left for the cotton and tobacco fields. Now Miss Edwina, she liked just fruit and tea up in her room, then after she dressed she'd come down the long stairs and *glorify in her repast*, as she said, usually all by herself. The table had to be set just so, and she expected fresh flowers and freshly starched linens every day.

Landress, her youngest, would usually join her toward the end, as he was a late riser, but her older son, Marshall, would have been in the fields checking on Blackie Turner, their top hired man, making sure he was doing his job. Miss Edwina's daughters, Nellie and Leeanne, had married and had moved from Fairlea to Live Oak, about sixty miles east and a two days' trip. They married the Fournier brothers and already had a bunch of children. Been nearly two years since they had come home to Fairlea for a visit, too long, Silvey could see.

Miss Edwina seemed so lonely. Why just the other day Ma Sarie said that she didn't know for sure if Miss Edwina would see another spring. She was so down that she almost never smiled anymore. "'member how she used ta laugh? My, she'd laugh at the drop of a hat - laugh and laugh at Miss Nellie's and Miss Leeanne's carryin' on. What fun we used ta have. Ain't nuttin' at Fairlea but long faces anymore."

"Now, Ma Sarie, don git goin' on de pas'. Don do no good - no good atall. Talmai! Git outta dose taters. Don ya bruise 'em. Go on out wid Aunt Mamie and de udder younguns. Always unduh mah feet. Now git!"

Talmai reluctantly put the sweet potatoes back in the wooden box underneath the long work table and went down the brick steps, not walking down, but bumping down one at a time on his bottom. He never did anything like the other children, his mammy said. Most would have walked or crawled, but not Talmai...bump...bump!

He kicked at the sand with his bare feet, then bored with that, joined Aunt Mamie and the quarters children. She had seven of them, all under eight years old. After they reached eight, they joined the others in the fields. Since Aunt Mamie was too old to work the cotton and wasn't a house person, it became her job to take care of them. Her sister, Amarine, would succeed her when she was no longer able. Everyone worked at Fairlea.

Talmai's ma, Silvey, was a full-blooded Guinea Negro and a house person, as was her Ma Sarie, and had been all her life. They did not often mingle with the field hands, and their quarters were separate and built closer to the main house and were twice as large as the others. His pa, Luther, was Marse Samuel's top Negro, much older than Silvey. His first wife died of the fever way back in '34 along with their two children. Silvey wasn't but fourteen when he bedded her and Talmai was born that first year.

She was a pretty girl, features just as fine as Nellie's or Leanne's, but was coal black. Couldn't find her in the dark if her eyes were closed and her mouth shut, Luther said, and Talmai looked just like her, except not as black. She was slight, not five feet nor a hundred pounds, and Luther loved every ounce of her.

Samuel Joseph Baker owned some of the best cotton land in the state of Florida, situated beside the Aucilla River, east of Monticello, and twenty three slaves, over half being children. Fairlea had been in his family since the early 1800's, before Florida became a state and was still a territory and grew not only cotton, but tobacco and peanuts on the high ground and rice in the lowlands. Samuel's father John Thomas had been very involved in the politics of the state, but Samuel was tied to the land and not Tallahassee, the capital.

If old John Thomas had had his way - the Lord played a trick on him, he always said - his first born, J.T. Jr., would have been master of Fairlea and not the quiet and solemn Samuel. He couldn't bring himself to call him Sammy Joe as did his wife, Lorna. He looked like a Samuel from birth - acted like a Samuel and had grown up to be just like Lorna's father, Samuel, for whom he was named. John Thomas had never got over J.T.'s death at age twelve during the yellow fever epidemic that almost destroyed Fairlea. Lost over half his people, and he never forgave the Lord for his part in it.

Lorna Leeanne Hill was one of the local beauties from a fine, though impoverished family, and John Thomas fell in love with her at first sight. He said that they complemented each other - he the fire and she the breeze to fan him. They were very social, and from the time that J.T.,Jr.,was off the breast they took him to all the political soirees all over the state. John Thomas was an advocate of the territory's becoming a state and worked endlessly toward that end. Then Samuel Joseph arrived, and Lorna just never seemed to regain her strength after his birth. When Lornalee was born prematurely five years later, she was so small that she had to be wrapped in warm flannel and kept inside a satin-lined feather pillow. Lorna never left her bed from that day and didn't live to see her daughter's first birthday.

John Thomas pined for over four years and then married Lorna's baby sister Elizabeth. It was not a happy marriage, no children were produced, and John Thomas soon followed his beloved Lorna. Elizabeth had never liked living at Fairlea. It was much too isolated for her taste, and when her share of the estate was settled, she immediately packed her bags and went to the big city, New Orleans, gladly leaving Samuel and Lornalee in John Thomas's widowed sister Hattie's care. Last time that any of them had heard about her she was reportedly happily ensconced in a beautiful townhouse in the heart of the city having champagne for breakfast and enjoying the other appetites of the prestigious New Orlean society.

Marse Samuel was a good man. He was firm but fair and had the respect, if not the love, of his people. Now Miss Edwina was loved by all of them, a warm, affable, compassionate woman. She loved her home, her garden and her children. Her husband she also loved but mostly tolerated in his later years, because Sammy, as she called him, seemed to change. Didn't get mean exactly, more like short tempered. She said it was brought on by his hearing loss, and because he couldn't hear, he'd shout angrily. Naturally, everyone would shout back.

When the girls moved away, seemed like the balance was gone out of Edwina's life, and there was nothing but shouting all day long. So she took to her room more or spent her time in her garden and was in the presence of her husband less and less.

Talmai had known that he didn't want to be a field hand, and when he became seven he'd prevailed upon his pa and Marse Samuel to allow him to train to be a groom. That was more to his liking, and he'd spend every waking minute in the stable. His favorite horse was Marse Samuel's little filly, Lucy B. Master Marshall never let anyone touch his stallion, Thunder, and that included Talmai, except to rub him down or feed him and only when he was around. Master Landress had rather sit on the porch doing nothing, just looking off into space, so Talmai got to ride and groom Pegasus, whom he loved, but not as much as he did that little Lucy B.

He was going on nine years when the fever hit Fairlea again, and this time it took not only his granny, but his pa and Miss Edwina and over a dozen of the other slaves. Marse Samuel's heart just went out of overseeing Fairlea. He spent most of his time rocking on the verandah and riding Lucy B. slowly up and down the land like a lost soul. Landress moved to New Orleans, and Marshall took over the running of the plantation.

Then the cotton blight with its deadly black arm swept the entire northern part of the state. From the Mississippi River to the Atlantic ocean it blackened and defoliated the fields of healthy plants. First the rains came, then came the high winds, and everywhere they traveled the black arm struck ruining plantation after plantation, Fairlea among them.

Silvey and Talmai, age eleven, had to be sold. Along with the few remaining field slaves they were bought by a Mister Sylvester Simpson from Louisiana, his plantation, Ridgeland, having been spared.

****

The trip to New Orleans with Sylvester Simpson's man, Durrance, was the most exciting thing that had ever happened to Silvey and Talmai. Fairlea had been the only home they'd known; neither had traveled for more than six miles from it, and then only at the insistence of Miss Edwina. Their yearly trip before Christmas, when they went into Monticello to select the store-bought items that she had had Mister Knight set aside for her people to choose from, was the only time that the Fairlea people left the plantation.

Durrance - he was never referred to as mister or marse..just Durrance - was an enigma to Silvey and Talmai. They did not know just what position he held with Marse Simpson, so they lowered their voices and mumbled more than usual just in case he was someone of great importance and would take offence at how they addressed him.

They were driven by wagon to the railhead in Tallahassee. Everything along the narrow, rutted road was of interest to the inquisitive Talmai. He had seen more wagons in just one mile than he saw in a year at Fairlea. The blight had created an exodus of people that that part of Florida had never seen. Some were going to north Georgia, others to Alabama or Louisiana, but all were escaping the devastation that surrounded them. Their wagons were piled high with their belongings, and their hungry livestock, following their creaking, laboring wheels, strained to get to the shoots of green grass beside the sandy paths but out of reach because of the ropes around their necks. Smaller carts, sometimes pulled by the children, held crates of chickens and hogs of the owners, who sought refuge from the fever and blight.

Along with the four other slaves Silvey and Talmai sat in the back of the wagon, jostled by the uneven road, its rough bottom digging into Silvey's smooth, black skin beneath the wash-tired dress. At every pothole, she wanted to moan, but could not. She could feel Durrance looking at her. She didn't like what his expression conveyed as he brazenly stared at her. Marse Samuel would have stropped anyone who had looked at her like that...but Marse Samuel was no longer her owner, her protector. Durrance was squat, fat, balding, and his pale eyes seemed to have extra layers of skin. "He looks just like a gopher," she thought. Sensing his lust she became afraid.

They finally arrived in Tallahassee. "Get outta the wagon and hurry about it," he said in a voice that lacked the authority they were used to. Talmai rolled his large eyes at his mammy as if to say, "Dis foreman cain't hold a candle to Marse Samuel's man, Blackie, can he mammy?" Silvey, frightened, squeezed his young hand and shook her head to let him know that he was to give no expression whatsoever and, of course, not a word.

She wanted nothing more than to be settled into Marse Simpson's plantation, Ridgeland, where she hoped they would have the same position as they had had at Fairlea. They were the house people, and Durrance wouldn't be messing with the house people...just like at Fairlea. Silvey had inherited her position from her Ma Sarie, but this Durrance treated her and Talmai just like the others. She feared that they were but field hands, now. Silvey shook her turbaned head dejectedly. "To think that we de same as dese niggers. Oh, my...oh, my." She shivered.

Marshall Baker had sold them as a group, no one having more value than the other. He had been so disheartened by the toll the fever had taken, and then the blight, that when his poor old father babbled nonsense, rocked on the porch and rode his filly all day long going nowhere and doing nothing, in desperation he took matters into his own hands.

Still holding Talmai's hand hard, Silvey followed the others into the box car, narrow and foul smelling. Talmai was so excited he was about to burst. A train ride! He'd heard of trains, of course, and had heard their low, moaning, lonesome whistle as they traveled on the heavy air across Fairlea, exciting him - making him curious, but to actually see one, and better yet, to ride on one almost made him forget Fairlea.

Durrance told them where to put their slops and handed them each a cornpone, about the size of his pudgy hand, and put Jimbo in charge of the water barrel. Then he slid the creaking door closed. Lord, it was dark. There was a sliding trap on the ceiling to let in some light, but if the rains came hard it would have to be closed.

Talmai huddled close to Silvey. Their backs leaned against the rough side of the car. Then it started jerking - then it would stop - start again with a jerk, metal on metal, the clinking noise of the wheels invading the darkness. Old Ruby, scared, started humming, then Jimbo added his bass, and soon Silvey joined in, and Talmai, soothed by the familiar singing, eased into sleep, his kinky head against his mammy's slight shoulder as the car swayed from side to side into the night.

They rode but one stop. The big door slid open, and Durrance shoved a lantern inside and asked Jimbo if everything was all right. "Yassuh," he said. Durrance volunteered that they'd be in New Orleans by the following evening. He moved the lantern all around until it got to Silvey. She could see his expression, and Jimbo saw it, too, but decided that she deserved whatever she got. "That uppity nigger ain't no better'n de res' of us now. She be gettin' hern." and he grinned at her as he thought it. She pulled Talmai closer and tried to figure out what she could do to prevent Durrance from having his way with her, but she couldn't think of a solution.

When Durrance next opened the door, Talmai was the first to jump from the box car. His dirty shirt was quickly grabbed by Durrance. "Where ya think ya goin', boy? Ya tryin' to cause me a problem, huh? Ya try just one thing, and Ah'll have yore kinky, black head dangling from a big ole tree, ya heah?"

Silvey was out of that car and holding on to Talmai quick as a cat. "Mah boy don want no trouble, Mister Durrance, suh. He's a good boy."

Durrance grinned. He now had the key to that gal's lock. He'd get her through that boy of hers. He knew just how to make things miserable for the likes of that one. He was unashamedly salivating. Silvey grabbed Talmai, pulling him into the mule-drawn wagon that was waiting for them.

Talmai couldn't be frightened. There was so much to see that his eyes were large with wonder at all that surrounded him. Something smelled so good, better'n his Ma Sarie's fried chicken, better'n hot peach pie. Oh, he was hungry! The vendors' carts containing everything imaginable lined the long street. The people happily bustled around serving food in paper cones to their customers. Some of the men even had on their top hats, and the women, it appeared to his inexperienced eyes, had on the most beautiful gowns he'd ever seen. "They be prettier than Miss Leeanne's and Miss Nellie's wedding dresses." All the excitement made him ignore his grumbling stomach.

There were wooden carts with dead chickens dangling from ropes all in a row, and he even saw a whole hog's head with its eyes just staring at him. One cart sold fish and crabs and wiggly things that he didn't recognize, their obvious odor happily mingling with the sweet aroma of the flowers in their brightly painted carts. "There be more flowers than in Miss Edwina's whole flower garden," he observed in amazement.

The buildings seemed to reach almost to the sky. They were pink and lavender and green and had brightly colored flowers in big pots hanging from oversized baskets, and people were peaking from behind lace-curtained windows. Some of them were laughing as they waved to friends across the busy street. The signs hanging from the buildings had funny writing on them, so he couldn't read them. Miss Leeanne would have been disappointed in him, for she had taught him well.

But the most exciting things of all were the horse-drawn street cars clanging up and down the brick-paved streets drawn by big horses like he'd never seen. The people were hanging on for dear life as the wooden cars rumbled past him.

Talmai knew that he'd never forget that sight nor those smells and sounds. He became puzzled when he saw his mammy's head down, her hands covering her face, trying to block out everything around her. The tears seeping through her fingers, stained her rose print, cotton blouse.

"What's de madder, mama? Why ya cryin' so hard?" She did not remove her hands but began humming low, trying to erase all that was foreign around her. Talmai patted her quivering back and said loudly, so they could all hear, "Ah'm gonna take care of you, mama. Ain't no harm gonna befall ya," and Jimbo laughed, the low sound coming from deep in his throat. "You sho gotta powerful job ahead of ya, Talmai," he said when he glanced up at the seat that held Durrance and the other white man Marse Simpson had sent to fetch them to Ridgeland.

CHAPTER II
RIDGELAND MANOR

Alicia Simpson was a plain woman in appearance only. Her nose was large enough for two faces, her eyes small, dark brown and close together, lips thin and constantly pursed, her sparse hair straight and pale, but she was bright, an excellent conversationalist, a perfect hostess, and she was fearless. She'd nursed the quarter's Negroes during three successive years of the fever and seen to their education and religious training just as any devoted mistress would. She had also reared five strong, intelligent, devoted children, three boys and two girls.

Alicia had supervised Ridgeland Manor since she'd inherited it from her family, the Rosamonds, formerly of Virginia, and even before she'd decided to marry one Sylvester Hartford Simpson. She married him for two reasons: he was handsome beyond belief and a gentleman throughout his being, the perfect counterpart to her personality. Where he was weak, she was strong - he pliable, she clever - he a plodder, she witty - she politically aware, he unbelievably ignorant. Sylvester was always a beat behind Alicia, but she loved him with reverence and total commitment. For his own good she'd tried to put an end to his philandering escapades in New Orleans.

Sylvester was almost loved to death, he determined early in their marriage, and soon sought the refuge of Madam Bourquin's upstairs haven whenever he could escape Ridgeland, which was not often enough. It wasn't that he didn't love Alicia, and it wasn't that he didn't appreciate her, for he did both. But even after twenty six years he still had difficulty looking at her. He'd avoid that whenever possible - the woman overwhelmed him. Her homeliness usurped his strength and purpose, and his poor mind needed frequent cleansing by all that was beautiful.

He'd take the *Delta Sun* pretending that he had pressing business in New Orleans and had almost become clever at deceit, but the cunning Alicia had seen through his guise. Although she knew she should be perturbed with him, she rather enjoyed his pathetic ruse. If he could just keep his visits quiet, there would be no problem, she decided.

Obvious he was not, nor flamboyant, and not given to excess, she thought. What Alicia didn't know was her husband's penchant for gambling - it simply was not in his character, she would have sworn, but a word here and a word there from their frequent guests made her suspicious. Added to that, the books did not show the profit that they should have after three years of bountiful harvests. But it wasn't until after Talmai's and Silvey's arrival at Ridgeland that she realized her suspicions were warranted.

It was Alicia's practice to inspect the new people Sylvester purchased, having always taken an interest in their welfare. She believed that everyone had a talent and that it should be developed to its fullest potential, even the Darkies. When Durrance and Lem Whitcomb rode up with the new people from Fairlea, she was at the quarters welcoming them as soon as they alighted from the wagon.

In a row they stood with their heads bowed...all except Talmai, who was openly staring at the homeliest woman he'd ever seen, but then she smiled down at him, and he responded with a face-wide smile, and he knew immediately that he had a friend.

"Mr. Durrance, I see that you have returned." She did not particularly care for Malcolm Durrance but had inherited him along with Ridgeland twenty seven years earlier and had become accustomed to him. She read him well, and although there was little respect between them, they tolerated each other, and he did his job adequately, or so she thought.

She began as she always did. "I am Mrs. Alicia Simpson, wife to Mr. Sylvester Simpson," and they could tell that she was proud of her position. "You are now at Ridgeland Manor, and my family and I want you to be with us for a long, long time. I am in need of a house woman. Do either of you have any training in that area?" she asked as she looked first at Imogene, Jimbo's woman, then at Silvey.

Neither spoke nor raised her turbaned head, but Imogene did shake her head no and Silvey yes. Talmai couldn't help but blurt out, "Mah Mama's been a house woman since she was borned, haven't ya, Mama?"

Durrance stepped forward and said as loudly as he could manage, "Don't ya talk less'n you're asked, boy."

Alicia patted Talmai's sun-dampened head and said, "He's just excited, Mr. Durrance. I'm sure he meant no disrespect."

Quickly Talmai latched onto Silvey's skirt and assured the missus that he didn't. When Alicia patted him, Durrance knew that she'd taken a liking to the boy and that he'd have to think of another way to get at that black wench. But have her he would.

"What is your name?" Alicia asked Silvey, lifting her chin. Silvey forced herself to open her frightened eyes and found them staring into beady, brown ones, but she could easily see the kindness shining through. "A'hm..A'hm called Silvey, ma'am."

"Is this your boy, Silvey?" She knew that he was but wanted to engage her in conversation so she wouldn't be so frightened. "Oh, yassum, Talmai's mine and Luther's, but he be taken wid de fever 'long wid mah Ma Sarie."

"I'm sorry to hear that, Silvey. It's terrible to lose your loved ones. We'll not be able to replace them nor their love here at Ridgeland," She looked at all of them as they stared at her, "But you'll be treated with respect if it's respect you deserve and earn, and you'll always be treated fairly. Is that not so, Mr. Durrance and Mr. Whitcomb?" They shook their heads in the affirmative, and there was not one of the five adults nor Talmai who believed them.

"Silvey, you come with me. Yes, you may bring your boy along. I want you to meet Ada and Snow. They've been running Ridgeland Manor since before I inherited it. They will teach you a great deal and, who knows, perhaps they can learn from you as well."

"Talmai, is it?" He shook his head and responded, "Yassum" with gusto. She liked the boy and knew she'd have use of him.

"Talmai, Mr. Simpson, or Mr. Sylvester, however you choose to address him, has need of a body servant to assist Caleb, who is getting along in years and can no longer stand those long, tiresome trips to New Orleans. Would you like to be trained for that position?"

"Oh, yassum, and I'se good wid hosses, too. Why, Marse Samuel let me groom Lucy B. and Mistah Landress let me tend to Pegasus."

"We already have several grooms, Talmai, but I'm sure that Mr. Sylvester would be able to spare you from time to time so you could assist at the stable."

"Ah'd lak dat, ma'am..uh..Missus.." "You may call me Alicia Ma'am, as do the others."

"Yes, Miss Alicia Ma'am. Dat would be fine." He was quick and bright and, she thought, probably ten or eleven years, a good age to train for her purpose. His expectant face was raised to her, waiting, when she turned toward him and said, "Miss Estelle, my youngest daughter, has classes on the side verandah every morning after first bell, and I'd like for you and your mother to attend. Would you like that?"

He was going to agree with everything Alicia suggested and with enthusiasm. "Good. I thought you would. Since you're so young, about ten?" she questioned. "I'se 'leb'm," he interjected. "I'll ask you to help Silvey with her lessons. You'll have more time to practice than she. Promise?"

"Oh, yassum, Miss Alicia Ma'am..Yassum."

"That's yes ma'am, Talmai, not yassum. Say after me - yes, ma'am," and he did.

Estelle, who was going on sixteen and almost as homely as her mother, took a special interest in him from the beginning. He was quick to learn, just as Alicia had suspected, and he took to his new job of body servant to Sylvester in no time at all. Caleb would have been jealous a few years before, but now, with his arthritis so bad in his bent back, he was just plain grateful.

The mister was fastidious to a fault about his appearance as was Alicia. It seemed to Caleb that he was forever having to go up and down those long stairs, and now he had him a fetch-boy. He referred to Talmai as the boy, never by his given name. It was, "Fetch this or that, Boy," or "Boy, fetch Mr. Sylvester's shirt from Snow," or "Boy, go to the laundry room and fetch Mr. Sylvester's clean handkerchiefs, and you best make sure that Snow's got them folded just so. You hear me, Boy?"

Talmai always said, "Yes, Mister," and refused to use Caleb's given name as well. He had decided that when Caleb started calling him Talmai, he would call him Caleb, but not until.

Down that long, curved stairway his skinny legs would dash, past the vestibule, through the dining room, onto the side porch and into the laundry room, that was situated off the kitchen, separated from the house, just like at Fairlea. Snow kept half a dozen flat irons all in a row in front of the open fire. She was ironing painstakingly the fourteen-foot, white linen tablecloth that had to be washed and ironed after but one sitting. Alicia was a stickler for cleanliness, and Snow took great pride in her work. Must have been about thirty of those tablecloths, Talmai observed.

"Snow, Caleb wants Mr. Sylvester's handkerchiefs, and he said that you bettah make sure that they folded jes right."

"What'd he say, Talmai? What'd that uppity nigger say fur ya to tell me? Why, Ah been at Ridgeland jes as long as dat uppity, no-count man has, an' ain't evah been de day dat Ah'd evah han' Mistah Sylvester a unproper handkerchief...not evah!"

Talmai loved it when Snow got all riled up, because she forgot all the learning that Miss Estelle taught her, and besides, he could calm her down with his sweet talk and patting her and agreeing with every little thing she said, and she'd for sure slip him some dark syrup candy. Never failed. It became a game, and Snow knew and loved it.

Alicia had watched Sylvester's frequent trips for over two years with growing alarm, when she decided that Talmai was trained well enough to accompany him. Caleb was surely relieved. She had Ada summon

Talmai to her in the morning room. She had been promising him this position for the last seven months and continued to encourage his efforts, but he was beginning to think that his time would never come.

When Ada first approached him, he was sure that it was to be chastised about something or other, but the nearer they got to the morning room the broader her smile became. He was sure that he was going to be told by Miss Alicia Ma'am that he had earned the right to accompany Mr. Sylvester on the big boat to New Orleans, the most fascinating place in the whole, entire world. He babbled excitedly to Ada about the sights he'd seen when just a youngster before he came to Ridgeland as they approached the morning room.

Talmai was tall for his age, and Alicia was sure that looking older and with his quickness he'd be able to handle the job she had planned for him.

She began, "Talmai, you're going on fourteen now, approaching manhood, and it is a man's job that I have in mind for you, and I now believe that you'll be capable of handling it. This is between you and me, Talmai. No one else must know what I am about to confide in you. Is that understood?"

"I'm glad you understand, because it is of the utmost importance. The preservation of Ridgeland is at stake. I entrust this mountainous responsibility into your young hands, and you must have lessons about this poker."

He was very sober. What on earth was she talking about? He thought that he'd be accompanying Mr. Sylvester on the big boat to the city to see that his clothes were brushed and laid out and his toilet as he expected. What on earth was so all-fired important about that? He'd been doing just that for two years now. But he listened, and when she got to the part about his accompanying Mr. Sylvester to the men's saloon on board the *Delta Sun*, and said he would be in charge of all the money used in the games, he was flabbergasted. She said that he was to receive instruction in the game of *poker*, because that was the game that Mr. Sylvester seemed most fond of.

"Talmai," she said, "Sit down here. No dear, here beside me," she patted the fluffy cushion. "Now, as I told you, no one must know about this. It would appear that my dear husband has fallen victim to this game, *poker*, and has gambled away a great deal of money. I plan to bring this to his attention. You see, he is not aware that I know of this, shall we say, weakness. I want him to allow you to accompany him to the men's saloon, and when he has reached a certain amount of money that we have agreed to, you are to inform him that it is time for him to retire."

"Now, he must agree to this arrangement. If he does not, then I'm fearful of how long we can maintain our standard of living and protect our other interests."

"Are you agreeable to this arrangement if Mr. Simpson is in accord?"

An adventure of this magnitude had him gulping uncontrollably. Just being in the men's saloon would be excitement enough for anyone, but to be in charge of all that money, well...

"Oh, yes, Miss Alicia Ma'am, I am indeed, but as you suggested, I'll certainly need to know something about this poker. I want to thank you for having such faith in me. It makes me very proud," and he stretched to his fullest height.

"You've come along just fine, my dear, just as I knew you would. You've always known on which side of your bread had the butter," she said as she looked at how handsome he had become.

"I would have entrusted this mission to Jessup or Henry, but I do not want them to think less of their father. Do you understand my decision?"

"Oh, yes, Alicia Ma'am. I think it was wise of you," but he wanted to say that those two didn't have the gumption for such a scary mission. "And, I'll do my very best for you and Mr. Sylvester. When do I begin my lessons?" he asked, trying to hide the eagerness in his voice but not succeeding.

"A Mr. Conner O'Farrell of New Orleans has agreed to take on the job of teaching you. I have been told by, shall we say, my associate that he is versed in the game and is fairly new in New Orleans and that Mr. Simpson does not know him. He will arrive and present himself as our guest, and I'll introduce him as a prospective cotton buyer, so that dear Syl does not become suspicious."

He could tell that she was deeply concerned. She lowered her head and continued. "I am afraid that he is being cheated in this *poker*, and you will certainly need to be expert in all its phases to assure me that he is not. This Mr. O'Farrell guaranteed my associate that he would be able to instruct you thoroughly in only a few weeks' time. Do you understand, Talmai?"

Sylvester was very upset when Alicia approached him, telling him of her knowledge of his heavy losses at poker and that she had been aware of his debts for a very long time, that they simply could not afford his extravagance and what she proposed so that he could continue to enjoy the game but with a reasonable expenditure. He saw the wisdom in her argument and had to agree with her proposal of allowing Talmai to dole out the money. He simply had no choice. He was not told about the poker lessons or that Talmai was also to police the games.

He seemed relieved that his wife would allow him to continue his pleasure and that she hadn't mentioned his frequent visits to Madam Bourquin's in the city. Quickly he escaped her presence with his oft-used excuses, and she, contributing it to his guilt, never realized that his escape was to avoid having to look at her.

Conner O'Farrell arrived at Ridgeland Manor early on a Saturday afternoon. There was a slight drizzle, and Talmai had the umbrella over the buggy door even before Conner had opened it. Instant communication transpired between them, and Conner thought, "This is the boy, I'm sure. I wonder just how much they've told him. Maeve would have a fit if she knew what I'm up to, but when I return with enough currency so she can stock her own shop, she'll not ask another question. Wonder, she will, but she'll not ask. I know my Maeve."

He took the umbrella that Talmai was trying his best to keep over his head, but his young arms were just not long enough. He started to ask for the boy's mistress when Alicia came out onto the second floor balcony, that was directly above the pillared entrance way. She wore her black bombazine dress with a white lace collar, as she did every day except Sunday, when she'd change to more colorful dress and would lead her people in prayer on the side porch.

Conner was only seventeen, but no one would have believed it. Alicia thought him to be in his late twenties and was surprised that her associate had sent one so young. She stood beside the French doors and placed her hand over her mouth as she thought, "What a delightful-looking young man, but I do hope that he's not too young and that he has the experience I require." He removed his grey felt hat and bowed gracefully, and she smiled her most ingratiating smile and raised her white gloved hand.

"Mr. O'Farrell, welcome to Ridgeland Manor. Talmai, show Mr. O'Farrell into the morning room, and I'll join him directly." His manners were impeccable and his dove grey wool suit perfectly tailored. When he removed his gloves she sighed loudly. She had never seen such beautiful hands on a man. Alicia Rosamond Simpson appreciated beauty. She had noticed Talmai studying Conner's costume and manners and knew that he'd apply both to himself if he were in a similar position.

Conner rose as she entered the sun-filled room and noticed that she had added a frilled lace cap, and that told him that she, as homely as she was, was a vain woman. Conner understood vanity.

"How very nice of you to answer my summons, Mr. O'Farrell. I do hope that it has not inconvenienced you in any way."

"Mrs. Simpson," he bowed, "No inconvenience at all. I was enchanted by the beautiful Louisiana country side, and the drive leading to Ridgeland Manor was breathtaking. You have a lovely estate. I am delighted to be here," and he raised her extended hand gently to his lips.

"He is so polished. We're going to have a delightful two weeks ahead of us. Perhaps I can prevail upon him to extend his visit for a longer period," but she said aloud, "It is lovely, isn't it? We are very fortunate. I do hope that the arrangement Mr. Coutant made with you is satisfactory?"

"But of course, Mrs. Simpson."

"Please call me Alicia, Mr. O'Farrell," she said almost coquettishly. He was amused and began to enjoy mesmerizing the mistress of Ridgeland Manor.

"And you, Alicia, must call me Conner," he added as he followed her to the soft rose, damask love seat placed strategically inside the deep bay window. The morning light streamed brazenly into the rather small room, that was Alicia's favorite. The walls were book lined, and a small spinet was against the west wall beside the French doors that led to the more formal parlor. Two deeply cushioned floral chairs faced the love seat, and the room was filled with flowering plants and ferns.

"Such a lovely room, Alicia. Lovely." She gestured to the floral chair opposite her and rang for Ada to come draw the curtains on the bay window, as the light was too strong for her guest. "And, Ada, please bring our guest some tea, or would you prefer lemonade, Conner?"

"Lemonade would be fine."

They chatted, and his quick wit and ability to turn a phrase left her speechless. She was delighted to find that he was not married. She immediately thought of dear Estelle but, realizing her shyness, knew that she would surely get tongue tied, as she always did around young men. Charlotte would have been a more likely candidate but had insisted on marrying that Howard Beasley, so beneath her station, but it did seem to be a happy union, even Alicia had to admit.

"Conner, should we proceed with the business at hand?" He nodded in the affirmative. She repeated the information that he had been given by Henri Coutant and emphasized the importance of teaching Talmai to distinguish between an honest player and a cheat. He was quickly warming to the task before him.

When Conner first arrived in New Orleans, not quite two years earlier, he had helped his cousin Denis at his hotel, La Paloma, but soon found that he'd not be able to return to Macon a rich man with the wages he received. In order to court Berta properly and to convince her father that he was worthy he would need to make a great deal of money.

It had not occurred to him that Wesley Norwood did not object so much to his lack of wealth but rather that he was an Irish Catholic and not a Protestant of the Old South. And why he thought that Berta had a romantic interest in him, his sister Maeve could not for the life of her understand. The girl hardly knew that he was alive as he mooned over her from afar. It almost broke Maeve's heart when she saw how he went to jelly whenever she had come into their millinery shop with her mother. His was indeed a one-sided infatuation. But Maeve knew Conner and knew his determination, so never even hinted at how foolish his dream was.

A frequent visitor to the hotel was Captain Elmore Quigley, a friend of long standing of Denis's. He piloted a sternwheeler on the Mississippi, the *River Queen*, and encouraged young Conner to work as his purser. Conner had the polish and education that the position required, and Quigley had noticed how well Conner handled the hotel guests.

Conner accepted the position but soon realized that a ship's purser was never to realize the kind of wealth he needed to impress the Norwoods, so when he was relieved of his duties in the early evening, he would wander toward the action in the men's saloon. He soon found the other gentlemen encouraging him to join them in the games. At first he was hesitant in his betting but very quickly overcame his timidity and eventually became a formidable player.

When Conner informed Elmore that there were professional gamblers who were cheating at his tables, Elmore, being a man of very high principal, became concerned and hired Conner to keep the games honest by informing him when he suspected an unreliable patron. Conner was soon making more money in the saloon than in the purser's office, so Quigley hired him, at his request, full time to police the games. He worked in that position until Alicia summoned him.

Henri Coutant was a frequent passenger on the *River Queen*, and he and Conner became as close as Conner allowed anyone to be. He was a studious man, well versed in a variety of subjects, and he and Conner would converse for hours over a brandy at the end of the long night. Being an insomniac, he appreciated the hours that Conner helped fill.

Alicia was a distant cousin of Henri, and when she determined that she would have to take Syl's gambling seriously, she immediately sent for him. It was he who decided on their course.

He sought passage on his return to New Orleans on the *River Queen* and approached Conner that very night with Alicia's proposal.

"Henri, you're indeed speaking to a novice...but, my dear man, not a fool." But when Conner was told the outlandish fee she was prepared to pay, he immediately asked Quigley for a leave of absence from the sternwheeler.

"Now I can help Maeve realize her dream of owning her own shop and have plenty left over to impress Wesley Norwood," he thought naively.

"Talmai, Ah don wan ya ta git so highfalutin' actin' wid me, young man," Silvey informed him as she pulled his shirt sleeve. He hadn't meant to get short with his mama, but he was in a hurry to get back to the game with the light supper that Conner had requested. They had been working very hard in the morning room.

Sylvester had been sent to New Orleans by Alicia with a promise that he would not frequent the poker tables and would tend only to the business that had been assigned him. Son Jessup had been asked to accompany his father for the two weeks, so she was comfortable with the situation. That should give Talmai plenty of time to learn and understand the game, she thought.

When Talmai started to protest Silvey's accusations, he caught a glimpse of Durrance at the corner of the laundry room. He put down the tray of sandwiches and questioned his mama.

"How long has he been hanging around here? Has he been bothering you?"

"Now, don git upset, son, he ain't caught me 'lone yet an ain't a-goin' ta. Ada an Snow heppin me know jes where he be. Don worry 'bout me. Now go on wid dees fur Mistuh Conner 'fore he come a-lookin' fur ya."

"I don't like that man hanging around here, Mama. Now you know how I feel about him," he said raising his voice.

"Ah knows. Now git! He ain't gonna try nuttin' wid me after all dis time." He was not convinced but decided that he'd not pursue the matter further until after his lesson with Conner.

When Talmai got back to the morning room, Conner could see that his mind wasn't on the game and questioned him. Talmai decided to tell him of his suspicions. He trusted Conner and felt that he'd believe and perhaps even advise him how to handle the matter.

"Do you mean that he's been after her since you arrived here? Well, the old reprobate! Why haven't you spoken to Sylvester or Alicia about him?"

He held his hand on Talmai's arm and quickly said, "Don't answer, lad. I understand. Do you want me to say something to her on your behalf? With you on the trips with Sylvester I'm sure you won't be able to keep your mind on the game if it's concerned you are with your mother's welfare. I'll speak to her immediately." And he did.

Alicia was not just perturbed about Durrance - she was down right angry. She called Silvey into the parlor and questioned her. Then she asked Ada and Snow to corroborate her story about how he was always hanging around and if it hadn't been for Talmai that she was sure that he would have had his way with her. Ada and Snow eventually confessed, after much prodding by Alicia, that he had done the same with a number of the other women and had indeed succeeded with some.

Finally, Silvey told Alicia what he had said to her numerous times, something that she hadn't dared tell Talmai, that he'd get a poke from her first chance he got. Alicia made up her mind. She'd have to let him go. It wouldn't upset her one bit, because she had never liked nor trusted him, but she simply could not have Talmai's young mind being concerned about his mama when he was supposed to be concentrating on her Syl's problems. She was proud of Ridgeland, and the fact that that man had molested those women, some just young girls, and misled her for all those years infuriated her. Alicia Rosamond Simpson did not like to be taken advantage of.

She decided not to wait for Syl's return and so asked Conner if he would be present when she dismissed Durrance. He happily agreed.

Durrance fidgeted and rolled his hat around and around between his sweaty hands as he stood just inside the door, his hooded eyes barely open. "What does that ugly old woman want? Hell, she ain't never called me into her fancy parlor before. Never!"

"Mr. Durrance, you have met my guest, Mr. O'Farrell, from New Orleans. I have asked him to be present during this meeting."

She continued in a very deliberate fashion choosing her words carefully. "I want you to pay close attention to what I am about to inform you, Mr. Durrance. I have been told by three members of Ridgeland Manor's house staff that you, shall we say, molested and attempted to molest a number of our women, and Mr. Durrance, do not interrupt...please let me continue..."

He drooled and taking one hand off his hat wiped the saliva with the back of his hand but did not utter a word.

"I have no recourse but to relieve you from your position as head foreman of Ridgeland. It is with great distress to me that I do so." She rose majestically to face him at eye level. "I must in all honesty after this long relationship, but with no regret, send you from Ridgeland to whatever life you can afford."

He did not respond. He just stood looking at her. "Mr. Durrance, are you aware of the enormity of this accusation?"

He could not seem to find his tongue, and his face began to grow red. "Why in hell's name should poking a couple of no-good nigger wenches get this old woman upset! Hell, that bastard husband of hers does it every time he goes to New Orleans. What's wrong with her, anyway?" He kept clearing his throat but could not speak.

Conner finally intervened. "Mr. Durrance," he turned toward Alicia and asked if she minded whether he spoke, and she, looking gratefully at him, assured him that she was appreciative of the intervention.

"Mr. Durrance," he began again. "Miss Alicia is being as direct as she can possibly be in her position as Mistress of Ridgeland Manor, and I can assure you that if Mr. Simpson were here it would be he who would be flogging you first and then be relieving you of your position."

Before Conner could continue, Malcolm Durrance found his voice.

"You don't hafta be talking for Miss Alicia or Mr. Simpson, Irishman. She done made it clear that she'd believe no-account nigger wenches over me, and I been here even before she got holt of Ridgeland. Why, hell, I worked for old man Rosamond, and me not more than fourteen at the time..."

"Mr. Durrance," Alicia interrupted, "If it were not a fact that you have mistreated my people and brought shame on them, I would not have brought you here and would not have been put in the position of having to dismiss you. But, it is indeed a fact!"

He was furious. His flustered face screwed up in every direction, the folds of fat not being able to find their rightful place. Hitting his rumpled hat on his big square hand, he glared his hatred at the two of them. Conner stood immediately, but his imposing size did not frighten Durrance.

"You ain't seen the last of me - not the last! Them nigger bitches been lying and you'd believe them over a white man, old woman!" he shouted. "You're in for a heap of trouble!" He turned, then whirled around, "And you, Mr. Smart-ass Irishman, you best be looking over your shoulder every minute 'cause Durrance is gonna be in New Orleans with a long, shiny knife just waiting to cut out your yeller nigger-lovin' gizzard!"

He slammed out of the front door before Conner could react to his tirade. When he did, Conner abruptly left the room calling over his shoulder, "Alicia, do not follow!" and ran after the fat pig of a man.

Conner would and could not accept a threat against his person without putting the man in his place. Durrance had not counted on the Irishman's temper, that was as uncontrollable as his.

With his long stride he quickly caught up with him and, grabbing his shoulder, turned him around roughly. Durrance was off guard. He had been cursing so loudly that he hadn't heard Conner. Conner knew that mere words would not penetrate the man's anger but didn't want to waste time on the low-life so shouted, "Durrance!" He was close to his face, "Do not, I repeat, do not threaten me unless you're capable of carrying it out. Now get your fat ass out of here, and you'd better take only your own belongings. Do you understand me? Only - your - own belongings. And Durrance, while you're prowling the streets of New Orleans with your shiny knife, just what do you think I'll be doing? Do you think I'll be on the verandah holding my Mum's knitting yarn? Well, do you? No, my man, I'll have ready a shiny knife of my own to plunge into your pig belly...or better yet, how big a hole does a Colt make?"

He let that sink in and added in a threatening voice, "Now remember this, I have eyes like a hawk and ears like a bat, and never have I received a scratch from the likes of you. But, you should see my adversaries, Durrance. You should see them!"

"You're to be off Ridgeland before nightfall, and you, sir, are the one who had better be keeping a sharp lookout."

He watched Durrance waddle past the chinaberry tree. His face had gone from red to white before he left the path. He was still mumbling obscenities about how he was going to let light into that bastard Irishman. Conner had not heard Alicia follow him out to the front porch, and when she touched him lightly on the shoulder, he jumped and whirled around ready to do battle.

"Oh, Alicia..."

"Mr. O'Farrell...I mean Conner, you were magnificent. I wish that Sylvester had been here. Oh, my dear, you were superb. I do so hope his threats were not sincere. I do not want to cause you any harm."

"Alicia, I think it wise that Lem Whitcomb see to Durrance. He is the second in command, so to speak, is he not?"

"Well, yes, actually he is. But is he to be trusted? I do wish Syl were here. This is so distressing..."

"Now, don't. Here, let me have Talmai bring you a nice glass of sherry to calm you, and you should rest and put this unfortunate episode out of your mind." He took her arm firmly and led her to the morning room and summoned Ada.

"Ada, your mistress is weary, and I'd like you to have Talmai bring her a glass of sherry. Here, Alicia, let me assist you." She did not protest - she was loving every minute of his attention. How gallant he was. If only Estelle had more, well, charm, but she did not. She allowed Conner to hold her gloved hand and sighed contentedly.

Talmai, Snow, Silvey and Ada were hovering just inside the vestibule and had not missed the show. They were overjoyed at how Conner had put the riffraff in his place. Snow had already got word to Jimbo that Durrance was leaving, and that the quarters' people had best keep an eye out for what he might be doing over at his house.

****

"That son of a bitch ain't gonna scare me. Who the hell does he think he is coming here strutting like a peacock with his fancy foreign talk! He might fool that ugly old witch, but he don't fool me, not for a minute. Hell, he probably ain't even a gentleman, just a scoundrel fooling that old woman."

"Serve that bitch right!" He slammed into the foul-smelling room. There wasn't a foot-wide spot free from clutter. Everything from rags to wadded-up paper to dirty clothes was strewn around. It'd sure take more than a bresh broom and dust cloth to take care of the filth. Alicia had asked him repeatedly whether he had had one of the quarters women clean for him, and he always grunted something unintelligible. So she figured that if he was satisfied with the conditions, then she would interfere no further.

Lem Whitcomb, the number two man, shared the square, two-bedroom house with Durrance. There was a long front porch, two parlors, one large and a smaller one. They took their meals in the small room off the laundry at the big house. He and Whit were not really friends, but because of their positions took up for each other - at least they had in the past.

Whitcomb had been at Ridgeland less than ten years. He was as good a cotton man as there was in Louisiana and took pride in his work and appreciated being associated with a fine plantation such as Ridgeland. He'd married a girl much younger than he when he worked up at Oak Manor, but she ran off - couldn't stand the loneliness of plantation life. They were together less than a year. Whit understood why she ran away but couldn't seem to adjust to being without her. When he heard that Sylvester had need of a number two man, he came down to Ridgeland, twenty miles south of Oak Manor.

He was not an unhappy man because he loved his work, and the Simpsons allowed him time off for fishing and hunting. If Whit had a passion for anything besides the cotton fields, it was drowning a worm in the river or pond and hunting for quail, rabbit or deer. Durrance didn't do either but used his leisure time sitting on the front porch or sleeping or trying to figure out how he was going to get at one of the black gals without the Simpsons' finding out. Until now he had been successful.

Sylvester saw that they got their pleasure time in New Orleans, but Whit was the only one to take advantage of it. Durrance had rather force himself on one of the quarters' gals. Whit didn't have much respect for him but had less for the Blacks, so he never let on to Sylvester about Durrance's doings.

Whit even saw him entice that little high-yeller daughter of Naomie's into the shed back of their house, and her not more than eleven or twelve. He had his pockets bulging with molasses candy, and that fool gal followed him just like a lamb going to slaughter. Whit thought about stopping him or at least saying something to him, but he never did. He just got his pole and headed for Dead Tree Pond to fish and tried to forget about it.

Alicia sent Talmai down to the field to summon Whit. Talmai was cautioned to give him the message and nothing more, for he loved to talk and elaborate, and Alicia knew his penchant for telling stories.

"Mr. Whitcomb, sir, Miss Alicia Ma'am wants to see you at the big house this minute, and I'm not to say another word." Whit raised his brows and began to quiz Talmai. He'd never, not once, been summoned to the main house, not in the ten years he'd been at Ridgeland.

He was curious and a little bit frightened. The boy didn't seem concerned, so he assumed that nothing tragic had occurred. He knew that he'd not be brought to task about his work. He worked the hands hard but was fair, and they seemed to respect him much more than they did Durrance. What on earth could she want with him, he wondered.

Alicia and Conner were sitting on the back verandah, that looked down from its high perch onto the Mississippi River about a half mile away. He was having a bourbon and water, and she her afternoon cup of tea. They seemed very relaxed, and Whit noticed that she was dressed in a colorful blue and mauve printed sateen dress, one that she usually wore for church services, that he and Durrance were obliged to attend along with the Darkies. "Something is for sure up," he said to himself.

"Oh, Mr. Whitcomb, thank you for coming so promptly. Talmai, you're excused, dear." She waved him away with her white-gloved hand, and he reluctantly joined Ada and Snow and his mama as they listened inside the parlor door. Conner stood when he addressed Whitcomb, and when the Irishman started speaking, Whit became uneasy.

When Conner finished, Alicia asked Whit if he understood the responsibilities that he'd have to assume as number one man and if he thought that he'd be capable of carrying out such a tremendous job. Conner had now taken his place beside Alicia.

Whit assured her that he understood and that he saw no reason not to accept the position. The only thing that he might have a problem with was seeing that Durrance cleared out of there without causing trouble, but he was smart enough not to mention this to them.

"Mr. Whitcomb," Conner said, sensing his concern. "Do you envision any problems with Durrance? And if you do, you need only to say so. I would be most willing to assist you in removing him from Ridgeland. As a matter of fact, it would give me great pleasure," he smiled at the captivated Alicia, her homeliness not bothering him in the least, as she was one of the few women Conner had met who could carry on an intelligent conversation.

"Oh, no sir, I don't," he lied. "Me and Durrance always got along fine. But, Ma'am, he's not to be trusted. Now I'll carry out your orders, and between Jimbo and me we'll make sure that he leaves Ridgeland right away." To himself he thought, "I don't know how in hell I'm going to get that bastard off, but do it I will. He's as mean as any White man I ever seen."

"Excuse me Ma'am - Sir." He bowed slightly and did not know any other way to leave the room, so he backed out. When he got to the side porch, he loudly sighed and proceeded to make the long walk back to his and Durrance's house. He stopped. He decided on another course of action and headed for the stable to get Rasputin, Sylvester's black stallion. He was allowed to ride him when Sylvester was away. He headed for the fields and Jimbo, his mind working hard trying to figure out how he could get Durrance off peacefully. The man had a short fuse. He had been witness to it before.

Whit did most of the work at Ridgeland, work that was Durrance's job. He never complained because he liked to stay busy. That man slept more than anyone Whit had ever seen and spent most of his energy avoiding work. He'd sometimes sleep fourteen hours a day. Oh, he'd be up at first light to get the hands to the fields, but then he'd go back to the main house to eat breakfast, return to his own house and sleep 'til time for the dinner bell, and then go to the fields to make sure Naomie and some of the children had taken the dinner pails to the fields and toted the water. Back to the main house he'd go for his big meal, and then he'd nap 'til most time for the hands to leave the fields close to dark.

He'd get on poor old swaybacked Jupiter, who was so old that he could hardly trot, but he suited Durrance. He'd yell out some orders very important-like, then head back to the main house for his supper, sit a while on his porch 'til the bugs got too bad, then turn in for the night. The next day he'd do the very same thing.

Whit never saw the man bathe, and from his odor knew that soap and water didn't like him either. Naomie did the washing, and if she hadn't come around to gather up their clothes every week, he figured that Durrance would probably not change them for months.

Jimbo saw Whit coming and knew why. Ada and Snow had got word to him that there was gonna be hell to pay when Whit had his say to number one, and that he was to make sure that number one didn't cause Miss Alicia Ma'am any trouble. Jimbo had worked close to the south field so he could be on ready when Whit summoned him. He was getting anxious.

Jimbo didn't like Durrance, but he'd always treated him fine. He knew about his having at Naomie's gal, Blossom, but if Durrance hadn't got at her, probably that long-legged boy of Pearl's would've. Hell, there wasn't a single quarters gal that he hadn't had by the time they were on the rag. His name was Humphrey, but the men all called him Hump. Didn't have to worry about that high-faluting Talmai. He thought he was too good for the quarters girls just 'cause he was the son of that stuck-up house girl Silvey.

One thing Jimbo hated though - he'd sure hoped Durrance would've got a poke from that bitch. That'd bring her down a notch or two. She really thought she was something, looking down on him like she did just 'cause she was a Guinea nigger. He just might have to take over where number one failed, he just might. He smiled as he thought of her fighting and struggling and digging those long fingernails into his back, trying her best to keep him off her. "Yes, oh yes. Jes might hafta poke that nigger 'til she cain't hardly walk. That'd put her in her place."

"Jimbo," Whit called. "Gotta chore for you that don't have nothin' to do with cotton." He proceeded to tell him about how Alicia had promoted him to number one and instructed him to get rid of Durrance without any commotion. Jimbo allowed as how he'd do the best he could to help him, and they left the field together with Whit astride Rasputin and Jimbo walking alongside - they didn't hurry.

Durrance saw them coming up the path even before they got to the grove of hickory trees. "If that Whit thinks he's gonna take my place without a fight, he'd better think again!" He laughed when he thought, "Had to go get Jimbo to help, did he? Well, it'll take more'n them to get me off my place!"

He dropped the dingy curtain and went toward his room. "Ain't nothin' in here I want or need but these," he said kneeling down, hardly able to bend over his bulging belly. He pulled two long knives out of their box from beneath the high bed. Stroking them lovingly he remembered when Sylvester had offered him his side arms, but he told him that he'd rather work a knife or whip. He'd only had to use the whip a dozen times or so in all the years he'd been number one, and hadn't used the knives since '54.

That New Orlean's bastard wasn't alive to tell about it. He got excited just thinking about the dark Cajun he'd relieved of his stinking soul with his pleading in that stupid foreign tongue of his. Durrance didn't pay him any mind and plunged his knife clean up to its guard. His Cajun blood was spurting all over that dark alley. "That'll teach you, you dumb bastard, making fun of me, calling me a fat-assed prong!"

Durrance slipped just outside the back door. He knew Whit would look all over the house first. He could read him like a book. Then he'd come out back, big as you please, not suspecting a thing. "Take my place 'cause of some lying, stinkin' nigger wenches! It ain't gonna happen. Not to Durrance! I'm *number one*, you hear?"

Crouching down behind the tall weeds that grew thick beside the back steps, he waited. Jupiter was tied to a tree not six feet away, his old tail swishing flies, his eyes half closed. He wasn't fast, but he'd get him to New Orleans, Durrance thought. He checked him, making sure that he was still tied, then looked at the door again nervously waiting. The sweat drops were so large that they poured off the rolls of fat and then bounced off his dirty blue shirt.

He knew by Whit's nature that he'd ease open the door, and was probably even dumb enough to call him. Probably thought that he'd give up being number one peaceful-like.

Durrance heard the door creak open. He was on ready, and even before the foot touched the second step, he lumbered up and laughed as he plunged the six-inch blade into the stomach just above the rope belt. When he saw the rope he realized that he'd made a mistake. He'd stuck Jimbo.!

"Gawd almighty - what the hell!" is all he could say. When he looked up into Jimbo's disbelieving, bulging eyes, he jumped back out of the way as Jimbo pitched forward into the dirt, not saying a word - he made just a gurgling sound.

Durrance didn't take time to look back. He untied Jupiter and was gone by the time Whit got to the back door. Whit had taken time to look underneath Durrance's bed to see if the knives he was always bragging about were gone, knowing that if they were, Durrance was also gone.

It never crossed Whit's mind that Durrance would be stupid enough to go after him. Mr. Simpson would have had him tracked down, no matter where he tried to hide, and would have strung him up high even before a judge gave the word. You just didn't kill a good cotton man in Louisiana and live to tell it.

Durrance high-tailed it to New Orleans and buried himself in the dark alleys of the French Quarter. "This beauty," he said as he caressed his knife, "Will easily find the throat of that Goddamned Irishman - on that you can lay a wager." He drooled as he thought on it.

CHAPTER III
LA PALOMA

The purple bouganvilla lazily draped over the green wooden gate that led to the alley beside the pink stucco of the La Paloma Hotel. Conner had used the side entrance many times as he made his way to his room in the back of the building. He knew his mum suspected his nightly escapades when he was off the *River Queen* for a few days, but she did no more than raise her graying eyebrows, looking directly into his pale eyes, and he, avoiding her questioning gaze, would either give her an affectionate hug or kiss, or he'd be so stimulated by his evening's excitement that he'd get her a cup of tea and regale her with the sights and sounds of the city, never going into detail as to his own activities.

Una, or Agnes, as she preferred to be called now that she was in America, seldom left the hotel except for daily Mass at St. Ignatious, only three blocks down La Salle Street. She no longer attended evening devotionals, as she had in Macon, using her arthritic knees as an excuse, but if she had been honest, she'd have acknowledged that the unruly people on the streets at dusk made her uneasy. The only person to whom she had confided her discomfort was Monsignor Haut, who had, upon her arrival in New Orleans, taken an immediate liking to the devout Agnes.

Vincent Haut was quite young to have achieved the rank of monsignor, she thought, but he was such a warm and caring man, whose laughing eyes could never mask his true feelings, that she soon warmed to him, and he became her confidant outside the confessional as well as in. Her concern for her children and the welfare of Denis's young ones gave them a great deal to talk about, for he was especially fond of children and they of him. Vincent was a frequent guest at the La Paloma, having been welcomed into Agnes's kitchen for a good meal almost every Thursday evening, an event that they both looked forward to.

Miraculously, Maeve finished with her work at Madam Colette's on those evenings and would join them, and when Conner was in port, he too would show up earlier than on any other night, for he found Vincent intelligent with a ready wit, not as stuffy as some of the priests he had known in Macon.

Conner had noticed that Maeve's coloring, that was usually quite pale, allowing her pale ginger freckles to shine through, would heighten, and she was more talkative and animated when around Vincent.

Agnes did not notice. Had she done so she would have immediately stopped extending the weekly invitations to protect both of them, for Vincent had become like a son to her, and she would have died rather than have him tempted by her own daughter with herself playing a part in the breaking of his vows. Oh, she had seen how the young women of the church eyed him lovingly, and it sickened her. He was a tall, handsome man, clean shaven with thick dark golden hair that refused to be tamed and would curl brazenly through the hair wax he used. He carried himself in an almost military manner...straight, but with not too much pride, just a hint, she observed.

The La Paloma was not in the best section of town. It had been at one time, when Denis first bought it, but the neighborhood seemed to be deteriorating, and Agnes was more comfortable helping the Sheehan children with their catechism lessons of an evening than being jostled on La Salle St.

Once in a while she'd accompany Maeve to Collette's and assist them with the hats, but her eyesight had failed in the past few years, so the intricate work that she had loved since she was a young colleen in Ireland had to be done by others. She didn't miss it like she had the first year that they were at the La Paloma. That had been a difficult adjustment, but she had been heartened by Conner's happiness. The darkness that he'd displayed that last year in Macon seemed to have lifted and been replaced by a new purpose, especially since he'd been on the *River Queen*.

Collette promoted Maeve to an assistant at her exclusive shop in less than six months after their arrival and had also accepted her as an apprentice in dress making. She had been told by Collette herself that she had a unique eye for design and color. Agnes had never seen her so happy, and Maeve even accompanied her to Mass, no longer displaying the rebellion she had shown in Macon.

Agnes also noticed that she had taken more of an interest in her own appearance. She was not a beautiful girl - lovely was a better description. She wore her thick auburn hair in a more fashionable style now, and though her freckles had faded somewhat, they were still noticeable across her straight nose. Agnes had always told her that her greatest asset was how her big gray eyes would light up when she allowed herself to give into joy, or when she looked at Conner. Had Agnes noticed, she could have added Vincent to the list, too.

Daily, Agnes prayed that Maeve would find a nice young man to light up her eyes, as Agnes had found in her Nolan. He would have to be Catholic, of course, but so far she had not found one, and Agnes worried and lit another candle. She would have worried even more had she known of Maeve's affection for Vincent and his for her, but since they were not fully conscious of it themselves, Conner, the observant one, was not about to inform on his Maeve. He wanted for her only happiness, and if he had thought she could find it with Vincent, he'd have intervened. He liked the man, and there were few he could say that about.

It seemed that Maeve's life was filled with her work, but Agnes knew that being Collette's assistant would never satisfy the ambition she saw in her tall daughter. She was unaware of the quiet conversations Maeve and Conner shared in the La Paloma kitchen after she had retired for the night. How those gray eyes would sparkle with her dada's fire for life as she shared with Conner her dreams, her ambitions, and he, sipping his bourbon, would listen and encourage her as he had from childhood. Theirs was a unique bond.

Maeve, in turn, heard the tales of shipboard and how the rich women were dressed when Conner described their gowns in minute detail, the type of lace, buttons and fabric and Maeve with her pad and pencil would sketch the designs to be incorporated later into her own creations. He had become quite expert in his observations and even suggested the type of fabric and colors for the gowns. Conner had a flamboyant style, as did his father before him, and his mother's studied sense of composition. He never missed a thing.

This aptitude was used as well in the games he played in the men's saloon. His unique ability to distinguish a player's weakness, a raise of an eyebrow, the flutter of his lashes, the ripple of his fingers on the polished table when he had a good hand. Conner would be cautious at first, but by the fifth or sixth hand he'd have his opponents figured. Oh, their eyes could hood their anxieties and frustrations, but the shuffle of their boots underneath the table and their handling of their cigars as they rolled them around in their sweaty hands soon gave away their holdings, and Conner would ultimately capitalize on their nervous mannerisms.

By the time Sylvester Simpson and Talmai Harrison made their maiden voyage on the *Delta Sun*, Talmai had been thoroughly trained in reading the players. Conner had taught him how to distinguish a player who was cheating, and how best to inform Sylvester, who was truly a poor player, though enthusiastic, almost childlike, without giving away Talmai's knowledge of the game, and therefore Alicia's part in the scheme. Her interference would have hurt him terribly. Talmai had to be very discrete in how he handled him.

Conner had been amazed at Talmai's insight. For a lad barely fourteen he was unusually mature. He would have thought that the controlled life he led on the plantation would have dulled his instincts, but it had not. Conner wasn't aware of how Talmai had had to play Caleb and Snow and his Ma Silvey, and even Ada, and he also had to be on the alert at all times with Durrance and that Jimbo hanging around. He'd had to be very skillful in handling the adults around him since his Pa Luther had been taken with the fever, and he had to assume the adult role when they left Fairlea. Silvey was so frightened by the turn her life had taken that Talmai's childhood ended abruptly when they arrived at Ridgeland.

The *Delta Sun* was a magnificent steamer. Talmai, or rather Harrison - Conner and Alicia had decided to call him by his last name because they felt it sounded older - should have been unnerved by the ship's size and elegance, but he was not. The only sign that he was impressed by it at all was in his eyes - they just got bigger and bigger. He could hardly wait for Mr. Simpson to get settled in their suite and rushed around the rather small room hurriedly laying out Sylvester's evening clothes. As Conner would have said, "The games await," and he was having difficulty containing himself. He was about to pop!

"Mr. Simpson, sir, if you'd like, I'll order your tea to be delivered to our suite immediately after you've napped," he said running his words together. He was so excited as he brushed away at the suit.

"What did you say, Talmai? Boy, slow down. You're speaking so rapidly that I can't make heads or tails out of you." Harrison repeated slowly, and Sylvester calmed down, too. "That would be fine, Talmai, I mean Harrison. I don't know if I'll ever be able to remember that blasted name. I don't know why Alicia insisted on getting me confused," and on he babbled, nervously.

Harrison wasn't nervous, he thought. He did everything by habit, but after he had taken care of his duties, he allowed himself to ponder his situation. He was unaware that Conner planned to board at the next river landing. He simply had to see how Harrison handled the situation and had before he left Ridgeland assured Alicia that he would look in on him. Sylvester knew him as a cotton buyer, so he shouldn't become suspicious and, if he engaged in a little poker while on shipboard, well, that was normal.

Alicia had tipped Conner handsomely and expressed a genuine

desire for him to visit Ridgeland again. He reconsidered accepting her invitation when he realized that she would immediately begin to groom poor, dull Estelle in preparation for his return visit, so instead he assured Alicia that he would at least write and that perhaps he'd be able to visit Ridgeland Manor at a later date.

She seemed satisfied by his promise, but before he left cautioned him, "Please, my dear friend, you must be on the alert for Durrance." Conner could tell that she was truly concerned and smiled his most devilish grin and replied as he took her extended hand to kiss, "Dear, Alicia, I'm touched by your concern, and you can be assured that I'll be very careful in the *big bad city*." Had he not made light of the situation and been honest with her, she would have seen that he too was concerned. Durrance was not the type to threaten a person and not carry out the threat, and Conner knew it.

Rushing alongside the polished railing of the first deck and rounding the stern, Conner then ran up the narrow stairs. He wanted to alert Harrison of his presence before Harrison accompanied Sylvester to the men's saloon. He had been told their suite number by the purser, whom he knew. He saw the napkin-covered tray containing Syl's tea and rolls outside their cabin and knew that Sylvester was still napping when he rapped lightly on the door.

Harrison opened the door, his forefinger pressed to his lips to warn the intruder to be quiet because his master was asleep. When he saw Conner, the hand dropped and his perturbed expression evaporated, replaced by a wide grin that spread from one side of his animated face to the other. He stared up into the familiar, crooked grin of Conner's and slipped outside, pulling the door quietly shut behind him.

Conner rested his hand on Harrison's young shoulder and in a low whisper asked, "Did you think I'd be letting you have all the fun, lad? Did you now?"

"Thank you for coming, Mr. Conner, sir. I haven't had time to get nervous yet, but now that you're here, I'm sure I'll do much better."

Looking around to make sure that they were not observed, Conner saw a man who he recognized from the *River Queen*, an ill-tempered gambler, who he knew had been cheating, and whom Captain Quigley had removed from the games at Conner's suggestion. The man saw Conner and bristled as he recognized him. There was no way that the man could have been positive that Conner was the informant, but Conner had known by his attitude that he suspected him.

Conner could feel the man's hatred as he approached and decided to not show that he recognized him. Instead he pretended to be looking for someone else, and when he looked directly at the man, he allowed disappointment to register as if to say, "Oh, I thought you were so and so, but I see that you are not." He turned back to Harrison and said in a loud voice, "No, that is not Mr. Johnson, as I had hoped. Please inform your master that I'll continue searching for him. Good day to you."

Conner left Harrison and followed behind the man, who had slowed down to make sure what the Irishman was saying and had breathed an obvious sigh of relief when he realized that he had not been recognized. Conner walked to the outside rail, flicked his cheroot into the swirling, brown river water and began humming to himself as he lackadaisically walked past the man.

Conner knew that they were in for trouble, for he was sure that the man would be at the tables.

"Damn...damn...damn! We couldn't have hit it at a worse time. The man is a trouble maker and as clever as any I've ever seen. I'll have to be on my guard this night."

Harrison could smell the smoke and hear the noise as they approached the men's saloon, he a few steps behind Mr. Simpson. He had noticed Sylvester's excitement while he was brushing the blue gabardine frock coat and straightening the grey satin vest. "I'll have clothes like this some day," he thought. His thoughts were interrupted by Sylvester.

"Talmai...dagblast it! I mean Harrison. I know Miss Alicia told you what your function is to be. Now don't you be nervous, Lad." He placed his veined, manicured hand on Harrison's shoulder. "You must stand directly behind me - just lean against the wall and relax. Mr. Montoya always brings his body servant along with him, for his eyesight is so poor, and no one has ever commented on it."

Sylvester chuckled. "Montoya's fair game, so to speak. Almost never wins a pot," and he continued to chuckle. Harrison wondered at the intelligence of the man - it would appear that he too was fair game, the same as this Mr. Montoya, except that he obviously had the excuse of poor eyesight. It never ceased to amaze Harrison, this stupidity. Take Durrance for instance. He was determined to get at his Ma Silvey and ended up losing his job and becoming a wanted man when he stabbed that dumb Jimbo. "Whew!" he said aloud.

"What, boy?"

"Oh, I was just thinking about what you said, Mr. Simpson, sir.

About how that poor Mr. what's-his-name does something in a pot." Sylvester bent double with laughter. "That's a good one, Talmai...a good one. Must remember to tell the men that one. Does something in a pot, is it," and he continued to laugh.

Conner was the only smart man Harrison had ever met except for his Pa Luther, and maybe Conner was even smarter than he. Harrison didn't feel guilty about his summation of Conner's being more intelligent than his dead father. It was truthful, and he realized that he could learn a great deal from him. He could hardly wait to get to the tables, so he could observe Conner in action. As Miss Alicia Ma'am always said, "Talmai knows which side of his bread has the butter." He laughed as he thought, "Yes, Miss Alicia Ma'am, I surely do," and followed close behind Sylvester into the smoke-filled, noisy room.

There were at least ten round tables in the large room, most surrounded by well dressed men already engaged in a game or just laughing and talking and drinking schooners of ale or sipping brandy. The only women present were obviously ladies of the night from New Orleans, expensively dressed, with face rouge on their expressive, laughing faces. Harrison had to keep reminding himself not to stare, but it was becoming very difficult; they were so beautiful to him. But he knew that if he was caught staring at one of them, there would be hell to pay, and he'd be just as dumb as that stupid Durrance. So he lowered his head and followed Sylvester, who paid them no heed, as he headed in a direct line to the back table, where he gestured to Harrison to lean on the wall as instructed.

The ladies just wandered around the room hugging and kissing the men as they teased them and accepted the drinks they were offered. When the most beautiful one of all sidled up to Mr. Simpson and inquired of him, "Who is the handsome boy with you, Sylvester, honey?" Harrison's mouth fell open totally out of control as he lowered his eyes, trying to look past her partially exposed breasts, all pink and white, that he was sure were on the verge of tumbling over the edge of the lavender brocade dress's low neckline right in front of him.

Harrison managed to force his eyes past his shaking knees and focussed them on his feet, hoping that they'd stay there forever, when she said, "Oh, Syl darlin', please let me and Trucilla have him for the night. What's he doin' in here, anyway? We won't let him come to any harm, now will we, Trucilla? We promise, Syl." The dark-haired Trucilla just stood there smiling, not saying a word and licking the frothy ale from her open mouth.

Sylvester looked up from his cards at the girl, who wasn't more than seventeen or eighteen, and sternly said, "Taffy, you best be minding your manners 'bout my black boy. You know Captain Foley doesn't like you girls to be causing a commotion, now does he?"

She dropped her hand from his shoulder and sheepishly said, "Oh, for heaven's sake, Syl, now y'all know I'm just a foolin'.". She looked around the table at the other players and gave them her most dazzling smile. "Gracious me, what would me and Trucilla do with a little old black boy, anyway, when we could have one of you big handsome men? Huh? Now what would we?" and she turned very slowly around and put her long, slender arm around the shoulder of the man in the brown suit. "Dancy, how much longer you gonna play? I haven't had a visit with you in, gracious me, I don't remember when. I've been missing you." He smiled up at her teasing face and pulled her down as he ran his hand inside her bodice, pinching the nipple of her full breast until she yelped delightedly. "Oh, Dancy, you old thing you!" He whispered loud enough for the curious men to hear, "I could go wid ya right now, Taffy, but it'd hafta be a quick one, 'cause these cards have been speaking to me tonight."

She kissed his hand and nibbled his fingers and said triumphantly, "G'night gentlemen. See you in a little bit. You want Trucilla to come with us, honey?" she asked Dancy. He kissed her bare shoulder and said, "You're all I have time for tonight, my sweet. Maybe on my return trip." and as she turned Harrison noticed her glancing at the bulge in his crotch, and she smiled as if to say, " *you're next*," licked her full, red lips and left with Dancy. Harrison hadn't realized what was happening, and had he not been so dark, a blush would have alerted the men of his problem, and they'd have had his head on a platter for sure.

He was so embarrassed when he realized his lack of control that all he could think was, "I'm surely glad Conner isn't here to see this. He'd know my condition for sure. He doesn't miss a thing. Whew!"

"Gentlemen," Mr. Simpson said strongly and with great expectations, as he always did, "Shall we turn our attention to the games?" They cut for deal and the game began. Harrison kept glancing through the smokey haze for Conner, but he was no where to be seen. He noticed, seated at the table next to them, the man who had passed their cabin earlier, and he wore such a serious expression on his swarthy face that Harrison began to watch him. He wasn't sure, but he could have sworn that the man was cheating when he dealt. He tried to avoid staring at the man's left hand as he was missing a finger.

"I must be mistaken," he thought, "but I'll watch him more closely when I get a chance." He wanted to use his new skills so he could impress Conner.

Sylvester seemed to be playing very well. He turned to Harrison and smiled and said loudly, "Harrison, I think you've brought me luck," and indicated with his hand the large amount of coins before him. Harrison grinned and replied delightedly, "Yes sir, Mr. Simpson, sir. I'm real glad." The other men paid no attention to him whatsoever until Sylvester foolishly over bid two hands, and the mound of coins dwindled before him.

Sylvester slightly turned toward Harrison, and he was by his side immediately. Sylvester excused himself with, "Gentlemen, I'll return shortly. One must relinquish the bourbon consumed in order to replace it, eh?" Harrison noticed several of the men raise their brows questioningly, and one said low, "Is our friend from Ridgeland taking lessons from his body servant now?" He got a laugh from them, and Sylvester turned red with humiliation. Sylvester turned to the man and related the story about the pot, that Harrison had told him earlier, and added, "Mr Randall, if my body servant does not know what a pot is, then I'm indeed taking lessons from the wrong source, wouldn't you say?" He grabbed Harrison's arm as he rushed to the outside door, not waiting for the man to apologize.

On their way out Harrison saw Conner. He was leaning against the opposite wall from where Harrison had stood, and through the thick smoke he had not seen him, or perhaps he had just arrived. Sylvester was so anxious to find out how much money he had left, that he did not see Conner. When Sylvester closed the door behind him, he asked, "How much do I have left? The evening's so young, and I do truly want to continue playing, Harrison."

"Mr. Simpson, I suggest that we go up to our suite and attempt to adjust our plan as much as possible." He wanted to suggest that he bet more conservatively against the man opposite him, because the man was excellent at bluffing. He had noticed his mouth twitching every time he bluffed, but Mr. Simpson was so intent on his own holdings that he was totally unaware. Of course, Harrison was in no position to mention it. It was very frustrating.

Sylvester was so upset by this new arrangement of a set amount of money for him to use that he bombarded Harrison's ears all the way up the stairs, while in their suite and continued on their return. Harrison had seldom heard the usually docile man even raise his voice while at

Ridgeland. This was a caged man before him.

Harrison wondered when Conner was going to make his move to join them. He need not have been concerned, for on their return Conner had taken Sylvester's place at their table, "Just to fill in until Mr. Simpson returns," he said. When Sylvester saw him, he said to Harrison, "My luck is bound to have turned. Look, our friend Mr. O'Farrell has joined us."

"Yes, sir," is all Harrison allowed himself to reply, because he knew that Sylvester was pleading for him to be more lenient with the purse strings. But his luck did not turn, and by the time Dancy rejoined them, Sylvester had had to drop out with the excuse, "Gentlemen, I'm near exhaustion in this hot room. I think I'll retire for the evening," but he hesitated, glancing toward Harrison, hoping that he could prevail upon him to ignore Alicia's edicts. But when he saw him standing very erectly with such a sober face, he knew that there would be no more stake. He rationalized, "Better this amount of pleasure than none at all."

With Harrison in tow they passed by Conner. He stopped Sylvester, his hand on his arm, and asked, "Mr. Simpson, would you join me for a bourbon and cigar while I finish this hand?"

"Well, I would be delighted, Mr. O'Farrell."

"Conner, Mr. Simpson. Call me Conner. There's no need to be so formal."

"And you must call me Syl, Conner. I'll observe for a short while only, though." He feigned weariness with a sigh, and Harrison smiled slightly at Conner, his expression of gratitude obvious. He was beside himself with excitement. He was going to see his teacher at work, now that Mr. Simpson was out of the game.

He was mesmerized as was Sylvester. When Conner threw in a hand of two pairs, queen high, Syl almost blurted out his incredulity, restraining himself just in time. The gentleman with the twitch was not twitching, so Conner was positive that he had at least three of a kind...and he did, three jacks. He beat out Dancy, who had two pairs, kings over sixes, and was sure the two pairs would take the pot.

Harrison stood away from the light beside the darkened wall and restrained any emotion. He realized that he'd have done the same as Conner and was grateful for even a vicarious game. Sylvester was so amazed that he babbled too much, and Harrison was afraid that Conner might ask them to leave. But he didn't. Instead he said, "Syl, I must caution you. In your exuberance, my good man, you might give away my trade secrets." He said it with a laugh, but Sylvester got the message and made no move to leave.

Dancy soon threw in his hand and exclaimed, "Well, gentlemen, the only thing I got out of this evenin' was a poke with Miss Taffy, and, hell, I could've got that without you guy's stripping my money belt. G'nite."

Dancy was an affable, middle-aged man, portly, with a full red mustache and long sideburns that were also red, whereas his other hair was brown. Harrison found that strange. He had never heard of the henna dye that was commonly used by the Whites and some of the Creole ladies.

When Dancy left, the man from the next table rose and asked if he might sit in, that his luck could only improve, and a definite change was needed. Conner again showed no signs of recognition, and Harrison, wanting to warn Conner of his suspicions of the man's cheating, did not know what to do.

"He'll be on to him in jig time if he's cheating, and he'll not let that missing finger throw him. I'm not believing this! Never thought I'd see this my very first time at the tables," he nervously thought while anxiously waiting for the game to begin so he could see how Conner handled the situation.

Unbeknownst to Harrison, Conner had already alerted his friend, John Malloy, the former purser on the *River Queen*, of the man's cheating habit and asked that he have someone notified. John knew of Conner's love of the game and his growing reputation as an expert player, so he had alerted the first mate, Glenn, to the situation.

The man pulled the oak chair that Dancy had just vacated back from the table as Conner sat relaxed, leaning back in his chair, his white Panama rakishly on the back of his head, and smoked his cigar. The game resumed. Harrison had to keep wiping his mouth - the saliva just wouldn't stop seeping out of the corners, no matter how hard he tried to stop it.

When Dancy passed by him, he whispered in his ear, "Miss Taffy said she was goin' to have at ya, boy." He bent over, his hand covering his laughter, his head bouncing up and down, as he gestured toward Harrison's bug-eyed expression. Harrison thought he'd die on the spot. Never in his fourteen years had anything this exciting happened to him.

He remembered the ride in the wagon to Tallahassee and then the ride on the train to New Orleans and how he felt, and he thought then that nothing could have been more exciting than that. But there was nothing as thrilling as this game, poker. "Not even a poke with Miss Taffy." He laughed to himself and blushed as he thought of it, not that he could even imagine what that would be like, but he quickly diverted his face for fear someone in the room could read his mind as he pondered his unusual situation.

He need not have been concerned. They were all intent on their own pleasure, and by now Miss Taffy had already succeeded in enticing yet another gentleman into leaving with her and Trucilla, who was not nearly as pretty to Harrison and on the plump side. She did have pretty, shiny, dark brown hair and high coloring that her royal blue, taffeta gown set off just right. Harrison could hear her gown and petticoats rustle all the way across the room when she walked out with Miss Taffy and their gentleman friend. He liked the sound. Sounded like lots of money to him, and he knew that he'd certainly like the sound of that, just as Conner did.

Conner was relaxed, although on the alert. He was anxious to show off his skills to his protege. He had been very proud of how Harrison had handled himself earlier, when Dancy had obviously said something to him causing Harrison to almost mess his pants, but he'd remained calm. He'd find out what he said later after Syl was asleep and he and Harrison went over the evening's events, he decided, spreading the deck of cards with an exaggerated flourish face down in a crescent shape on the table.

"Gentlemen, let the game begin," he said looking at the gambler from the *River Queen* sitting opposite him. "I don't believe we've met, sir," he said formally as he rose to shake his hand. The man did not rise, but extended his hand, the left hand with the forefinger missing, and Conner could see the other men react and try not to look at it.

"My friends call me Sago, but my name's Palmer."

"So it's Sago, is it now? Welcome," Conner said sitting back down. The white-haired man won the deal, and they began. Harrison was cautiously watching Sago's expression, but the man did not flinch, nor did he react in any way. Nothing! It was as if his face had been painted on. Harrison studied and studied but could see no body movement nor repeated gestures. He was baffled because he was sure the man was cheating. He won almost every pot when he dealt. Conner was winning his share, but the white-haired gentleman threw in his hand and quit in disgust at his sudden turn of luck, and the two other gentlemen from Natchez quit as well. Only Conner and Sago remained.

Harrison had been so intent on the game, that he had not noticed the man who came and stood beside him and was just as interested as he. The crowd had left its own game and had gathered around Conner and Sago. Sylvester's face was so red that Harrison was concerned for him. He sat glued to his chair, rubbing his sweaty palms in anticipation. The air was electric, and the men surrounding the table were unusually quiet. Even the giggling girls were silent.

Sago shuffled the cards, dropping a few to get sympathy for his deformity, feigned embarrassment for his clumsiness, then picked them up and began again. Harrison looked around and noticed the observers were avoiding looking at the missing finger. "Look for the obvious," Conner had told him, over and over. Sago, who insisted on checking the cards before dealing, very methodically checked each card and was unusually jocular, keeping up a constant patter. Harrison made himself stare at the missing finger. He didn't like to, but he did anyway. He noticed that Sago was rubbing the cards with the stump and realized why no one had suspected him before.

"So, that's it! He's smart enough to know that people avert their eyes to avoid looking at his stump. He's marking the cards. Bet he's got a needle embedded in it. I just bet he does. I wonder if Conner knows!"

Conner had had difficulty figuring out Sago's cheating when on the *River Queen* but had noticed that when he dealt he consistently got a good hand. There had been no doubt in his mind that the man was cheating. But how? Capt. Quigley kicked him off the steamer before Conner had a chance to really observe him.

"A game of draw, sir?" Sago asked, and Conner responded, "A good no-nonsense game, Sago." The first four cards dealt to Conner were three sixes and an ace. His fifth card a deuce. Syl's was definitely not a poker face, as Sago had determined from the beginning. When Conner threw in the ace instead of the deuce and asked for a card, Syl's mouth dropped open, his reaction confusing Sago, just as Conner had hoped. But when Conner picked up the second deuce, giving him a full house, Syl was flabbergasted, and his expression was misinterpreted by Sago.

What could the Irishman have? The chances of four of a kind or a full house were slim. Was he working on a straight and drew the wrong card? Was that why the man reacted in disbelief? Maybe he was working on a flush. Sago knew that he had only one face card, because he had marked them. What could beat his three queens? He determined that Conner was bluffing.

Sago had planned to bet cautiously at first, but when Syl reacted in that manner, he changed his mind and raised Conner heavily. He was positive that the most he could have was three of a kind and knew that his three queens were higher. Conner saw him and hesitated before raising him modestly. Sago raised him again confidently and was surprised when Conner saw him. "Might as well go for broke," Conner said with a nervous laugh. It was the largest pot of the evening, and the crowd gathered around was dead quiet, and Harrison, his mouth now wide open, was panting.

Sago's barrel chest heaved. "So the goddamned Irishman thinks he can bluff Sago, does he? I can't believe he's so stupid. Didn't even recognize me, him with his high and mighty airs. I'll just fix his shanty Irish ass!"

Sago said triumphantly, "Lets see 'em, Irishman."

When Conner laid down his full house slowly, card by card, Sago stared in disbelief, then became furious, snorting like an angry bull. He lunged across the table at him tilting the table on Conner, the money and cards sliding off onto the floor. But First Mate Glenn was by Conner's side and shoved Sago backwards. Conner stood looking down at the red-faced man, but only his mouth was smiling - his eyes were stone cold. He whispered something to Glenn, who turned to Harrison and motioned for him to approach. Harrison told him about the needle that he was sure was imbedded in the stump. Conner had been right. Harrison's satisfied expression had told him that he had Sago figured out.

Then Conner said calmly, holding up a handful of marked face cards, "Sago, this is First Mate Glenn, and I believe he'd like to have a word with you."

"Mr. Sago, may I please see your left hand? I believe, sir, that imbedded in your...eh...eh finger is a needle marker, and there is no cheating allowed on the *Delta Sun*. Captain Foley wishes to see you immediately."

Sago knocked over his chair and rushed past the men behind him, pushing them out of his way as he tried to escape, but Glenn had his men posted at both exits, and he was quickly apprehended. They held him kicking and screaming, but not before he yelled at Conner, "You son of a bitch! I'll git ya, Irish! I'll fry yore gizzard, you son of a bitch!"

Syl sat motionless in his chair, disbelief frozen across his face. Harrison, totally without control, began hitting Conner on his back, and the two of them laughed like school boys. "Harrison, you were very astute," and in his excitement Harrison blurted out, "Thank you, Conner," forgetting to address him as *Mister*. He would learn to not make that mistake in the future, but everyone was so excited that only a few of the men noticed their intimate exchange.

After Harrison saw to his master, he and Conner stood on the deck. A stiff breeze whipped past them. Conner broke the silence, "When did you pick up on the needle?"

"I didn't at first, then I remembered what you told me, 'Look for the obvious.' So I looked at the stump finger I'd been avoiding, and sure enough, he rubbed every face card in the deck and left his mark," he said, pleased by his ability.

Conner leaned against the smooth railing looking at the lights on the banks along the riverside. They passed the small river towns slowly. Finally, he said, "You're a good student, Harrison."

"And you're a good teacher, Conner." They bid each other goodnight with a firm handshake. But Harrison had to know one more thing. "Conner, just one thing. Why did you throw in the ace?"

"Harrison, one of the first rules of poker - *Know and confuse your opponents*. I knew Syl's reaction would change drastically when I threw in the ace instead of the deuce. That obviously would confuse Sago. Of course, I had no way of knowing that I'd draw a deuce for a full house, and Syl's reaction furthered the confusion and truly set the scene. Sago knew that I had only one face card, because he had marked them. He figured I was shooting for a straight, a flush or a full house, because I drew only one card, but because of Syl's reaction, he figured I must have ended up with only two pairs or three of a kind, which had to be lower than his three queens. If I'd drawn a card giving me four of a kind or a full house, Syl would have had a heart attack. So Sago thought I was bluffing, especially when I saw him, then hesitated before raising him."

"I have a lot to learn, Conner."

****

Sylvester Simpson stayed at the elegant Hotel St. Charles on the first floor, because Caleb had had such difficulty executing the stairs for the past few years. But with Harrison's strong legs, they could now stay on the third floor and have a balcony suite overlooking Dauphine St.

When they entered the lobby, Harrison looked at his surroundings in amazement: Italian rose-colored marble floors, tall, stately pillars, urns holding dancing palms, Louis XIV furnishings in rich blue velvet and heavily encrusted gold leaf. He'd never seen such a large, ornate mirror as the one that hung over the settee at the end of the sitting area.

"I'd certainly be concerned that thing might fall," knowing full well that he'd not be the one sitting underneath it, not a body servant.

The rectangular table placed in front of the settee had a gold leaf base shaped like dolphins, that held the long glass top. The crystal-globed gas lights, surrounded by tiny prisms, were hung on the maroon brocade-covered walls. He had thought that Marse Samuel's sprawling plantation, Fairlea, in Monticello, was the largest and grandest house in the entire world until he had arrived at Ridgeland Manor. But the St. Charles was the ultimate, he now realized.

Sylvester was hurrying him through the lobby. Harrison was having a problem trying to move his feet as fast as Sylvester expected him to while gawking. His kinky head turned as fast as it could, taking in all the beauty that surrounded him.

"Ummm...I sure wish Ma Silvey could see all this. I just hope that some day I can bring her here," but he knew that was impossible. When he thought of all the money that Conner had won from Sago, he thought, "Maybe when I get rich like Conner, I can buy our freedom. Or maybe Mr. Simpson would let me bring her for one visit. Just one, that's all I ask." But he knew he was just dreaming.

Conner had told Harrison the address of the La Paloma, where he lived, and also where Maeve worked at Madam Collette's on St. Ann Street. Of course, he knew that Harrison did not have the freedom to walk the streets of New Orleans at will, since he was owned by Mr. Simpson, and because this was his first visit, he would probably not venture away from the hotel.

Sylvester was very generous with his praise of Harrison's performance on shipboard and nervously told him that he expected the same quality while in the city. Frankly, he just wanted to be rid of him so he could pursue his own pleasures. He had trained Caleb beautifully, but he was unsure about Harrison. Alicia probably sent the boy to spy on him. After all, she had found out about his gambling so she probably knew about his frequent trips to Madam Bourquin's.

"Harrison, I'd like to wear the dark blue velvet coat tonight. Think I'll dine at Armand's with Randolph Wallace to celebrate Conner's putting that riffraff in his place. Champagne for everyone, eh? I'm astonished that you noticed that the man was cheating. How on earth did pick up on that, my boy? Very astute...very astute, indeed."

Harrison said that he was so busy looking at the man's missing finger and wondering how he lost it that he saw him mark the cards and alerted Mr. Conner. Sylvester patted him and said, "You have this day earned yourself a treat, Harrison. While I'm at Armand's, I'll allow you to roam around this magnificent hotel. Would you like that?"

Harrison assured him that he thought it a splendid idea, and Sylvester reminded him that he was to be in their suite by his return, that he was not to tarry, and he mustn't leave the hotel because he had no papers, and no telling what would happen to him if the authorities caught him.

Sylvester was not concerned because he could see that the boy was frightened at being away from Ridgeland. His hands had literally shaken as he brushed his coat earlier. He smiled to himself and thought, "My Alicia sent one much too young and inexperienced to spy on me. Ha!"

Harrison did not know what to do with himself. It was the very first time in fourteen years that he'd been alone. Always before there had been someone he could turn to. He knew no one at the hotel but had noticed how friendly the young Negro boy, about his own age, had been when they arrived, and Mr. Simpson had called him Strut. He had helped with the trunk while Harrison carried the traps.

Not being able to stand it any longer, he pulled on his black funeral coat, the only one he owned, and that his Ma Silvey had made for his fourteenth birthday. Being very brave, he added Mr. Sylvester's rose satin vest and his dark grey trousers. When he saw his image in the long, oval mirror he was pleased. "I look like a real dandy!" he exclaimed out loud.

"I think I'll just wander down to the main lobby and look for Strut. He'll be able to tell me what a dandy can find to do in New Orleans." He began his descent down those imposing stairs not looking right nor left, but dead ahead, for fear he'd lose his nerve. As he clung to the marble balustrade he wondered what he'd do if Strut weren't there. What if someone asked for his papers? He belonged to Mr. Simpson, but would anyone in the big city know of Ridgeland?

Harrison stopped mid-way down the stairs and got his bearings. "I'll go to the main desk and alert them as to who my master is. At least then they'll vouch for me. Surely they'll remember Caleb, and I'll inform them that I am taking his place. That should satisfy them." But he shivered nevertheless as he approached the long desk.

When Harrison saw the man behind the desk rise from his high stool, he almost broke out laughing. He wore the smallest eye glasses he had ever seen. They had a straight silver arm on one side, that he fingered in an effeminate manner. He was slight in build, narrow shouldered, small-boned like a woman, and wore his fingernails long and polished and smelled like every flower in Miss Alicia's garden.

From behind the glasses, that sat precariously on the very tip of his long, straight nose, peered vapid blue eyes as they questioned the intruder who had the audacity to approach him. His nostrils flared, and Harrison almost laughed out loud. "He acts like I just farted. I wish I had, then that'd give him a reason to act like that. I almost wish I were White like Conner; then I'd put the lily pad in his place. I'll at least ask him about Strut."

Harrison cleared his throat as he looked around the almost empty room. The man did not look up. Again Harrison cleared his throat and started to speak, but the man interrupted him. "What, may I inquire, do you want, boy?" in an unexpectedly low voice. Harrison was surprised, but did not react. He had expected his voice to be high. He asked very politely, "I wonder, sir, if you perhaps know the whereabouts of a person known as "Strut"?

The man was taken aback by Harrison's diction and showed it when he looked up with his eyes only, his chin still down in his starched white collar. After studying Harrison, going from his handsome head to as far down as the desk allowed, then back up again, he too cleared his throat before inquiring in his practiced, dulcet tones, "And what may I ask could you possibly desire of the boy Strut?"

Harrison didn't know what to reply, so he hesitated. The night clerk said impatiently and loudly enough for the few people who were in the lobby to hear, "I asked you, boy, what do you want with Strut?" and the way he said Strut made Harrison realize that the name was offensive to him, and he could hardly wait to spit it out.

Harrison decided to do what Conner had taught him, *know and confuse your opponent.* So he did. He had already figured the man out. He gave him three S's: Scared - Sanctimonious - Strange. He had given Conner three A's: Awesome - Aware - Articulate. It was a game he played when he studied people. Miss Alicia had introduced it to him to enable him to improve his vocabulary. Now Mr. Simpson received three G's: Generous - Gracious - Gad-about. He felt he knew the man's type, and the time to confuse him was now.

He put on his fanciest airs. "Mr. Sylvester Simpson of Ridgeland Manor - I believe that he is one of your best patrons - well, I am traveling with him, and he suggested that I engage this person called Strut to accompany me around your beautiful city. You see, sir, I am a stranger in New Orleans." Before he finished, the clerk had quickly gone from bent over to up straight and respectfully interrupted, "Oh, I see. I did not know that you were traveling with Mr. Simpson."

He nervously continued. "The boy you seek works the day shift only, but I will be happy to suggest a replacement. Please wait here and I'll return in a moment.

Harrison wanted to laugh. He had confused the pompous ass into thinking he was Mr. Simpson's companion and not his body servant. But at least, if he had any problems, the man would vouch for him. The clerk returned after only a few minutes but had been unsuccessful in finding a guide for him.

"It is of no consequence," Harrison said. "If you will direct me to the La Paloma Hotel and the shop, Collette's, I would appreciate it. I have friends there, and if you wouldn't mind, sir, I'd appreciate it if you would write the directions for me."

With that accomplished Harrison stopped outside the main door and in the lamp light wrote the man's name underneath the directions. He decided that he looked just like his name on the brass plate on the desk - Night Clerk, Horatio Longue, Hotel St. Charles.

The gas-lit streets put Harrison in a festive mood. The fact that he had no money for a carriage or street car made him soon realize that New Orleans was a large city, and it might be some time before he arrived at the La Paloma.

He looked up and around, enjoying the activity of the city, listening to the music that seemed to be coming out of every doorway and window, where people were laughing and talking as they sat on the fancy wrought-iron balconies that seemed to be suspended in mid-air.

Having no watch, he had no idea of the time when he finally arrived at the La Paloma. Realizing the necessity of arriving back at the hotel before Mr. Simpson, he planned on a short visit. About four blocks before he turned onto La Salle St., the buildings had become less attractive, in need of paint and care, and the brick streets were littered and the small yards overgrown. He began to worry. He had not thought of Durrance much since he left Ridgeland and threatened Conner. He thought of him now.

"Durrance said he was going to be in New Orleans with his long, shiny knife and..." The alley ways suddenly became shadowy, and Harrison got more anxious with every step. "I wonder if Conner is concerned about Durrance? Surely he is...I surely hope he's at the hotel..." and on and on he worried.

He saw the La Paloma sign in the soft light before him. Sighing with relief, he passed the strangers, not daring to look at their faces for fear one would be Durrance.

The lobby of the La Paloma was small but comfortable. White wicker furniture, colorfully cushioned, was placed strategically underneath the lamps on the black and white marble floor. The two large floor-to-ceiling windows were shuttered and closed against the night. Magazines and newspapers were piled on the tables, and several people were reading and chatting. It was a warm and cozy room. Harrison approached the long, mahogany desk. There was no one there, but he saw a bell on the desk and rang it. The portly man, whose once-red hair was now mostly white, rose from one of the chairs and approached him.

"Can I be helping you, lad?"

"Oh, yes indeed you may. I'm looking for Mr. Conner O'Farrell."

The man raised his reddish brows, and Harrison saw concern in his faded blue eyes.

"So, it's my cousin you're looking for, is it? Now, well, Cousin Conner is out for the evening, but I'll be takin' a message if you'd care to leave one. The other man who came earlier had not wished to when he came lookin' for Conner, not an hour gone past."

"I'm sorry I missed him. Would you please tell him that Talmai Harrison, who is staying at the Hotel St. Charles, asked for him? Thank you, sir. I'll be there until day after tomorrow, and again, thank you."

"No trouble a'tall, Lad." When Harrison mentioned the Hotel, the man had difficulty hiding his surprise. "What's a black boy doing staying at the St. Charles, even one who talks so fancy. Just what has Conner gone and got himself into now?" Denis Sheehan wondered. Two people had inquired for him in one night. First that rough looking man with the bulging, turtle eyes and now a well spoken black boy. Surely, for Agnes's sake, the boy'll not get himself into some kind of trouble. I'd best say something to Maeve when she arrives home."

He looked at his pocket watch and realized that she was late, later than usual. It was after nine o'clock, and she was usually home by eight, even when she worked late. Maybe Conner had stopped by for her, as he sometimes did, and they had gone to Clancy's for an ale before coming home."

Denis returned to his chair and again picked up the evening paper. Had the shutters not been closed, he'd have seen Durrance crouched behind the vine-covered, wrought-iron fence and seen him follow

Harrison as he left. Durrance was salivating with anticipation and could not believe his good luck. It had taken him over a week to find out where Conner lived, inquiring at the docks of the *River Queen*. He was not hard to describe, and several knew of him, but where he lived they knew not. Wasn't until one of 'em said that he thought he stayed at the same hotel as Capt. Quigley that Durrance followed Quigley to the La Paloma.

He went to the desk to inquire for Conner so the manager could alert him. No fun stalking him unless he was scared. Durrance wanted him on the alert. He wanted him to wake up in the dead of night swimming in his own sweat, as he had when he dreamed of sticking the Irish bastard. He had had to keep low, surfacing only when necessary, and had disguised himself, placing a patch over one eye, and dying his fringe of hair black, because Sylvester had alerted the New Orleans police about Jimbo. Durrance had cost Ridgeland a pretty penny, and Sylvester wanted Durrance to pay for his transgressions and pay dearly.

If he could just stick the Irishman, he'd go to his grave gladly, Durrance had decided, even before he had arrived in New Orleans. Miss Alicia wouldn't have been so anxious to get rid of him if she hadn't been encouraged by that uppity, smart-talking foreigner. He laughed at her, ugly as home made sin, showing off in front of Irish with her high and mighty airs. Nigger-loving old woman!

Durrance wiped the back of his hand across his wet mouth, pulled the patch down over his eye and followed Harrison, not more than half a block behind him. The streets were busy with the laughing people. A drunk fancy-Dan almost knocked Harrison off the path, and as he was recovering his footing he saw Durrance in the lamp light. Durrance stopped when Harrison did, but although he whirled around trying to get out of the light, Harrison recognized him. He had studied him enough at Ridgeland that even with the patch his facial expressions remained the same.

"Oh, Lordy!" is all Harrison could think to say. He thought that the hotel was about six to eight blocks away, but he was not sure. The streets were better lighted now, and there were more people around than there had been on La Salle St., so that was in his favor. He began to walk on the side closest to the street and away from the shadowy buildings and alleys and increased his pace. "I'm sure he was at the La Paloma. That means he knows Conner stays there. How will I get word to him? I have to warn him. But now he'll know where I am, too."

He walked through the courtyard of the St. Charles, where the gaslights were plentiful. He had made it! Relieved, he turned to look down Dauphine, and sure enough, Durrance was there, leaning up against a tree trying to appear nonchalant. "He must take me for a fool! How could I not recognize that ugly toad? Three D's! I give him three D's: DIABOLICAL... DEMENTED... DASTARDLY!" He felt better for having labeled him and turned the ornate brass door knob. When he went to the desk, Mr. Horatio Longue acknowledged his presence by a slight nod and handed him the key to the suite of rooms.

Harrison asked if Mr. Simpson had returned and was relieved to find that he had not. Quickly, he ran up the marble stairway and, arriving at the first landing, turned, and waited for at least five minutes until he was sure that Durrance did not enter. He swung around, caught his breath and tiredly climbed to their third-floor suite.

First, he removed Mr. Simpson's vest, checking it for odor, then carefully placed it in the armoire with his others. It was damp, but Harrison would suggest that he wear the coffee-colored, plain satin one for morning. He left the mirrored door of the armoire open to give it a chance to air. Again he went to the door to check it. It was locked but he was sure that he'd not be sleeping much that night.

When he heard Sylvester return, he went to him. He was more than a little inebriated, and Harrison had difficulty removing his clothes, that were still neat. He wondered how on earth old Caleb had managed. Finally, he said his goodnights and climbed wearily onto his own small cot, but before he gave in to slumber, he again got up, checked the door, then decided for further protection to push the side chair underneath the door handle. He placed the tray holding the crystal decanter and glasses on its cushion. As tired as he was, he'd need their noise to awaken him if Durrance decided to come in the door. He didn't believe he would, but the man was wily and unpredictable. He slept soundly.

Light was streaming through the partially-closed shutters when he awakened. Yawning and stretching his slight arms upward, he got his bearings and got up and in his night shirt went to Sylvester's room to check on him. He noticed that the chair was no longer underneath the door knob. It had been pushed aside, and the tray holding the crystal decanter and glasses had been removed and placed back on the table. Perplexed, he looked at Sylvester, but he was in a deep sleep snoring steadily.

He shook his head trying to make sense out of it, then went back to his room to get dressed before awakening Sylvester. "Mr. Simpson must have got up during the night and removed the chair. He likes everything so neat..."

"Oh my God!" he screamed. "He was here!" On the table beside his cot was a black eye patch. He stared at it. "How on earth did he get in here? He must've been looking right at me while I was sleeping! Oh, sweet Jesus!"

****

Conner felt rocky. "I should've declined that last one. Ohhh...may the saints be merciful!" he said as he held his head, pouring the tepid water onto it, not bothering to see whether it splashed into the white wash bowl. He went to Collette's early in the evening for Maeve, but when he got there she had an order that had to be finished by the morrow. So he asked Collette's man Slidel if he'd see to making sure that she got home safely, and he proceeded to the Vieux Carre and the bars on Bourbon and Dauphine streets, ending up at Clancy's before he rolled into the alley beside the La Paloma. He remembered removing the note Denis had pinned on his door but didn't bother to read it.

As he lay on his disheveled bed, he read the note again and again. *Conner, you had two visitors. One was white and ugly, eyes like a turtle, and the other a young Black named Harrison. The White gave no name. Denis.*

"Mum'll have cooked mush and will expect me to eat and visit," he thought. But he continued to lie flat on his back, simply because his legs were wobbly, and it felt so good not to stir as he sorted out his thoughts about Durrance. "So the knife-wielding bastard has found me...Well, well. I'll take my own sweet time and hope Mum'll give up on me and go on her way to Mass. Then I can slip out and have coffee and rolls at Dauphine's." The idea of having to eat mush under the suspicious eye of Agnes made him head hurriedly for the wash bowl and retch noisily.

"Best that I have a steaming cup of coffee with a sweetening of brandy to placate the wee man who's playing the pipes inside my poor head. Then I can address my problems," he declared as he reached for his morning clothes.

****

Durrance stirred slowly, not wanting to meet the bright morning sun. When he remembered the frightened look on Silvey's boy's face, his stained, broken teeth grinned up from under the newspapers that he had used for a cover. The back of the alley off St. Charles St. with the draping ivy and bouganvilla hanging to the ground gave him a perfect sanctuary if there was no rain.

There was a water spigot behind the Hotel Baronne, that he used to rinse his face then cup his dirty hands to hold the water that he slurped noisily. He decided to use the same ruse that he'd been using for a handout. It had worked very well ever since his arrival in New Orleans. He tied the dirty rag around his head and over one eye, retrieved the gnarled cane from underneath the vines and hunched over, he proceeded to the kitchen door of the hotel and rapped loudly until the colored cook answered. Pretending to be deaf and dumb, he went into his act. He'd usually get a heel of bread and even a piece of fish, meat or cheese. The peach tree behind the house next door was heavy with ripened fruit, and the servant had given him the nod to pick some.

Durrance always took very good care of his stomach; even the street vendors had taken pity on the unfortunate man and shared their unsold meat pastries with him at the end of their long day. He was perfectly at home in his new surroundings and decided that after he had taken care of that bastard Irishman and the wench's boy, he'd have to concentrate on going to another section of the city for his handouts and also find a more comfortable place before winter set in. It never crossed his mind that he could look for honest work.

****

Conner approached the desk of the St. Charles. The day man, Mr. Robert Aubuson, an older man, probably in his late fifties, answered his inquiries and summoned Strut to the desk. Strut gave Conner the once-over and decided that his tip would be sufficient for him to go into his middle-priced act. He smiled pleasantly up at Conner and said, "I'll be back in a moment, suh, wid Mistah Simpson's man servant's ansuh." Lowering his head just a tad to show respect he then backed up, turned abruptly and scurried up the marble stairway. Conner smiled after him and decided that the affable young man deserved a handsome tip. "He's astute in his summation of me, very much like Harrison."

Strut returned with the message from Harrison even before Conner had a chance to settle in with the morning paper. "Mr. O'Farrell, suh, Mr. Simpson's body servant suggested dat dey receive ya in der suite for coffee. Ah'm ta lead ya der."

"Sure you are," Conner thought. "You want to extract a tip from both of us," but he answered Strut with, "That would indeed be delightful," and rose to follow him.

Harrison grabbed Conner's coat sleeve the minute Strut left. He was wearing a broad smile on his black face. Strut had figured both of them right and quickly added the coins to the other tips he had received earlier in the morning.

"He was here, Conner! Durrance was here!" Harrison held up the black patch and in a low muffled voice proceeded to tell him about the previous night's experiences, only to be interrupted by Sylvester's moaning. His aching head was held between his shaking hands as he called softly, "Talmai, where on earth are you, boy? Talmai!"

"Mr. Simpson, I'm right here with your nice, cool, seltzer, sir, and I've ordered your coffee and croissants and a nice bowl of fruit for you." He didn't want to announce Conner until Mr. Simpson had finished his morning toilet and was more fully awake. He could be a real bear in the morning. Normally, he was a very pleasant man, but Caleb had cautioned Harrison about the change he could expect when in New Orleans. Harrison decided that he had indeed been accurate in his warning.

Harrison slipped Conner a roll and a cup of coffee in his own room and went to Sylvester to assist him while he squirmed and tried to put on his morning coat. The cool seltzer water seemed to quicken his alertness, and Harrison said, "Mr. Simpson, I think it would be nice to have your breakfast on the balcony, sir. Would you enjoy that?"

"Why, Talmai, that would be lovely indeed," he managed to say. Harrison got him seated on the cushioned chair, his fruit sliced and coffee poured. When he glanced at the balcony railing he saw the broken ivy on the tile floor and realized how Durrance had come into their suite. Durrance was so lazy and fat that Harrison knew he'd not attempt to climb up the outside of the hotel. Probably sneaked into the adjacent room and climbed over its balcony, that joined their own. Harrison edged over toward the balcony, and sure enough, he could see the broken ivy on the other balcony railing. He had neglected to lock the French doors that lead to the balcony the night before. "I'll know better tonight," he said aloud.

"What, Talmai? I didn't understand you."

"Oh, Mr. Simpson, I was just talking to myself, sir," then said, "I think I hear someone at the door. Excuse me. I'll be right back."

"I didn't hear anyone. Your hearing must be very acute, Talmai."

"Not acute enough," he wanted to say, "or I'd have heard that fat Durrance. God! He could have knifed me as I slept!"

"Well, if it isn't Mr. O'Farrell. Come right on in, sir. Mr. Simpson will be delighted to see you. Here, let me take your coat. Mr. Simpson is on the balcony having his breakfast. Would you care to join him?"

He led Conner to the balcony, and Sylvester felt Conner's hand on his shoulder, restraining him. "No, don't bother to rise, Syl. Only a moment shall I take, and Harrison, I'll have to decline the invitation, for I have some disturbing news. It has come to my attention that Durrance is indeed in the city and that he intends to make good his threat to *do me in*. He came calling at my hotel last night. Fortunately, I was, shall we say, otherwise engaged and out for the evening." He laughed, as did Syl, who responded, "As was I, Conner, as was I," and moaned as he held his head.

"I'll pay a visit to the constable, so he'll be on the alert for our Mr. Durrance. Alicia has led me to believe that the man has been misusing his position for years, and I do not like for anyone to take advantage of our people at Ridgeland." He stopped long enough to break his croissant, dunked it into the sweetened, black coffee and continued. "Would you be so kind as to accompany Talmai and me to the constable's office, Conner? Since you reside here and it is you whom the man has threatened, it would seem the fitting thing to do. Do you agree?"

"But of course, Syl. I have a description of at least one of his disguises and believe I know his character well enough to alert the constable's men. He's a dangerous one, Syl. On guard we'd all better be." He and Harrison had decided not to tell Sylvester about the previous night's escapade and certainly not about discovering the eye patch right beside Harrison's bed.

Constable Poirret assured them that his men would track the scoundrel down and that he would leave messages at the La Paloma and St. Charles to inform them of his capture. But neither Harrison nor Conner had any faith in the ability of the New Orleans police and had already decided that they would have to take matters into their own hands. They knew that their position was to *watch and wait* until Sylvester took his afternoon nap or went to the Vieux Carre for his afternoon's entertainment.

Conner had figured that Durrance would not show until the dark of night. He was correct. Durrance had found the vendors along Jackson

Square to be very generous, and as he sat in the doorway of the abandoned warehouse on Canal St. he ate the cold but still succulent pastry and finished the nearly full bottle of wine, that he'd lifted from a sleeping sailor in the alley beside the Blue Parrot Bar. As he downed the remaining swallow, he wiped his wet mouth with the back of his hand and smiled at his good fortune.

"Now is the time," he decided, full of his ability to complete his mission. "Old man Simpson will be having a cold supper, then Talmai will be dressing him for his night out, so's he can poke every black wench he can find, high priced whores all of 'em, but he'd deny his number one man even one little poke from that Guinea nigger. Hell, all I ever wanted was one, just one, and he couldn't even let me have that. I'll fix ever' last one of 'em," he declared feeling brave from the effects of the wine.

He pulled on another black eye patch and got his cane. Hunched over, he left the shadows of the poorly lit doorway and proceeded toward the St. Charles to watch for Sylvester to leave in the fancy carriage. He knew that Sylvester would not be gone long before Talmai would follow like he'd done the night before. He'd get rid of him first, then go after Irish, who he suspected would be out 'til the wee hours. Oh, Irish'd be on the alert alright, so he'd have to be especially careful, but he wasn't concerned about that smart-assed Black boy of Silvey's.

Things went just as Durrance thought they would. He was across the street from the St. Charles hidden behind the clipped privet hedge, squatting almost inside it, but he could see the well lighted entrance. Sylvester came out all decked out in a white linen suit and waited for only a few minutes before the carriage arrived. The hotel doorman assisted him into the carriage, and the groomed horse with its brown, shiny coat snorted then trotted toward the Vieux Carre. Durrance knew he'd not have to wait long before Talmai was out of there and on his way to the La Paloma in search of Conner, where he had gone the previous evening. If he had not been set on killing Talmai, he'd have alerted the law and told them that he was a runaway. But that was not his style.

Durrance knew for a fact that he was a virgin, never touching the quarters gals. Hell, by the time Durrance was Talmai's age he'd had at least a dozen of 'em, and old man Rosamond didn't even care. But that Guinea nigger's boy was just too good for quarters wenches - too good. Durrance spat on the ground. He was only a slave, no matter that he was Simpson's body servant and highly thought of, and was new to New Orleans, so Durrance knew that he'd not frequent the river front, the seamy part of town. Durrance would have been more comfortable sticking him there, where Durrance blended in with the other riffraff.

Talmai came out onto the steps of the entrance. He looked left, then quickly to the right. Durrance's hand went to his mouth restraining his laughter, delighted by Talmai's fear. "He's lookin' fer me. I've got that little black boy messing his pants. He's afraid to even stay in his room. Ha! I've got him right where I want him!" and his hand eased down until he felt his knife, stroking it, patting it. Getting to an upright position, he followed Talmai.

Sure enough, Talmai began going in the direction of the La Paloma just like Durrance had figured. Durrance waited just long enough to make sure that he was not detected, then crossing to the opposite side of the street, he began to follow. He was so intent on his own pursuit that he hadn't noticed Conner come around the side of the St. Charles to follow him. He wore a black, long-sleeved shirt and trousers and light-weight boots, no hat. His black hair needed no cover. He had even darkened his face with soot, and when Durrance nervously looked around, Conner quickly ducked into a doorway, or if he was near a lamp, he'd get behind a pedestrian or lean against it with his face turned away from Durrance.

Harrison continued walking slowly, taking his time, toward the La Paloma, as they had decided he should. When he got to Villere Street, a much darker and virtually isolated street, about six blocks before the La Paloma, he was to turn onto it, forcing Durrance to cross the street in order to follow. Conner was to have crossed the street earlier and hidden behind the iron-grilled fence in front of the Three Lions Inn, and as Durrance passed it, Conner would step out behind him and force him into the dark alley that ran behind the Inn. At least that had been their plan.

The Inn was small and had been lovely at one time but was now run down and frequented mostly by foreign sailors off their ships with their lady friends for the night. You could barely make out the small sign above the columned entry, the light was so dim, so Conner knew he had good cover. He also knew that Durrance would make his move before Harrison got to the La Paloma but would probably wait until Villere crossed Canal Street, because it was almost pitch black at that point.

Conner waited for Harrison to pass, when suddenly the door of the Inn opened, and four laughing sailors came out. He ducked into the tall bushes beside the north corner of the Inn, but from there could not see when Harrison walked by.

"Sweet Jesus, what should I do? In this get up they'll probably jump me - then that pig will knife Harrison!" He couldn't go around to the back of the inn because it was fenced in all the way to the alley, and he'd miss seeing Durrance altogether. He decided to take a chance and come out of hiding, and if the sailors said anything he'd tell them that he was looking for someone who'd jumped ship, that he was undercover and worked with the New Orleans police.

But as he listened to the sailors speak he realized that they were Portuguese and probably couldn't understand English. Suddenly, they left the lighted entry, and Conner sighed with relief. They rounded the fence and almost knocked one Malcolm Durrance over. Conner gratefully took that opportunity to slip behind the hedge and position himself at the entry of the dark alley.

He listened to the sailors trying to apologize to the infuriated Durrance and grinned at his response as the men tried in vain to brush the dirt off him. Durrance grumbled angrily, "Why the hell you foreigners taking up the goddamned walk? Can't you see where your stinking asses are goin'? Get your goddamned hands off a me!"

Conner was now in position, his derringer on ready. But with the men so close they'd hear the report and perhaps act before he had the opportunity to try to explain who he was.

He had never killed a man. The threat he'd made Durrance at Ridgeland was a bluff, but he was looking forward to this job. He'd become very protective of Harrison and was especially fond of Alicia, and if ever a man needed killing, Durrance did, he rationalized. Besides, he knew that he'd have need of Harrison and Alicia in the future if he was ever to have enough money to return to Macon to claim his Berta.

He could hear Durrance as he came closer, no longer trying to be quiet, grumbling loudly. "Those damned foreigners gonna take over the whole country...goddamned stinking Portuguese..." Conner hated to use the knife and so went for his pistol. Durrance was there - right there!

Conner, catlike, eased up behind him. Swiftly his arm encircled Durrance's protruding belly, his arms tight around him, removing any chance for Durrance to go for his knife. He dragged him kicking, yelling, struggling just inside the alley. He would have liked to see his face before he pulled the trigger, and he wanted Durrance to see who had the last word, but it was much too dark. He hated to be denied that pleasure.

Harrison heard the report of the bullet and stopped dead in his tracks. He heard running feet behind him, and when he turned he saw the sailors run into the alley. What should he do? Should he try to help Conner, or should he run to the La Paloma for Conner's cousin Denis? He decided on Denis. His long legs passed no one as he ran the short distance to the hotel, burst into the lobby and was so out of breath and frightened that he could only manage to whisper, Conner.

Denis Sheehan didn't bother to close the door behind him as he followed Harrison, nor did he hear Agnes call after him, her concern etched on her distorted face. He and Harrison weren't two blocks down La Salle Street when they heard, "Top o the evenin' to ya, mates," and Denis suddenly stopped, his rotund body heaving for its next breath as he declared to the saints and all the angels, "Conner O'Farrell, you'll be the death o me and your dear mum 'fore the morn!" and leaned up against the elm tree and shook as Agnes came running toward them.

"Denis, is my boyo...oh, Denis, is he ...?"

Conner stepped out of the shadows. "Mum, it's alive and well I am. Don't Mum...don't fret yourself," and he took the sobbing Agnes in his arms. Harrison saw the tender side of Conner that night and knew that there was more to the Irishman than he'd figured... much more.

CHAPTER IV
AVALON MANOR

The Year 1861

    Conner had just turned an old twenty years. His life was over. His Berta had wed another and moved to Florida, and there was no longer a purpose to his life. His mum, Maeve and Cousin Denis were at their wits' end with him. The only time he showed his old fervor for life was when Harrison arrived in New Orleans with Syl, and he and Conner got in their games on the *Delta Sun*.

    Conner had made more money than he thought possible, and when he answered Claire's summons to visit the ailing John in Macon, he arrived there a wealthy young man. The news of Berta's marriage and move to Florida was so unexpected that the devastated Conner no longer cared for the money and played the games merely for the sake of besting his opponents.

    Maeve believed that his depression was due to Berta, but as close as they were, she was hesitant to inquire of him, so she wrote their Uncle John and received his answer about Berta's marriage to another and her subsequent move. She at last understood Conner's attitude and set out to remedy the situation.

    Being a take-charge person she brought Harrison into her confidence, and even though he was young, he seemed to understand Conner and have a genuine concern for him. He and Conner had become partners when on board the *Delta Sun*. Conner had continued working the *River Queen* the past two years, but the last week of every month he'd join Syl and Harrison on board the *Delta Sun*.

    Maeve and Harrison proceeded with their plan. She knew her brother's nature, and the fact that he couldn't have Berta as his bride was disheartening - she understood that. But to be near Berta, to watch over her, to make sure that she was well taken care of and happy would fill his need somewhat. Of this she was positive.

    Louisiana followed Georgia in seceding and joined the Confederacy in its fight against the Union. The War's arrival played into their hands perfectly. The Simpsons gave their people their freedom as soon as Louisiana joined the Confederacy, thus enabling Harrison the freedom to travel. Alicia put them on shares and gave each a parcel of land to be worked for five years, and at the end of that time it would become theirs.

Only two of her people decided to go north, Imogene, Jimbo's woman, and their oldest son, Maurice. All the others remained at Ridgeland.

Harrison stayed on as Syl's body servant receiving a wage and a portion of their winnings plus twenty acres of good bottom land, and Silvey was guaranteed a paid position for life. Harrison was satisfied with the arrangement, but when Maeve made her proposal, he was beside himself with excitement.

Her proposal was this: he was to create an incident that was of such a grave nature that he and Conner would be forced to leave New Orleans. She knew that Conner would not leave her or their Mum unless it was absolutely necessary. Conner had decided to bide his time and not join the cause, as had Denis's older sons, but he was well aware that the boats he worked would soon be used for the war effort and not for the pleasure of the passengers, so it was just a matter of time until their last run.

Harrison had noticed that Mr. Ed Longwood's young, buxom wife, Sophie, had on previous trips been especially attentive to Conner, but he, in his depressed state, had barely acknowledged her presence. Sophie was persistent and managed to be on the upper deck whenever Conner was there or in the grand saloon at the same time, etc. Harrison knew that she was ripe and ready and would, with the tiniest bit of maneuvering on his part, fit into his and Maeve's plan. It was time to act.

She had followed Conner to the upper deck. He was leaning against the railing and, as usual, looking off into space ignoring the peaceful countryside pass by and not noticing Sophie, who had placed herself a comfortable distance from him. She was close enough to smile invitingly in case he glanced her way. Her silvery blond hair was worn in a fashionable style, and her low cut, soft blue gown barely managed to contain her full breasts. With each hesitant breath they rose invitingly, but Conner did not take advantage of her obvious invitation. The situation would have been amusing to Harrison had he not been so concerned for his friend.

He leaned on the ship's rail beside Conner. Sophie was trying to appear nonchalant, unsuccessfully, but was not brazen enough to approach Conner. "Guess I'll have to do her work for her," Harrison thought as he softly spoke to Conner. "That buxom Mrs. Longwood has been after you the last few trips. This'll be your last chance to have her. You want me to keep a lookout for her old man?"

Conner was amused at his young friend's perception. He was well aware of her intent but had until now ignored her.

"Oh, what the hell! Life does go on Harrison, and you're right. This will be my last chance."

"*What would be the use of immortality to a person who cannot use well a half hour.*"

Harrison quickly identified the quote. "Ralph Waldo Emerson, right?"

"Right you are, my good man."

Conner turned in Sophie's direction, removed his hat confidently, smiled and walked toward her. She was wiggling nervously, and Harrison thought that she was going to tumble right out of her gown, she was so excited. He sure hated to miss seeing Conner in operation, but he had his job to do. He stayed as long as he dared, then left when Conner took her arm firmly, with her fluttering like a little bird, and opened the door to his cabin. He nodded to Harrison. Harrison nodded back and headed for the men's saloon to keep his eye on Sophie's old man, Conner thought.

Ed Longwood, his long, thin face dripping with perspiration, was obviously in over his head at the tables. Harrison could tell by his tautness, fingers drumming nervously on the polished table. Harrison wanted to give Conner at least fifteen minutes before he approached Longwood. No need in Conner's not having some fun, he thought. But all changed when Longwood lost the bet, and disgusted with the results, slammed his cards down and said, "This is obviously not my day, gentlemen. Think I'll get some air. Perhaps it'll clear my poor brain," and he smiled as he said it, if you could call it a smile.

Harrison had to do some fast calculating. His black skin was beaded in sweat. As he approached Longwood, he pushed his chair underneath the table and headed for the door leading to the open deck. Harrison followed and caught up with him, his mind churning. "Forgive me, Conner, but this is for your own good, at least I hope it's for your own good."

"Mr. Longwood, sir. I know it is none of my business, but I'd do the same for Mr. Simpson if he were in the same situation..."

"What on earth are you babbling about, boy?"

Harrison hurriedly pulled him aside and away from the strolling passengers. "As I said, Mr. Longwood, it is none of my business but..."

"She's where?" he shouted. "In his cabin? Which one?"

Abruptly he turned and headed for his own cabin. He emerged, slamming the door behind him, waving his pistol in the air and yelling, "I'll call the blackguard out! He has gone too far!" not caring one whit who heard him.

He rushed toward Conner's cabin with Harrison right behind him. Pounding on the door he called, "Sophie, are you in there? Answer me this minute, woman!" The deck was now filled with the curious passengers. Harrison heard a muffled response, and when Longwood pushed the door hard with a jolt, Conner jumped out, knocking him flat on his rear end, and grabbed Harrison's extended arm with one hand, trying desperately to pull up his pants with the other. They ran to the bow and dived headlong into the river.

"I hope to hell you can swim, friend," Conner yelled as they paddled for the nearby shore. They could hear Longwood shouting, and when they heard the report of his pistol, Conner told Denis later that he would swear on his Mum's bible that Harrison actually ran on water.

Ed Longwood did, as threatened, visit the La Paloma and call Conner out, swearing that he'd kill the Irishman and not caring if he got killed in the process. As Maeve had hoped, Conner and Harrison decided that it was time to leave New Orleans, to make a fresh start. Harrison insisted that they head for Florida, for he knew that Marse Samuel, if he were still alive, would take them in at Fairlea.

Conner left his savings and a note for his mum and Maeve explaining his decision.

My dear Mum and Maeve,
It is indeed sorry I am to leave you so hurriedly, but I feel it is time to embark on a new life. I am leaving my savings and would be pleased if you, Maeve, would put it toward your new shop. I know, now that we're in the middle of the Conflict, that it is perhaps not the most propitious timing, but I have faith that the War will be short lived.
I'll write you from Florida, as Harrison has friends there, and we've decided to join them in their time of need."

As he wrote that he thought, "Mum'll like that. It'll ease her concern for me if she thinks I'm helping others." What he didn't say was that he wanted to put as much distance between himself and one Ed Longwood, not that he was afraid of the man, but he just didn't want nor need any more distress in his life. It never occurred to him that he wouldn't kill Longwood, and the idea of being in Florida was very appealing - his love was there.

Maeve smiled when she read the note. She smiled through streaming tears. She already missed the boyo. Now, she could tell Vincent what she and Harrison had done.

****

"Harrison, I'll not be walking another step! We need horses."

"We wouldn't be needing horses if you hadn't removed yourself from your life savings, Conner. What on earth possessed you, I'll never know," he spat out. Harrison knew him to be smart and clever, but foolishness he'd never attributed to Conner O'Farrell.

They had crossed the Perdido River that separated Florida from Alabama, and it had taken them over two weeks to get that far, and then another week to get to the Escambia, catching rides on carts, buggies, fishing boats, anything at all, but mostly on foot. Their biggest problem had been in securing food, their provisions brought from New Orleans having been eaten long before. Harrison had managed to kill a few quail and some squirrels, and from time to time they had gathered vegetables and fruit, but their grumbling stomachs reminded them that they were without sufficient food.

Harrison had thought that they'd have no problem getting to Fairlea, twenty miles or so east of Tallahassee, and near the town of Monticello. They'd take the train from New Orleans to Pensacola, then on to the state capital, purchase a buggy and arrive at Fairlea in style. He was getting anxious to see his birth place. At least that had been his plan, but all changed when Conner informed him that he had given his life's savings to Maeve and his Mum.

Harrison had known that Conner had exchanged his paper money for gold long before the firing on Ft. Sumpter and the subsequent secession of the southern states, but after his debilitating visit to Macon it would have appeared that his good sense had evaporated into the atmosphere.

Harrison shook his kinky head disgustedly. Conner saw the gesture and said, "Oh, alright. I'll give you a lesson in human nature, lad. 'Never leave 'til tomorrow that which you can do today.'" Harrison was stumped, but didn't want to admit it, so he pretended to not have heard the quote. "Benjamin Franklin, Harrison. We can all learn from him."

"You surely could have, Conner. We wouldn't be in this mess if you'd listened to Mr. Franklin."

Conner ignored him and stopped underneath a linden tree on the bank of the trickling stream. A light breeze flipped its bright green leaves from front to back, and Harrison eased his weary body down onto the soft sand, resting his back against the smooth trunk. They were approaching a small settlement. They could see the buildings in the distance, where the flat, sandy, clay soil rose to meet rolling hills dotted with farms. The weedless, two-rut road was more heavily traveled the closer they got.

Conner reached into his bag and took out a neatly folded bundle. Harrison was observing his every move. "If I'm going to get a lesson in human nature, then perhaps I'd better pay close attention," he decided with a sigh. Conner went down the slight slope whistling and just as happy as Harrison had ever seen him.

Harrison rose to observe. "Heck, he's only washing his face." But then he began to strip off his clothing, his grey silk shirt, then his darker grey trousers, that had long ago lost their shape. He pulled a bottle out of his bundle and placed it carefully on the grassy slope, and buck-naked, singing an Irish ditty at the top of his lungs, proceeded to walk out into the stream. After using the soap and rinsing he splashed himself liberally with the toilet water. Its fragrance floated toward Harrison.

"What on earth is he up to?" Next, Conner pulled out a packet. Harrison couldn't see what it was, and when Conner energetically climbed up the slope looking as dapper as he did when in New Orleans in the pale blue suit, Harrison decided to not give the amused Conner any more cause for the satisfied smirk on his handsome face.

"I'll not ask about the packet. Oh, how evasive he'd be if I inquired. I can hear him. 'Harrison, my good man, the ingredients in this small, inconsequential packet have the power to enable us to acquire much desired transportation.' If he has money in there, I'll...I'll..."

Conner could see him squirm, then wrestle with his curiosity and decided to further Harrison's discomfort.

"Harrison, my man," he said smoothly. Harrison was alert now. "Aha, here he goes rubbing salt in my wounds, enjoying my discomfort."

Again..."Harrison, the contents of this small, inconspicuous packet are the end to our discomfort, the finality of our foot travel."

"Yes, Conner, I am sure you are correct," he answered as disinterestedly as he could manage. He was not going to give him any satisfaction, he decided, and proceeded down the red clay road at a good clip, ignoring him. They could see a large house in the distance, and coming toward them a young man riding a buckskin mare. Conner quickly caught up with Harrison and said, "I'll handle this."

"Handle what?"

"Just follow my lead. *The future is bought with the present.*' Samuel Johnson, Harrison"

"Follow your lead, indeed. I just hope Mr. Johnson knew what he was talking about. If I'd had the good sense I'd been born with, I'd be back at

Ridgeland with my feet not hurting, my belly full of fried chicken and biscuits and not in the middle of nowhere with no chance in hell of getting to Fairlea for at least another month. We'll probably become buzzard bait long before we get there. Follow your lead, indeed!"

Conner raised his arm and hailed the young man. He was about seventeen or eighteen years old and poorly dressed, but neat and clean. He trotted up to them and halted. He was giving them the once over, and Harrison could tell he was impressed by the cut of Conner's clothes and presence.

He spoke before Conner greeted him. "Are ya in some kinda trouble, sir?"

"You are very astute, lad. We are indeed in trouble. Some ne'er-do-wells have relieved my man, Harrison, and me of our money as well as our buggy and mounts, and we have been tracking them for over a month. As a matter of fact, when I saw you approach, I was sure that the mount you are riding was my mare, Guinevere."

The boy rolled his eyes at Conner, then looked at Harrison. "This here mare belongs to Jacob Turner over in the next town of Bagdad. He's the inn keeper there and let me borrow it so's I could ride to see Tilly 'fore I join up..."

Conner interrupted. "And how long has this Mr. Turner had Guinevere?"

"Well, I don't rightly know how long he's had Lady Bug, but I sure know it's his mare..."

"But do you have papers stating that, young man?"

"I don't hafta have no papers..."

He was getting very nervous. Conner held onto the mare's bridle. "Well, young man, if it's proof you need to determine the ownership of this mare, then it's proof I'll give you."

He turned to Harrison whose eyes were saucer sized. "Now what in tarnation is he up to? He knows full well that mare isn't..."

"Harrison, would you please assist the young man down from Guinevere, and, Harrison, so that the lad will believe that Guinevere is indeed mine, I'd like for you to be the arbiter..."

"The what?"

"I would like for you to ..."

"Now, wait a minute, mister. This here mare is named Lady Bug and belongs to Jacob Turner over in Bagdad!"

"And how long has this Mr. Turner had Guinevere? A week? A month?"

"Well, I don't rightly know, but he wouldn't have let me ride her if'n she wasn't his."

"That, young man, is just exactly what I intend to prove to you. Harrison would you please escort the lad to at least ten feet from Guinevere. Then we will have a little test to determine the true ownership of the mare. It's all right, lad. No harm'll befall you. Now, that's right. You're to stand there."

Conner took the packet out of the jacket pocket away from the boy's view and placed the contents in his hand. He pretended to be petting the mare. Then he stepped back.

"Now," he said, "I, too, will pace off ten feet, and then when Harrison counts to five, we will both call the mare. If the mare goes to you, then I'll be assured that she is this Lady Bug and belongs to a Mr. Turner. But, lad, if she comes to me, then you'll have to believe that she is my Guinevere, who was stolen from me by some scalawags. Is that not a fair assumption?"

The boy had no recourse. He was out-numbered, and the man spoke and was dressed like a gentleman, and, heck, he wasn't sure how long Jacob had had the mare or if he really owned it. He thought that he did but was no longer sure. So not knowing what else to do, he agreed by shaking his head up and down.

"Now Harrison, please give the count, and the lad and I will simultaneously beckon the mare. Are you ready, Harrison?"

He indicated that he was and began to count: one - two - three - four - five... Conner held out the same hand that he had previously rubbed on the mare's muzzle and called, "Guinevere"...the boy called loudly, "Lady Bug, come here to Jim, Lady Bug."

The mare didn't even look at the boy but walked directly to Conner, and when she reached him, he put his hand on her mouth and stroked her murmuring that he was so glad to have her back. The boy's mouth hung open, but he wasn't able to utter a word.

"As you can see, lad, she indeed knows her master. I do hope that you'll tell Mr. Turner that Guinevere's true master has been found, and whoever sold him the mare was a wretch of a thief. If my man and I were going to Bagdad, I would save you the trouble and tell him in person, but I have pressing business elsewhere. Good day to you, and know that your timely encounter has made me a very happy man to be reunited with my Guinevere. Up, Harrison."

Harrison leaped up on the mare's rump behind Conner and they rode off in a trot, but before they rounded the bend, Harrison took Conner's hand off the rein and examined it. The light tan grains still stuck to it, and

Harrison tasted them. "Sugar!" So that's what was in the packet.

"A fool and his mount are soon parted." Harrison said sheepishly. He'd made it up hoping to give Conner's brain a good workout, but Conner was so pleased by his ruse that he ignored him and happily burst into an Irish ditty, singing all the way down the tree-lined lane toward the strange looking house that they had seen in the distance. As they drew closer they were both taken aback. It looked like something right out of the *Arabian Nights*.

"Now, my man, I'll introduce you to the ways and means of securing lodging and a sumptuous meal," he said a little shaken by his surroundings. Harrison hit him a good one on his erect back and laughed nervously all the way to the front piazza. It was beautifully tiled in cobalt blue and rust and was lined with huge urns filled with colorful plants. Jumping down, he quickly took the reins, and out of the corner of his eye glimpsed a giant of a man walking toward them - he was over seven feet tall. Harrison gulped and quickly stepped behind Conner. "I hope this is a dream and I'll be waking up soon. Lets hear you talk yourself out of this one, master of mine. Let's just hear what that Irish mind of yours concocts!"

The giant stood in front of two massive, carved mahogany doors, his black skin shone in the noonday sun, his white uniform sashed with red. "God, all he needs is a turban and a sword, and he'd be right out of Morocco," Conner thought. "Bet his name's Sinbad," he almost laughed, and when the giant spoke in a high falsetto voice, both he and Harrison were too smart to crack even a tiny smile. "My God, he's a eunuch!" But Conner's expression remained the same.

The usually loquacious Conner finally found his voice. When it cracked on the first two words, Harrison was sure he was going to wet his britches. Again he began. "It is with... harumph... with...harumph...it is with great distress that I seek your master. My man, Harrison," he nodded toward Harrison, "and I have fallen victim to robbers and barely escaped with our lives. Unfortunately, they removed from us our buggy and trunk containing all our worldly possessions. Harrison had the presence of mind to unleash one of our horses and we were able to escape with our lives intact."

Conner could have droned on forever. He was just getting into the lengthy fabrication when the other door opened and out stepped one of the most beautiful women he had ever seen. She did not speak to the eunuch, just lowered her eyes, and he, who had not shown any expression whatsoever while Conner expounded on their unfortunate adventure, stepped aside as she glided past him.

When she spoke Conner thought of velvet, silk, pansies - everything soft he had ever felt or thought of. Her words slowly eased out of full, red lips. "I am Aurora Avalon. Welcome to Avalon Manor. I overheard," she lowered her black-fringed eyes, that were so dark that the irises were not discernable, "Actually I was just inside the doors eavesdroping."

She smiled then and raised her eyes to Conner, and he thought he was going to die on the spot, and when Harrison glanced his way, he was sure that he was. Her skin was alabaster white, and her thick hair as black as Conner's own, combed straight back and held with a giant silver clip restraining its tumbling to her waist. She looked to be about Conner's age but could have been somewhat older. Her deep violet morning dress had ecru lace primly surrounding the high collar, but Conner could detect her sense of mischief. She was not as sedate as her costume would have you believe. There was energy in her long frame - there was fire.

"A creature all too fair and good
For human nature's daily food."

"Wordsworth, Conner, Wordsworth. Oh, oh, we're in for a long stay," Harrison could see. "Not long enough for one Jacob Turner to come looking for his mare, I hope. That boy's going to have to join up sooner than he'd planned when old Jacob finds out about that mare."

Conner finally found his voice. "Miss," he began. She interrupted, "Madam, sir. I am Madam Aurora Avalon. My husband is First Lieutenant Ramon Avalon of the Marion Dragoons and has already seen action." She said it proudly. "He is serving with his friend, Captain John Martin." When Conner showed no recognition of neither the Dragoons or Capt. Martin she realized that he was not from Florida, for every Floridian who could read knew of their daring.

All Conner could think was, "So he's gone, is he now? Now very fortunate." He reached for her hand and brought it slowly up to his lips. The eunuch didn't miss a move. Harrison's kinky hair almost went straight every time he dared sneak a look at him. "Lordy, I've got to think of something! That fool Irishman's going to get us into a peck of trouble. Lordy!"

Conner continued. "Perhaps you overheard me telling your servant about our dilemma concerning our buggy and other possessions. We have been tracking the thieves for weeks and have at last reached the end of the rope, so to say, no food and no money, and, I am disquieted to say, no hope, until, you, madam, made your appearance. The light that had been rudely dimmed has now taken on a beautiful glow..."

Harrison felt like he was going to throw up. "If he says one more honey-coated phrase that giant is going to have done with us," but he instead mumbled, "Master, I feel faint." If the truth were known, he did feel weak, because he was sure the giant was going to squash the two of them between his oversized hands.

Conner reached for Harrison's arm before he sank to the ground, and Madam Avalon ordered Meshach to take the poor boy to the servants' entrance and to give him some food, then she turned to Conner, and with sad eyes, took his arm and led him to the brightly tiled dining room. There was no furniture. Colorful, plump cushions surrounded the open pit in the middle of the room, and Conner thought, "Looks like I'll have to cook my own." She clapped her hands and an ancient Negress shuffled in. "Miss Aurora, Ah'm comin' fas' as Ah can, ma'am."

Meshach returned, effortlessly carrying a large, tiled round table that fit over the pit, and the woman soon returned with a tray filled with cold biscuits, thick slices of pork, cold chicken, pickles, jam and a pot of steaming coffee. Conner knew he'd have a problem with his manners, he was so hungry. There were no plates and no utensils, just large linen napkins. He followed Aurora's lead. She was not a dainty eater, and as Conner watched her devour the chicken he hoped that her other appetites were as voracious. He had a feeling that they were, but with Meshach constantly by her side he'd have one helluva time reaffirming his suspicions.

Neither spoke. He decided to leave at least one piece of chicken and some of the pork, although he was still hungry. Aurora saw his hesitation. "Please, Mr. O'Farrell, finish. I'm sure it has been some time since you've eaten."

Conner declined and instead asked her, "May I call you Aurora? It is such a lovely name, and please call me Conner."

"Yes, of course you may. Actually my given name is Patricia, but Ramon preferred a more exotic name." Conner thought he detected a slight trace of a brogue and decided to pursue his curiosity. "Would your maiden name perhaps have been O'Toole, or Kennedy or Murphy, Aurora?"

She tilted her head back and laughed a low, musical, enticing laugh. "You have a good ear, Conner. Indeed it was. Mary Patricia Flannagan, it was, and from County Kerry originally. I thought I'd mastered my American speech as Ramon had wished, but wrong I am."

He lowered his voice. "In my presence please be Mary Patricia. It's a fine name, one to be proud of."

"My Mum and Da called me Keeta..." Her voice trailed off and she wore a faraway look.

"Keeta it is then," he interrupted her thoughts. "When did you come to America?"

"It was before I became a young lady, I was almost ten. Ramon's family brought me over after my family was taken by the plague, and I've been at Avalon Manor ever since. They've since passed on - the fever, you know, along with their other son, Frederick, and only daughter, Juliet. Only Ramon and I were spared. We're without servants now. Only Meshach and Aunt Thelma, who was too old to follow the others when they ran away, remain."

"If Harrison and I can be of help, Keeta, you have but to ask."

"Oh, Conner, I'm so glad you came. I was becoming frightened. Meshach is of no help in the garden and Aunt Thelma truly cannot assist me any longer. I'm really at my wits' end. If Ramon knew that the others had left, he'd be furious. I hesitate to write him of it, but I don't know what I am to do. Our food is getting low and it..."

She began to cry softly. Conner could not bear to hear her. He quickly glanced around for Meshach, and there he was on the other side of the high arch that Conner presumed led to the kitchen. Conner turned his back to him hoping that it would shield his hand that held Aurora's. Squeezing it, he said in a whisper, "You have but to ask, my dear Keeta, but to ask."

She brushed away the tears and saw Meshach. Taking her hand from Conner she clapped loudly and called to him. "Meshach, has Mr. O'Farrell's man been cared for?" He stepped forward and nodded in the affirmative. "Then would you please tend to Mr. O'Farrell's room. He has agreed to remain at Avalon Manor until we have received word from the Lieutenant as to the resolution of our dilemma. Is that not so, Mr. O'Farrell?"

"Of course, Madam Avalon. Whatever my man and I can do to accommodate you in your time of need..."

Meshach left while Conner was speaking, trudging reluctantly up the wide, marble stairway. It was obvious to Conner that he did not approve of his mistress's decision.

As in the other rooms in the house, Conner's room was bare except for the heavy tapestries that hung on the walls and the foot-deep pallet on the tile floor. Bright orange and blue tapestry-covered pillows were placed around the room, and in the alcove next to his balcony was an ornately carved trunk for his clothes and a marble wash basin with gold fixtures.

Keeta had mentioned that the Avalons had brought her to America after the second potato famine, but Conner found it strange that they had not accepted at least some of the American customs. He was curious about ther nationality. The house appeared to be right out of the *Arabian Nights*, and to have a eunuch as a servant furthered his curiosity. Keeta had said that Ramon had joined the Confederate army right after war was declared, but to have achieved the rank of Lieutenant in such a short time was unusual unless he had had prior service.

Conner was tired. Even a pallet looked inviting. He had decided when he bid Keeta good night that a visit to her room would not be advisable - he was sure that Meshach would be right outside her door. He had not seen Harrison since their arrival, but Keeta had told him that Thelma had fixed up a room in the servants' quarters for him. Conner wondered if he was fortunate enough to have a bed, but when he sat on the pallet he was amazed at its softness, his mind ceased to wander, he curled up and eased into a deep sleep.

Something awakened him. He could feel someone looking at him. When he rolled over the moonlight was streaming through the balcony doors, outlining her black, flowing hair. He reached toward her, she knelt down then curled up beside him holding his face in her slender hands.

"I need for you to hold me, Conner. Please...just hold me. I miss Ramon so very much."

He kissed her cheek and forehead and stroked her hair back from her tear-streaked face. "My little colleen - my Keeta. I'm here. The boyo is here for you," and they soon fell asleep.

He awakened long after the sun had been up. She was gone. The only sign of her presence was the unmistakable aroma of her rich, spicy perfume. Conner rested his head on his arms and said aloud, "I can't believe this night. God! I can't believe this entire place. I feel as if I'm in a dream and will awaken any moment and'll find I'm at the La Paloma."

He threw off the coverlet and anxiously went to turn on the gold faucet. There were fresh towels. Someone had already been there. He wondered if it was before or after Keeta had left his room. He'd not be able to tell by the eunuch's expression. Of that he was positive, and he hoped not to find out by his actions, as well.

The smell of smoked meat reached Conner even before he arrived in the dining room. No one was there, but a fresh napkin was beside the cushion along with a bowl of figs and oranges and a knife. Keeping hot over the charcoal fire were bacon and sausage and biscuits along with a pot of coffee.

When he had finished, he decided that he'd have to visit Harrison to tell him of his proposal. Beyond the tiled arch way was a long hall with marble columns and benches overlooking a well tended garden. On one side were very formal flower beds, but on the opposite side grew fall peas and beans and greens.

"Poor, sweet Keeta. So this is the garden she is desperately trying to maintain." He smiled at her efforts and bent down to pull the weeds that were attempting to strangle the peas. When he looked up, he saw Meshach's huge sandals, the white pants, then the red sash. His face was as stern as Conner had remembered.

"Madam is on the back piazza." He turned and Conner decided that he'd better follow him. She wore a flowing white robe with intricate beaded work around the high neckline, full sleeves of a sheer gossamer fabric, and her slender, white feet were sandaled. She rose from the marble bench and took his hand sweetly saying loud enough so Meshach could overhear, "Thank you for your kind understanding last night. Ramon would also thank you if he were here."

"My God! I can't believe she'd tell him. He must be one helluva man, even if all I did was hold her." Meshach showed no emotion. Conner asked for Harrison and also inquired about the town of Bagdad, where the young man, Jim, had come from when Conner had relieved him of the mare.

"Harrison, my man, it is with great relief that I have resolved our dilemma."

"Sure it is, Conner," he thought. "You eat smoked meat, and I get grits in a cup and sleep on a bed so lumpy that I'd prefer the ground, and you no doubt availed yourself of that seductive Aurora..." But he said simply, "I am very relieved, Master."

Old Thelma looked at the two of them and shook her turbaned head. "Dat boy sho don' talk right. Usin' dos fancy words 'round me, playin' de uppity nigger." She stood the brush broom up in the corner of the kitchen and proceeded with the preparation of their main meal.

Conner pulled Harrison outside, and they walked down the brick walk toward the stable and Guinevere. "Harrison, I want you to go to the roadway and wait for Jim when he returns from seeing his lady friend. I'm sure he's not anxious to return to the no doubt irate Jacob Turner. When you approach him, ask him to come with you to Avalon Manor, that your master will assist him in explaining to Mr. Turner about Guinevere. I'm sure he'll accompany you then."

"Now what good in tarnation will that do, Conner?"

"Harrison, just do what I ask, and you will know the answer to your question."

Harrison grumbled under his breath. "Why can't he answer me? Why does he enjoy making me miserable while I wait? He's enjoying my curiosity, so I'll not display any, and will be just as deadpan as Meshach."

Harrison did as Conner asked. It was almost noon when he saw Jim walking down the road toward him. When Harrison stepped out from under the shade of the water oak and held up his hand, Jim stopped and almost turned to run, but then decided against it when he saw that Harrison was alone. Harrison approached him slowly and gave him Conner's message. He reacted as Conner had predicted, but when Harrison explained the part where Conner would assist him, he acquiesced.

They approached the summer kitchen, and Conner, who had been in the shaded laundry area, stepped out. "Aunt Thelma has your dinner prepared, and there will be meat on your plate this day, Harrison." Harrison decided to pretend that he'd rather eat than listen to Conner's conversation with Jim. "He'll not know of my interest. I'll not give him that satisfaction," and he walked deliberately into the summer kitchen, that was attached to the main house by a columned walkway. Aunt Thelma had the pork on his tin plate. It was piled high, succulent and juicy, with collard greens and cornbread - he forgot about eavesdroping.

He drank the steaming coffee and thought, "I'll enjoy this more than usual. If the news is correct, most of what gets through the blockade will be going to the soldiers, and no telling when we'll be having it again." He thanked Aunt Thelma and patted her on her stooped back and thought of his Ma Sarie as he did.

"Ah guess he ain't so bad," Thelma thought. "Guess he was jes' hongry," and she went about cleaning up her kitchen, her domain. Humming to herself, she scraped the scraps into the cat's tin plate, placing it beside the cook stove, then when the grey, striped cat slinked out from behind the almost empty barrels of flour, Thelma took her brush broom and chased her out, exclaiming as she did, "What you doin' in mah kitchen, Mama Cat? Ya oughta know bettah dan ta be in mah kitchen. Go on and catch yore own dinner. Der's plenty o' mice in de stable. Go on, now git!" Mama Cat quickly grabbed a mouthful before retreating knowing full well that Thelma would leave the door ajar, and she could return for the rest later. It was a game that they both enjoyed. Thelma no longer had any Avalon people to impress with her authority, she being the head house woman. She missed it.

While Harrison was eating the first hot meal he'd had in over a week,

Conner was presenting his proposal to Jim. It was this: that he would go to Bagdad with him and together they'd tell Jacob Turner that they both had been attacked by robbers, that their horses had been stolen, and that they had taken refuge at Avalon Manor, where Miss Aurora had tended to them.

Keeta had told Conner a little history of the area the previous day, that is when Conner formulated his plan. This area of Florida had been known for its lawlessness even before it became a territory and had been a hangout for pirates and thieves, thus the name of Bagdad. He felt Turner would believe them.

Conner continued - Jim interrupted but was quickly told to wait until he had fully explained. "Jim, Lt. Avalon is in the thick of battle, and Miss Aurora is nearly beside herself with worry. Their slaves all ran away, except Aunt Thelma and the eunuch. She has no one to tend the fields or the stock. You understand?"

He shook his head no and began to question Conner. "Jim, please wait until I've finished. What this has to do with you is this. I shall accompany you to Bagdad to see Turner, and to tell him the lie about the robberies if you will promise me that you will return to Avalon Manor to stay with Miss Aurora, helping her in any way you can, until she receives word from the Lieutenant as to what she should do about the runaway slaves. Now Jim, don't interrupt again." Jim pursed his lips to control his outburst, grumbling to himself that there must be more to this than Conner was saying...

"I am positive that the Lieutenant is a Captain by now and will return to Avalon Manor immediately to attend its operation, and Miss Aurora will insist that he engage you as his orderly or at least see that you'll be reimbursed in some capacity for your invaluable help. Do you see the wisdom in this proposal?"

He seemed unsure to Conner, so he continued. "If you do not come to Avalon Manor to assist Miss Aurora in the running of the plantation, Jim, you will have to face one Jacob Turner by yourself and confess that you do not have his mare. Is he going to believe you if you say that you were attacked by robbers? Is he going to believe you if you tell him the truth of what happened? Jim..." He put his hand on Jim's slumped shoulder. "Would you not be better off if the two of us gave Mr. Turner the same story, return here for only a short time, I'm convinced, and then accompany the Lieutenant to his company to serve the Confederacy under his command?"

Jim shook his head up and down. "As I thought, Jim. As I thought."

Conner and Harrison rode Guinevere down the tree-lined lane as they had just two days previously, but this time they left Avalon Manor with a grateful worker, Jim Ramsey. When he and Conner told Turner the tale about their attack and the theft of their horses, he immediately sent word to the sheriff in Milton and was told that all would be done that was possible but he was only one man, that his deputies were already signed up for the cause and had headed for Tallahassee and their regiments, and therefore finding and returning their horses was doubtful.

Aunt Thelma had packed a bountiful meal, and Aurora and even Meshach were saddened by their departure. Jim had already begun plowing one small field, and he and Aurora had determined the needed crops to be planted. Cotton and tobacco, their money crops, were not even considered, what with the Conflict expanding on all fronts. Corn and hay would be needed for the remaining stock, and Aurora would expand their vegetable garden for their own use.

They headed for Fairlea.

****

Harrison was getting excited. When he had left Fairlea, he had been just a youngster. In his memory the white-columned main house had been majestic, but as he and Conner rode Guinevere up the overgrown path, he could see that all was not well there and the house not as pretentious as he had remembered. It paled in comparison to Ridgeland Manor.

There seemed to be no one around. Miss Edwina's flower gardens were no longer, and the weeds had overtaken even the tall azaleas. He got a catch in his throat as he and Conner made their way toward the stable.

"Stop!" he said hoarsely. "I hear something." But they heard nothing but bees buzzing around the flowers of the weeds, so they continued. Again, "Stop!" They both listened and Conner thought he heard humming. "It's coming from over there. Over by the quarters."

Harrison jumped off Guinevere and followed the sound. Sitting on an old oak stump beside the field hands' quarters was an ancient Negro man. He looked up when Harrison approached and said as big as you please, "Good mornin', Talmai. How's Silvey doin'?" Harrison didn't recognize the man.

"I'se Jonas, don' ya 'member me?"

Harrison's face began with a tiny smile, but by the time Conner joined him he was grinning broadly and patting old Jonas on his boney back.

"What's happened around here, Jonas? Where is everybody? This place looks deserted. Where's Marse Samuel and Mister Marshall? Are they all dead?"

"Nosiree, Talmai. Marse Samuel in mah care. Mistuh Marshall done gone to de War and lef' Marse Samuel wid me. He not been doin' too good dese pas' few days dough. Seems ta have de fever, but Ah'm takin' good care a him, jes lak Ah promised Mistuh Marshall Ah would."

Harrison looked at Conner, and they both asked, "Where is he?"

"Oh, Ah move him ta mah quarters. Dos long stairs jes too rough on mah poor ole legs," he laughed a toothless laugh and Harrison pushed past quickly walking to his quarters door.

Marse Samuel appeared to be asleep, at least Harrison hoped that he was. He studied the gaunt old man with his long white hair and scraggly, stained beard under the mound of dirty quilts. He saw a slight movement, so knew he was breathing. Putting his hand on the old man's forehead, he realized that he was burning up with fever, hot and dry.

Conner spoke from behind him. He sensed Harrison's fright and concern. "Here, let me see to him." Harrison, in a daze, moved aside, and Conner pulled the covers back and checked his pulse. His wrist was no larger than a small child's. He was very weak. He replaced the quilts and went out the only door toward Jonas.

"Jonas, when is the last time Marse Samuel had anything to eat?"

"Oh, Ah don give him breafus, mistuh."

"What was he able to eat?"

"He eat real good. Ah crumbled up the pone in de green's pot likkah, and he ate mos' of de bowlful. Real good. Now, yestiddy he won tetch nuttin'. Nuttin' atall. Jes hol' his mout' close up taght and won' eben let me git de spoon in. But, dis monin', he eat real good."

"Jonas, is there a doctor near by? Talmai and I could ride to get him."

"Don knows, mistuh. Ah nevah seed no doctah at Fairlea. Miss Edwina always take care all us, but de fevah done take her...long time ago." His voice trailed off, and they could see he was tired, just that little effort of explaining left him near exhaustion.

Harrison leaning against the weathered door spoke. "He's right, Conner. I don't remember a doctor ever coming to Fairlea. We could ride into Monticello to see if there's one there. It'd be a lot closer than Tallahassee, but first we've got to get more food in him. I think he's starving to death."

He squatted down in front of Jonas. "What other food do you have,

Jonas? Do you have any meat? How about chickens? I can't imagine Mister Marshall going off and leaving you without any food or money to purchase any."

"Oh, Mistuh Marshall left us plenty food. Why, de garden was full of good vegetables. Ah tried to catch dat rooster, but he too fas' fer me. Wees still got de bantams, and dey layin' real good."

Conner didn't wait for him to finish. He and Harrison headed for the coop. Within two hours they had a big pot with chicken and wild onions and cabbage boiling away in the side yard. Harrison had found a scythe in the barn and had cut down the tall weeds from around Jonas's shack and gathered limbs and cut logs from the stack of wood that Marshall had left for them over six months earlier.

Conner started to make the corn pones, but when he got the sack of meal out from the summer kitchen it was filled with weevils. "Jonas, do you have any kind of sifter? Nothing wrong with this meal if we rid it of these wigglers."

Jonas found a rectangular piece of wire and a piece of heavy, loose cloth that he tied onto the wire and began the job of sifting out the weevils. They found salt in the old kitchen and sugar that had almost turned to syrup. Harrison found a jar of pickled peaches and fig preserves on the high shelf, where his Ma Sarie had long ago stored them. By noontime they were sitting around Jonas's cabin on chairs that Harrison had brought from the main kitchen and eating the soup and pone piled high with fig preserves.

Between Jonas and Harrison they had managed to change Marse Samuel's bed. When Harrison lifted him, he realized that he couldn't have weighed a hundred pounds. His sunken eyes fluttered when Harrison spoke. He didn't recognize him but smiled when Harrison said his name. Conner brought the bowl of soup in and was blowing it trying to cool it. He had crumbled the pone into the broth to thicken it. Jonas took it from him, and Harrison held Marse Samuel on his lap, his arm protectively around him, while Jonas spooned the warm chicken broth through the dry, hot lips.

He ate slowly at first then with renewed gusto. "Dat's raght, Marse Samuel, eat up all yore soup so's ya can git well. Don' wan' Mistuh Marshall to come home an find Ah's let ya git all sick, now do we?"

When he mentioned Marshall's name, the old man closed his mouth tight and turned his head away. Harrison looked at Conner and they both realized what had happened. He obviously resented his son's leaving him for the War and had decided to starve himself to death to get even.

Conner spoke up. "Talmai and I think it very commendable that Marshall has joined the cause. If the Confederacy doesn't win its independence, there will be no Fairlea, and of course Marshall was aware of that. You're in good hands, Samuel. Talmai and I plan to go to Monticello to seek help for you and Jonas as soon as we get you on your feet again, and I'll write Marshall to let him know of your welfare. I'm sure he's concerned."

The old man turned his head back around and found his voice. "He's a God-damned traitor, that's what he is!" and said no more and turned toward the wall. He was soon fast asleep.

"Jonas, what did Marse Samuel mean when he called Marshall a traitor? Surely he didn't join the Union army!"

"Oh, no suh. Mistuh Marshall won't a done anything lak dat, not Mistuh Marshall. He up an married dat Sutton woman wid all dos younguns an moved over ta Monticello 'fore he join up to do his soldierin'. Marse Samuel don' lak dat woman. She won' live way out here in de country, an he tink dat Mistuh Marshall don' do raght by Fairlea. Mistuh Marshall did de bes' he could, wat wid no hep atall. Wen de blight hit, he had ta sell all de field people jes ta keep on goin', an' Marse Samuel tink dat he done give up on Fairlea. Dat's wat he mean."

He continued. "Marse Samuel won' move ta Monticello to live wid Mistah Marshall's wife so's Mistuh Marshall he done have ta go off an leave him wid me. Ah done tol' him dat A'hd take care of him real good, an' wen dat Sutton woman come 'round to see how he was doin', why he chase her off wid his big gun. She say she won' gonna be treated lak dat, and Ah ain't seed her since." He laughed as he said it, and Harrison and Conner realized that Jonas didn't take to Marshall's wife either.

Conner and Harrison went to the main house. When they went inside Harrison could see that a lot of the furniture was missing, probably in Marshall's house in Monticello, or maybe they had to sell it. Miss Edwina's spinet was missing from the parlor and the rosewood settee and side chairs also.

The one room that seemed intact was the dining room. He closed his eyes and could still see Miss Edwina sitting at the head of the table *glorying in her repast*, as she used to say. He had loved her and she him. He could feel her spirit still in this room. He knew she must be upset at her garden's condition. "If I can find the time I'm going to get it in good shape, Miss Edwina," he said aloud.

"What did you say, Harrison?"

"I said we should take a look upstairs, Conner." When they got to

Marse Samuel's room they found his furniture and trappings just as Jonas had said. Jonas had approved their idea of carrying the furniture to the parlor so he could take care of him without the long climb upstairs. They moved the heavy mahogany bed, wardrobe and tables. There was a narrow bed and dresser in another upstairs room, so they moved them down for Jonas and then proceeded to clean the summer kitchen and take inventory of the remaining food.

All the stock was gone now. Jonas had butchered their last hog and put the meat in the smoke house before Mistuh Marshall left for the War. There were only a few jars of fruit and beets, the remainder of the sugar, salt and meal and end-of-summer relish. Harrison held the jar of relish lovingly, remembering the happy kitchen with Ma Sarie and his Ma Silvey and even Miss Edwina working away at that relish. They had put everything they could gather from the garden in it, and it was a favorite of his. He blew the dust off the jar, and Conner saw a tear escape and roll down his cheek. Conner turned and busied himself so Harrison could visit his memories.

Conner and Harrison had no money for provisions, so they decided to ride Guinevere into town to speak to Marshall's wife to see if he had provided for his father. After careful consideration they decided to take the buckboard, that was in fair condition, just in case they were fortunate enough to bring back supplies.

Finding Marshall's wife was not difficult. The very first building they came to in the small town belonged to a relative of hers, and he told them that her house was only a few blocks past the main part of town with a white picket fence and a big oak tree in the front yard with a rope swing hanging from it.

A lovely looking lady of about forty years answered the door. When Conner explained his mission, she didn't question his identity or his motives and invited him in for tea. Harrison remained with the buckboard, and when he glanced up at the second floor it seemed that there was a child's face peering out of every window. He remembered old Jonas' saying that Mister Marshall's wife had a lot of children.

She told Conner that she had repeatedly sent someone to Fairlea to see about her father-in-law, but that he had run them off as well and that she was at her wits' end. She had promised Marshall that she'd see to his needs and had even gone to Mr. Stockman's Grocery to have his son Wilbur drive out to Fairlea with provisions. The old man had shot at the boy also, so her hands were tied. She felt that she'd done the best she could. She suggested that Conner go to Mr. Stockman's to purchase whatever he felt Mr. Sam needed and that she would take care of the bill as she had promised she would.

When Conner and Harrison rode up the lane to Fairlea Jonas was in the middle of the road waiting. They could tell by his expression that something was bad wrong. He blurted out, "Marse Samuel is now wid Miss Edwina. He jes' turn ovah and give up his soul ta de Lawd." He was ashen with grief. Harrison jumped out of the buckboard and went to him. They walked slowly back to the house, Harrison's arm around his bent shoulders.

They buried Marse Samuel beside his wife, and Conner was expected to say the words over him. Having been raised Catholic and having learned his prayers in Latin, he decided to recite Lord Byron and Shakespeare of whom he was most fond. Their words might not be as appropriate as a prayer, he realized, but they were beautiful none-the-less.

Now cracks a noble heart. Good night, sweet prince;
And flights of angels sing thee to thy rest!

Oh, God! it is a fearful thing
To see the human soul take wing.

Old Jonas and Harrison began to sing, and Conner could not continue, he was so moved by their grief.

They asked Jonas if he wanted to stay on at Fairlea or move into town. "Oh, no suh, Ah can't leave Marse Samuel and Miss Edwina. Deys de only kin Ah evah had, an' besides who gonna take care of der graves less'n ole Jonas do, huh? Who? 'Sides, de Lawd come a-callin' fer me soon."

Conner told him that he'd stop by Marshall's wife's house and tell her about Sam, so she could write Marshall, and that they'd make arrangements for Stockman's Grocery to deliver groceries at least every two weeks.

"Don' hafta worry 'bout old Jonas. Ah got mah garden, an' when de pears and peaches come in, Ah gots dem. 'Bout de onliest ting Ah needs is some side meat fer de greens and meal. Dem chickens lay real good, and de fish always hongry. Don' ya worry 'bout old Jonas."

They left him whittling the cross for Marse Samuel, sitting on the oak stump, just as they had found him, and humming contentedly to himself.

Harrison didn't utter a word until long after they had left Monticello. Then all he said was, *"So be it!"*, but Conner could see that he didn't want to leave just yet, and where were they going and why were they in a hurry.

He turned Guinevere around and headed back toward Fairlea. When they rode up to the quarters, old Jonas was still whittling on Marse

Samuel's cross and looked up and said, "Ah's got some greens inna pot and de makin's fuh pone, if'n ya wan' some, Talmai."

****

    Conner and Harrison stayed on at Fairlea until the summer of '62. They joined Captain John Jackson Dickison's Company "H", 2nd Florida Cavalry, and Harrison cooked Conner's mess throughout the War. Conner fought in every major skirmish, the Battle of Gainesville, Cedar Key, Olustee and was fighting beside Sergeant Charles Dickison, the Confederate Swamp Fox's son, when he was killed in Palatka. Florida supplied 15,000 soldiers to serve the Confederacy and another 2,000, who joined the Union forces, out of 78,000 White citizens, and was known as the bread basket of the War, keeping their soldiers' bellies full on beef and razorback hogs. Tallahassee was the only Confederate state capital not occupied by the Union.
    This was all made possible by the daring of *Dixie*, as the Union referred to Capt. Dickison, and his men; they were amazing. He used the swamps, the pine forests, the palmetto scrub and the thick cypress trees to screen his small force, never over 200 men at a time, and he never had over two pieces of artillery, and these only during the last year of the War. At one time or another his command ranged from Cedar Key on the Gulf to Smyrna on the Atlantic, and from Tampa Bay to near the Georgia border, where a spot known as Ocean Pond or Olustee was where the fiercest battle of the War was fought.
    Dickison's hit-and-run tactics, his ability to engage in a surprise attack on the enemy with comparatively few casualties, proved remarkable, and his men idolized him, Conner and Harrison among them. If Conner O'Farrell ever had love for anyone other than his family, Berta, and Harrison, it was for his beloved leader, Capt. John Jackson Dickison, *The Grey Fox, The War Eagle*, the most feared officer in Florida...his *Dixie*.
    It was while riding with *Dixie* that Conner discovered the wild, untamed beauty of the state. At the War's end he and Harrison decided to remain in Palatka and resumed their lives on the river, the beautiful St. Johns. He soon sent for Maeve and his Mum, but Agnes took a congestive chill and joined her beloved husband, Nolan, in his heavenly abode before she could accompany Maeve to Palatka.

BOOK FOUR:

THE KISSIMMEE VALLEY

CHAPTER I
CALLIE'S AND THOM'S HONEYMOON

February 1881

Callie's and Thom's delayed honeymoon to his parents' ranch, Bullseye, in northeast Florida, had been planned forever` it seemed, to impatient Callie. They hadn't even been able to go to the state fair in Gainesville in August, and that truly upset her. Seemed like all she had done since her wedding was supervise the building of the barn, look for bunch quitters and do all the other range work. Heck, she'd been doing all those things, except building a barn, ever since she could remember. Sure wasn't much difference since she had married. Somehow that didn't seem quite right to Callie.

They still ate up at the main house when not on the range. Thom let her know very early in their marriage that he liked her beside him in their feather bed, in their bed roll on the range and beside him when they hunted and fished, but he sure preferred to eat at Kate's and Mattie's table. That suited Callie just fine, because she didn't take to the kitchen or the brush broom either, even with all the trying she could conjure up. Somehow sweeping dirt off a floor wasn't nearly as exciting as waiting for a croaker to nibble unsuspectingly, then nibble again, and then just when he thought he was going to get the worm, she'd yank the pole, hook him and pull him up for their dinner. Now, that she liked, and so did Thom. Callie loved a challenge.

She had corresponded with Betty Sue Reynolds from south of Gainesville in the Micanopy area, whom she'd met at the one and only state fair she'd ever attended, so she knew who won the calf roping contest and other events. But she was getting antsy to get on the trail for Bullseye and, even more, for the steamboat trip all the way to Charleston.

Her mother-in-law and sisters-in-law had all written and told her of some of the sights she would see. Oh, they were glorious! She could hardly contain herself, and when Callie had that problem, she made sure that the entire ranch knew it. As Mattie said, "Miss Callie sho shoots straight. When she make up her min', watch out! Ain't no pig hidin' inna poke from her. Miss Callie know her druthers."

Betty Sue had mentioned Marthanne's fat baby boy and how Callie ought to see her traipsing after her husband, that Monti Fiske. Just like a sheep, she was, with him eyeing every girl at the fair and thinking he was some kind of special. Just because he got the high and mighty Marthanne Greer with child and had to marry her, didn't give him the right. She was the talk of the cow camps - boy, had she got fat! Callie had remembered how pretty she had been and how she'd made a play for Thom and how scared she'd been that she'd beat her time with Thom and the calf roping as well.

Betty Sue seemed to think that Marthanne deserved her fate, and Callie guessed that perhaps she did. But Callie did envy her her baby boy. She thought for sure that she'd be expecting by now - it was going on a year since she and Thom wed, and they'd been doing their most to beget a baby ever since. But her mother reminded her that she and her pa had been wed for over four years before Henry Parker was born, and then he lived for only a few days, so Callie realized that she was being impatient as usual.

But, oh, how she wanted a little boy. He'd have to look just like Thom, and she'd teach him how to ride and fish and hunt, all the things she liked to do. She knew that he'd have Thom's all-color eyes and dark brown curls springing every which-a-way and be just as full of life as his pa. She just knew it!

The long awaited day finally arrived, and she and Thom left Tall Ten right after first light. They had decided to ride BeeBee and Goldie instead of taking the buckboard. Mary had suggested that Callie take only one good dress and a morning dress, because she wanted to take her shopping in the fancy shops in Jacksonville and Palatka. Her bed roll and trap held the few items she needed, as did Thom's, so no need for the buckboard. Callie had never before got excited about shopping for anything other than a horse, but she found this venture out of her realm, therefore, thrilling.

When Mary had come to Tater Hill Bluff for the wedding, she had delighted the young women and their mothers with her descriptions of the beautiful shops along the river front in Palatka and the elegant steamships. The dining saloon on the *Robert E. Lee* steamer, with the violins playing and the ladies and gentlemen dressed in their finest, dancing to the lilting music, had them all enthralled. Callie was awed to think that she was going to witness it first hand.

Thom knew how excited she was and teased her unmercifully, but he, too, was looking forward to the trip. He had told Parker that one thing he was going to look into was the Kissimmee valley. Just how this millionaire saw maker, Hamilton Disston, and his associates thought that they could drain the swampy area that surrounded the river was a curiosity to him and every rancher in Florida, for most had driven their herds through that area many a time. They'd skirt the west side of the river, go around Lake Okeechobee and then would cross the Caloosahatchee at old Ft. Thompson or farther west in Alva. Wasn't anything in that valley but pure swamp, so he was curious.

Disston and his associates had saved Florida from bankruptcy when they bought the four million acres from the Internal Improvement Fund for only twenty-five cents an acre. They'd promised to reclaim the swamp and overflowed lands in the valley by cleaning and deepening the river all the way to Lake Okeechobee and to open shipping lanes to the tributary lakes. The *Tampa Tribune* said Disston was the largest individual landowner in the entire United States. Now Thom sure wanted to see just what this Yankee was up to. The final agreement would not be signed until summer, but there'd been rumors of Disston's already establishing a ship-building business in Kissimmee City. One of the cowmen told Thom that people had begun to move in there even before the dredges had got started on the river, and that they couldn't chop down the trees fast enough for their houses.

Well, they'd wanted the settlers to come in, and now that the Seminoles were peaceful and they no longer had to worry about raids and the War was but a memory, though a constant one, now did seem like the right time. There was also talk of the railroad's being completed to Kissimmee from up Orlando way. The legislature had granted charters to railroad companies just last year enabling them to build in the state. Governor Bloxham had seen to that. That's when the South Florida Railroad Company was formed and had already begun a line from Sanford to Orlando.

Callie and Thom talked almost non-stop all the way to Bullseye. They both agreed that they couldn't have been born in a more interesting time in history. One of the things that the railroads and the deepening of the Kissimmee would change - and they were all for that - was their ability to travel to places much faster. Callie lay awake at night, her mind racing to beat the band, dreaming of how some day she and Thom would get on the train right in Tater Hill Bluff and take young Thom all the way to Bullseye for a visit. She could hear the clickty clack of the wheels and, when she tried real hard, its moaning whistle.

She didn't like to think about not going on another drive to Punta Rassa, but the cowmen all agreed that with the trains it would no longer be necessary. The demand for their beef up north had increased substantially since the War's end. Layke Williams, who was running for the state senate, had explained it so well on the last drive. He had ridden as far as Tall Ten with the men from Old Town, the ranchers from Crescent City and the Big Lake spread. As they gathered, he announced his plans and told them that he'd miss the drives, but felt that his energy and time left on this earth could best be served from the halls in Tallahassee. Afterwards he returned to South Spring to be with Berta and the younger children while Young Reuben, Jonah and the deMoya brothers drove the South Spring beeves.

Callie's pa had said, "Now, isn't that just like Layke. Ride all this way just so's he could tell us in person about running for the senate. Yep, that's just like he'll be when he wins, too. Poor Berta won't see as much of him in Tallahassee as she does now," and he laughed, but they all knew that he was right. There was something inside Layke driving him - he never seemed to let up.

There wasn't a man around that camp fire from Layke's district who wouldn't vote for him. Why, he'd been a leader ever since Callie and Thom had known him, a take-charge kind of man. Callie was especially touched by how he handled Berta's sons. A person would have thought that they were his very own. Not bossy except when it was necessary, but it was how he did it, firmly but with understanding. She wished that she could vote - she'd surely vote for him.

Pierce Garvin laughed at his usually calm wife. "I can't believe you and Risa. Never in my entire life have I seen you so nervous. You'd think that the President of the United States and his first lady were coming for a week's visit instead of Callie and Thom."

"You get out of our kitchen, Mr. Smartie Pants!" Mary reached for the broom in the corner and began to shoosh Pierce out. Risa chuckled at the two of them. Seemed like they were the ones who were newlyweds to her, the way they had been carrying on these past few days. But Mr. Pierce was right. They did indeed have enough food cooked for everyone in Crescent City. She wiped her buttery hands on her apron and took the broom from Maam Mary, so she could chase that ornery rooster away while she checked the nests for more eggs. They needed only two more.

Mary sang softly as she finished creaming the sugar and butter together for the pound cake. Risa was sure that she'd find the extra eggs that they needed so it wouldn't be heavy. It was Thom's favorite cake, and she remembered how as just a little tyke he'd beg for more, even after a bout with a cold. They could always count on getting him to eat if there was pound cake. She knew he'd be expecting it.

That was the one thing that his Callie couldn't do, but he didn't fault her for it, and Mary was glad. Callie's few letters were short but filled with news of Thom - it was Thom this and Thom that. Mary smiled. Their young love had spilled over into her and Pierce's lives too. Or was he more loving because of the frequent trips that she and the older girls enjoyed every few months? No matter. She was just grateful that he'd become more affectionate.

Perhaps it was because of Berta and Layke. She and Berta had become very close since her honeymoon trip to Bullseye. Mary would be eternally grateful to her. She had suggested that Mary and the girls take the trips on the steamships to Savannah and Charleston and also had encouraged her to do her shopping in Jacksonville and Palatka. What fun they'd had, and what made it even more exciting was finding out about the Graves girl, Juanita.

Mary could hardly believe it when Berta told her that that girl had taken up with a riverboat gambler, and right on the St. Johns, too. She and the girls had seen the two of them - they were the talk of the steamer. She had her hair done up so fashionably and was wearing a very expensive dress. Mary was sure he must have bought it because it was so expensive looking. He was dressed all in white and was by far the handsomest man she had ever seen. And did he ever know it! She hoped that they'd be on board so she could point them out to Callie. After all, she and Thom had recovered some of the doubloons that that gang had stolen. Too bad that they'd missed the hanging in Old Town, she thought.

Pierce had even said that he'd be interested in accompanying them sometime, something that she'd thought she'd never hear. In the past all he'd ever wanted to do was ride the range and tend to the groves. She sighed and continued her daydreaming.

Mary had Berta's latest letter in her apron pocket. Lucinda had accused her of wearing it out, she had read it so many times, but she detected an undercurrent in it that concerned her. Berta was an open person, or had been in the past. Mary smiled. Maybe she is as I was two years ago. Maybe she, too, needs a change, but it is hard with the twins so young. Moving to Tallahassee should be exciting for her if Layke wins the election.

"I'll write her the minute we return from the trip. She seems so interested in Juanita and her gambler. Well, why not? She did live with them for months, and according to Berta, Etienne deMoya was so smitten by her that they were all afraid he'd end his own life. Poor thing. Pierce said he has a beautiful singing voice and makes the drive to Punta Rassa so pleasant, singing of an evening around the camp fire.

"Oh, you found more. Here, Risa. Put them in the bowl, and I'll get them beaten in no time." She continued to hum and Risa joined in with her island sing-song.

When Little Bit and Holden, the youngest Garvin children, came tearing into the kitchen, Mary grabbed Holden by his shirt collar and gave the two of them a real talking to. Risa realized that she was as Mr. Pierce had said, a nervous wreck.

"But, Mama, they're here! We can see them riding up the lane," Little Bit said breathlessly, and Holden, panting beside her, said, "Mama, we're not foolin', honest!"

"If you two are teasing me, I'll have your hide. Now I mean it! Risa, here, finish up these egg whites, and I'll just see for myself." Risa couldn't help but laugh at the three of them and had noticed that Maam Mary had removed her apron, so she must have believed them. Those two were always getting into some kind of mischief, not one bit like the other children, except maybe Thurmond. Maam Mary said that he was a little imp when he was small, always bedeviling someone or other, but he had grown up into an upstanding young man and had become Mr. Pierce's right arm since Thom moved away.

Risa could hear the shouting, so knew that they had not been teasing their mama. She took the blue-ringed earthen bowl out onto the side porch to finish beating the egg whites. From around the barn and up from the garden ran long legs. Lucinda and Sarah, now thirteen and fifteen years old, came bounding down the stairs out the screen door to the front porch and joined the others. Mary had said to Risa just yesterday that she was anxious to witness Thom's and Thurmond's reunion. They had been so close, and she knew that Thurmond missed him terribly. He had been especially quiet lately, she had noticed.

Thom hadn't even got off of Goldie when Thurm got to him. He was hitting him on his thigh before he could get his foot out of the stirrup, and Callie sat there laughing at the two of them. She had noticed their bond on the drive to Punta Rassa, the first one Thurm had been allowed to go on. He was so unlike Thom in appearance and temperament, but she liked him right off, as he did her. Anyone'd be better than that Marthanne Greer, he had decided long ago.

"Hey, Thurm, don't I get a hug?" she said as she slid off BeeBee. "Would you ever, Thom. Here we ride half way across Florida, and your brother just ignores me."

Callie was tall for a girl and slender like her pa. Thurm's broad shoulders and barrel chest dwarfed her in a bear hug as they went round and round.

"Hey, you two, better save some for everyone else," Thom shouted. Mary detected a little edge in Thom's voice. "Well, he's tired. They've been on those horses for over a week." She hoped that that was all it was. Kate had written her that Callie was already fretting about not being with child yet, and she wondered if Thom was concerned about it, too.

"Why do I do this to myself? Pierce is right. I must love to worry, or why on earth would I do so much of it. I'm going to enjoy their visit, every minute of it, and'll put my suspicions to sleep. And that's the end of it."

"I don't know who're the best cooks, you and Risa or Kate and Mattie, Ma..."

"If you're smart, son, you'll say your Ma and Risa, 'cause they've been working on your favorite cake all morning."

"Oh boy! Callie, you haven't lived 'til you've tasted Ma's pound cake. Whew!" he laughingly exclaimed, rubbing his stomach. "Don't worry, Ma, I'll find a place for it."

It was a happy table. Mary looked around and thought, "Guess Thurmond will be next to wed, then Sarah. Oh my," she looked up and saw Pierce looking at her, reading her mind. He smiled that crooked grin that he seemed to save just for her. Callie saw it and got almost teary eyed. They acted just like her ma and pa.

"Grief! I'm already homesick." She asked if she could be excused, and Thom looked at her to see what was wrong. She patted his shoulder and said, "Think I'll go check on BeeBee," and he knew that that meant she needed to be alone.

"Wonder what's bugging her?" He turned back to Thurm and said, "Hey, brother mine, you wanta go for a ride?"

"For heavens sake, Thom! You just rode for over a week and already want to get back on Goldie," Kate fussed at him.

Pierce spoke up, "I think you might find some peace away from this rowdy bunch over by Two Fork Creek, boys. Now if this doesn't suit your Ma, then maybe she has another suggestion, like maybe helping the ladies in the kitchen with this mountain of dishes..."

"Now, Pierce Garvin, did I even suggest such a thing? Now did I? I just thought he'd be sick and tired of riding on an old horse, that's all."

"Hey, you two, don't lets have a fight now. Gotta set a good example for my bride." Thom hugged the two of them around the shoulders and walked them out to the front porch. He and Thurm decided to walk to

Two Fork Creek instead of riding. They needed to talk and began even before they were out of earshot.

"I think Thurm needs to talk to his older brother, Honey," Pierce said lovingly to Mary. "I haven't mentioned it 'cause I know how you would fuss over it, but I think he's sweet on Harriett and Milton's daughter Charlotte..."

"Who? You don't mean Lotte MacIntosh? Well, I just don't believe it, Pierce Garvin! I just don't! Why, she isn't much older than Sarah. And just when did all this happen? Tell me when! I never even saw him give her the time..."

"See. That's just why I didn't mention it. You're already having a conniption fit, just like I thought you would."

"Men!"

She retreated to her kitchen, as hot as it was. She wanted to be in her own domain away from prying eyes. "This I'll have to sort out, Mr. Garvin. I just gave up Thom, and now I'm expected to give up Thurm as well. I don't believe I'm ready for that. My family is dwindling too fast. I just bet that Milton MacIntosh'll want him to go into business with him at the hotel, and he'll leave Pierce high and dry. I'll just bet that's what!" and she stewed and stewed and enjoyed every minute of it.

Pierce sat on the porch and laughed to himself. "She's in that kitchen giving us what for, I bet, and loving it. He lit his pipe and watched Little Bit's long, blond braids fly out behind her as she rounded the big live oak and hid from Holden. "Won't that boy ever learn that he can't catch her? I do wonder about that one. Mary says he's good with his numbers, and I for one hope so. He'll never outsmart even a cow, I'm afraid."

He rocked and smoked, and pretty soon Mary joined him. They didn't speak, but Pierce found her hand on his shoulder and she squeezed it. He put his hand over hers, and she drew up the other rocker and began crocheting. When he looked at her, she was smiling. Then he saw what she was working on - it was a baby bootie.

"Why didn't you tell me, Miss? So you've been keeping secrets, too!"

"Oh, Honey, now don't get too excited," she said restraining him. "This is just an *in case*, as my Ma used to say. No, I'm afraid there is no news there. Kate said that Callie is concerned. I believe Thom is too."

"Now where did you get that idea? Did he say anything to indicate that he was?"

"Well, no, but I can tell."

"Women!"

****

Callie had on her morning dress, blue checked gingham with a deep yoke edged with ruffled eyelet and long sleeves. No matter how hot it was, a southern lady never exposed her arms to the sun, and although she wore no hat, she did consent to a parasol to ward off the sun's rays. She, Sarah, Lucinda, Mary and Thom had boarded the steamship, *Savannah*, at the dock in Georgetown that morning. Callie was sure she was going to die before they got there, she was so excited. Pierce had had Maccaw drive them in the buckboard while Thom rode Goldie.

It was just as Mary had described it. The sea birds were flying all around the deck waiting for a handout while the creaking paddle wheel dipped into the amber water turning it to light gold with the froth an even lighter yellow, and the verdant countryside glided by, sometimes with high bluffs and majestic homes or stretches of orange groves almost to the water's edge.

"Are you happy that we came, Hon?" Thom asked, holding her hand. "Honey, I love it. It's just as Sarah and your Ma described. I can hardly wait to eat in the dining saloon. Did you see the waiters in their white uniforms? And the women! Why, I've never seen such dresses, not even in the *Godet* magazine at Jeeters'."

He laughed at her. "Callie Meade, as I said when I asked you to marry me, 'marry me and I'll show you the world...'"

"You never did such, Thom Garvin! Not ever!"

"I love you. Do you still love me, maybe just a little bit?"

"Why, Thomas Pierce Garvin, you rightly know I do," and she giggled up at him, the red glints of her brown ringlets shone in the noonday sun. "Thomas Pierce Garvin the third, that would be a nice name," she thought.

Mary and the girls were resting on the deck chairs watching. "I hope that whatever's bothering them can be eased on this trip," Mary thought, studying them.

Out of the corner of her eye she saw the man in the white suit approach. His white Panama and black cheroot just as she had remembered. Conner O'Farrell, the gambler, the man that that Juanita Graves had taken up with. She had just written Berta and told her about talking to the girl in Monique's shop in Palatka. It would appear that she had a position there, but she couldn't figure out just what it was. Monique referred to her as Cherie and treated her differently than she would just an employee, and Mary was positive that she was not kin. What really puzzled her was that Juanita's accent was French, too. Berta had never mentioned that. She thought that she was just a LaBelle girl, country through and through.

When Conner got to where Thom and Callie stood beside the railing, he stopped and doffed his hat, big as you please. They were both taken aback, but Callie said as she had been brought up to do, "Howdy."

He responded, "And a good day to you and your..husband?"

Mary thought that Thom was going to punch him a good one, he was so mad at how he said it, like he was asking her if she was married to Thom. But instead Thom grabbed Callie by the arm and practically dragged her away toward the stern. The gambler actually laughed aloud as he strolled on past her while smoking slowly on his cheroot.

"Good for Thom! That man simply has no manners, but I've never seen Thom show any jealousy. This is a new wrinkle in my son's character. Heavens, Callie meant nothing by her greeting. Something's going on. Well, there I go again. Just as Pierce said, loving to find something to worry about."

CHAPTER II
MONIQUE'S

Juanita heard the steamship's whistle..once..then again, its loud cry riding the warm February breeze toward Monique's small shop on the boardwalk beside the St. Johns. She hurriedly placed the ribbons that she had been wrapping around the cardboard up on the shelf above the work table. "I wonder if it's the *Savannah*?" She hoped that it was, as that was the steamship that Conner worked, and leaning back with a sigh, she thought of the night, the night that she hoped would be filled with music and laughter. She was afraid that she was indeed dreaming, for if Conner didn't invite her to join him on board, she'd spend another dull night with Maeve.

They'd probably just sit in the upstairs parlor and do more hand work, or she'd turn to her books for entertainment and escape, curling up on her narrow bed under a thin sheet with the window wide open, hoping for a breeze off the river and a full moon to dream by.

She opened the beautifully bound book of Jane Austen's *Pride And Prejudice*, that Harrison had given her for Christmas. She'd read it twice and had not tired of it, loving the sparring between the characters Darcy and Elizabeth. Conner insisted that she read Shakespeare's *Much Ado About Nothing*, explaining to her in that superior attitude of his, that only he could effect, the similarities of the two works, but she got so angry that she put the book down, declaring that she'd never read it or Shakespeare again. He called her an ignorant girl and stalked off toward the ship. She decided to not tell him of her love of *Little Women* - oh, how she did love Jo - or he'd no doubt find some of Shakespeare's works to compare it to. That she couldn't bear to think of.

Frankly she was getting sick of this waiting....waiting for his majesty to decide to include her in on the *Savannah's* festivities. He had been in one of his moods before he left for Sanford. She had finally learned to ignore him at those times, but his moods seemed to come more frequently than when she first arrived in Palatka. He seemed to take great delight in putting her down of late.

She had been so unsure of herself and of Conner upon her arrival, not knowing whether he felt for her as she did for him. Preacher Catlett would have accused her of lusting after him. She giggled, for that was exactly what she was doing, but Hell's fire and damnation seemed so very far away. It was a silly thing for her to do, showing up in Palatka unannounced, she now knew. "But I go with my instincts always have, or why on earth would I have run away with R.J. and Joe Bob. Why?"

She had bought a new dress, hat and almost everything she had tried on at Monique's that beautiful summer morning. She could still see Maeve's surprised expression when she told her that she'd take everything, even the slippers that were really much too tight. Oh, Juanita could tell what Maeve thought of her, that the country girl was just wasting her time trying on everything in her shop. She was sure that Juanita couldn't afford such expensive things. How could Maeve have known about the doubloons R.J. had given her and about all the money that she had earned with the medicine show? Her attitude had been so superior. It tickled Juanita.

Later, when Harrison found her in Conner's cabin on the *Savannah* and brought her to Monique's, he asked Maeve if she would take her in. She did not even question his motives. She was as contradictory as her brother, but Juanita had learned to respect her, and at least Maeve she could understand. Conner remained an enigma...but oh, so fascinating - she still thrilled at the thought of him.

But she was grateful to Maeve, or as she was called in Palatka, Monique, for taking her in and allowing her to apprentice in her shop, Monique's, the most exclusive shop in all of Palatka. Every time Juanita thought of being associated with Monique's she wished that she could flaunt it in the face of her sister Bonnie and her Ma in La Belle. My, how they would have carried on!

Juanita heard the tinkling of the little brass door bell and rushed from the back room expecting it to be Conner. "Oh, I'm sorry," she said, hastening to change her flushed expression to a more business-like attitude when she stared at the four ladies. She and Maeve both affected a French accent when speaking to a customer or when around the other townspeople. She went into her act.

"How may I help you, madame and mademoiselles?" she addressed the foursome. She had seen them in the shop and knew that they either lived in Palatka or in a nearby town, because she had also seen them on shipboard, all except the tall, brown-haired, pretty one.

They had bought a number of items in the past, so she was almost assured of a sale. Maeve would be pleased, because business had been unusually slow. Maeve had not returned from Mrs. Ahern's, where she took tea every Wednesday afternoon. She was one of the few real friends Maeve had made since arriving in Palatka. They were both active in St. Monica's Church and every morning they walked together to Mass.

Juanita did appreciate that Maeve had not insisted that she accompany them. She just didn't understand any of it, all the kneeling and making the sign of the cross, but she'd tried real hard on her own, thinking that becoming Catholic would be a way to Conner's heart, not that he ever attended Mass, but gave up after a few times. She did enjoy looking at the candles flicker brightly in their tall, gold, ornately carved candle sticks and the blue and pink statue of Mary, her golden hair wearing a crown of stars. She also appreciated the church's beauty with its pungent aroma of incense, and the mysterious sound of Latin the priest mumbled fascinated her. Although she didn't understood it she liked how it sounded. But it was all so foreign that it scared her half to death.

Mary spoke. "We'd like very much to see some hats. My house guest - actually she's my daughter-in-law from down Tater Hill Bluff way - also would like to see something in a morning dress, wouldn't you, Callie?"

Callie couldn't take her eyes off Juanita. She knew that she was staring and felt like a fool, but her eyes were somehow riveted. Mary asked again, "Wouldn't you, Callie?"

"Yes, ma'am," she finally got out. They had told Callie that she'd probably get to see Juanita Jane Graves from La Belle, the one who had run away with the Skinners, but Callie had not been prepared for this. She was so beautiful that she could readily understand why Etienne deMoya and the gambler she had seen on the *Savannah* were so taken with her. She'd already had more excitement in one day than she'd have had at Tall Ten in a blooming month. Whew! And she could hardly wait to get back so she could tell Jam and Slick about seeing the Golden Girl in person and that she didn't have horns or a forked tail. She laughed at some of the descriptions that had been painted of Juanita. Heck, she looked like everyone else, except she was a lot prettier.

Juanita brought out several dresses from the back work-room where Maeve stored the finished gowns. Maeve designed the gowns, cut them out, pieced them together, and then turned them over to hired seamstresses to complete. Things were so different in Palatka. Finding experienced seamstresses was next to impossible. In New Orleans there were trained garment workers who were expert, but as she had said to Annie Ahern just last week at tea, "Cherie seems to have been born to the trade, although she has never even done hand work. She is really an amazing girl in many ways. I just wish she were Catholic - then I wouldn't be so concerned." Mary and the girls gushed over the peach sateen morning dress with dark brown accents, that Juanita held up, and enthusiastically talked Callie into trying it on. "Do you think Thom will like it?" she asked her mother-in-law. Mary could tell she was unsure of herself in the elaborate surroundings and was not sophisticated enough to hide her discomfort in front of the Graves girl, so she quickly assured her that anything she wore would be pleasing to her husband. Callie was not convinced. The girl looking back from the full length mirror didn't look a bit like Callie Meade Garvin. Callie wasn't sure that she liked what she saw. Oh, she liked the dress, all right, but she was not quite ready to give up the old Callie for the image in the mirror.

"I can't think of a single place I'd be able to wear this in Tater Hill," she looked around at the admiring faces, then back at Juanita. "Oh, it's very pretty, I've never had on a prettier dress, except maybe my wedding dress. What I mean is, I live in a cow town, and we don't have a lot of fancy places to go and..."

"My, Callie, you won't always be traipsing after Thom on the range. Before you know it you'll be able to ride the train up to see us or up to Kissimmee when the shops are built. Rumor is that Kissimmee will be *the town* in Florida, what with its becoming a ship-building center and everything. Why that Mr. Disston has promised that the President of the United States will be down for the grand opening of the waterway. I'm sure there'll be lots of places you can wear it. It's so right with your coloring, my dear, isn't it ...I'm sorry, I didn't catch your name," she lied, turning to Juanita. Lucinda and Sarah turned their heads and smiled sheepishly.

"Cherie. Just call me Cherie."

"So, she's going by the name she used when doing the tight rope act, is she," Mary thought. "I must remember to write Berta."

Juanita continued. "And of course you're right. A mademoiselle was een the shop only yesterday. Her family was moving to Kissimmee, and she wanted to be prepared for the many social functions she expected to attend. She said that there were plans for fifty houses to be built right in Kissimmee City, and until last year there was only one. Imagine!"

Callie wanted to appear as sure of herself as Juanita was. Heck, even Lucinda and Sarah knew how to act better than she did. She gulped and said quickly, "You're right. I really do like it, and Thom did say to buy what I wanted... I'll take it." And having finally made up her mind she sat down hard on the little gilt chair and sighed loudly.

Juanita saw her relief. "I was like her only a year ago, scared and unsophisticated. Conner and Maeve and even Harrison have all taught me a lot, but I've got a lot to learn yet." Wanting to put Callie more at ease, she whispered to her that she was so pleased that she'd decided on that particular dress, because it was one of her very own designs. Callie was beside herself. "Wait'll I tell Maida and Marta and all the ladies at Aunt Beulah's about her. Grief! I've never had such a day!" she thought. "Juanita Jane Graves, *The Golden Girl*, and R.J. Skinner's accomplice in crime." That was how the newspapers referred to her.

The back door of the shop closed with a bang. Thinking it was Maeve returning, Juanita didn't even bother to peek around the satin striped curtain that separated the workroom from the showroom. When Maeve didn't join her, she went to the back and called up stairs. "Maeve...Maeve." No answer at first, but then Harrison appeared at the top of the stairs with his finger on his lips to caution her to be quiet. She realized that Conner had come back and was resting in his room. At least she hoped that he was resting and not just nursing a hangover.

Juanita ran upstairs and said to Harrison, "I'll fix us a cup of tea." He followed her into the small upstairs kitchen. It was one of four rooms where Maeve and Juanita lived and Conner spent his time when on shore. Harrison saw her concern and hastened to assure her that Conner was indeed resting.

They sat quietly, not speaking, when all of a sudden Harrison blurted out, "We had an exhilarating evening, Cherie. This is one trip that I'm sorry you missed. Hamilton Disston was a passenger on the trip to Sanford, and he and Conner spent the larger part of the evening in Conner's cabin discussing Disston's venture. I do not wish to spoil Conner's account of the evening, but I do want you to know that he offered Conner a job in Kissimmee after he sets up his office there." Having said it, he sat back in the chair and waited for Juanita's response.

"What was his reaction, Harrison?. I mean did he show any interest, or could you tell?" She was not overly excited, more cautious, he noticed.

"I was surprised, I truly was. Never did I expect Conner would even consider leaving the river..never! But he asked question after question and ...he had only a brandy with Disston, nothing more," he said as much for himself as for Juanita, for Conner's drinking had become a concern for all of them.

Juanita wore such a perplexed look that Harrison added, "He hasn't made up his mind, Cherie. I'm sure that he'll discuss it with Maeve and, of course, you," he added knowing full well that Cherie knew better. Conner O'Farrell did just what he pleased without regard for anyone but Maeve and, once in a while Harrison, but Cherie, well, she was taken for granted just as all the other women in his life had been.

Harrison knew that Conner cared for her, or she wouldn't have been tolerated for such a long time. But she wasn't his true love, his Berta, and to actually consider Juanita's opinion regarding his future, that would never be entertained.

When she pursed her lips and jumped up practically knocking her cup off the table, Harrison was not sure he had done the right thing by telling her. "I'm in for trouble - am I ever. Conner's going to have my head!"

Juanita was positive that he'd go to Kissimmee without her. She immediately began to plan, and if there was one thing that she was expert in, it was planning. She had allowed self doubt to entrap her after she became Conner's mistress, but her self preservation was as strong now as it had been when she was just a sixteen-year-old girl in La Belle. Her determination returned that day.

"I'll not be shoved around any longer. Who does he think he is, anyway, going off without me. And what do I care if he does? I've got my doubloons, and I can design and make dresses and hats with the best of 'em! I'll just show Mr. Conner O'Farrell, that's what I'll do!"

And so she did...

Maeve looked up from the letter she was writing when Juanita came into the back room. Juanita wondered why she always chose the workroom in which to do her writing while she had a perfectly beautiful desk in her own room upstairs with the morning light shining in the bay window, but here she sits holed up in near darkness writing. "Guess she's writing her secret letters to that Vincent again. Why in the world doesn't she just accept the fact that she loves him and either go back to New Orleans or have him come here. I don't understand either one of those Irish, I declare I don't." Juanita had seen Vincent's name on letters addressed to Maeve but knew nothing of their relationship.

"Maeve, I'm going to the *Savannah* for the evening. I'll return in the morning in time to open up."

"I'm sorry, Cherie, what did you say?"

"What did I say, indeed?" she thought. "She's just surprised that I'll go when that brother of hers is still upstairs sound asleep, that's what."

"I said that I'm going to the *Savannah*, but I'll return in time to open up so you can go to Mass with Mrs. Ahern."

"Don't bother to rush, Cherie. I can have Mrs. Sullivan open tomorrow. Why don't you take off for a few days - we can manage, I'm sure." Maeve knew that something was up. She'd seen Juanita in a snit before, but it had been a very long time ago.

"That sounds like a splendid idea. I'll just run upstairs and pack a few things and shall return after the Charleston run. Oh, thank you, Maeve," and with that she turned and actually ran up the stairs.

"Yes, something is definitely up. I wonder what Conner's done this time. Is it another woman? I wouldn't be a bit surprised. He's been with Cherie for over a year, and that's an eternity for him. I can hardly wait to share it with Vincent, but I'll have to make sure of the boyo's indiscretions before I do. He is so wise. He'll know how I should handle the situation." She glowed. She always did when she thought of Vincent.

She reached behind the business ledgers and took out his picture, that had become yellow with age, and rubbed it lovingly with her forefinger. Then she removed his latest letter from inside her skirt pocket and read it again. She missed him so.

She felt someone staring, but when she looked around there was no one there. Juanita had ducked into the showroom so Maeve couldn't see her. The look on Maeve's face had not been for another's eyes. "She must love him very much." Juanita brushed a tear away. "I know that I love Conner, but I'll simply not let him pull me around by my nose any longer. Never again! Why, I'm just like an old catch dog past my prime."

She called to Maeve before opening the front door. "Maeve, do you want me to go to Mr. Coates' for any notions while I'm in Charleston?" She heard the chair scrape on the bare floor. Maeve put her head around the curtain and said, "That would be wonderful of you, Cherie. Here, I've had the order written out for over a week but wanted to wait until business improved. I've never seen it so slow. Your sales this morning certainly helped."

She went to the workroom and returned with the order, and while they were standing talking, Juanita heard Conner call Maeve from the stairway. She hurriedly took the order from Maeve and dashed out the front door, her trap in hand.

"Yes, something is definitely going on." Conner called again. "I'm coming, Conner. I'll only be a minute."

He walked up the gangplank, head held high seemingly with great purpose, always with great purpose, sparkling white suit and panama - his trademarks. There were other gamblers that plied the St. Johns, but none with the reputation of Conner. He was colorful, known for his fascinating stories, his wit and his honesty at the tables. He was also envied by those less handsome, less articulate and less charming, and he gloried in their inadequacies.

Since his association with Juanita, his reputation as a ladies' man had lessened, and those who had known him for a long time felt that he was actually settling down. It was good that Conner O'Farrell was unaware of their observation.

Juanita stood back in the shadow watching him. "I wonder if Maeve told him that I was on board? I bet she didn't. Why do I always get a catch in my throat when I see him? I wish that I didn't love him, that I was bored with him...but I'm not and might as well admit it. But doggone you, Conner O'Farrell, I'm not going to let you walk all over me...I'm not!" She turned, and when she did, saw the girls who had been in the shop earlier. She smiled, acknowledging them, and rounded the corner almost at a trot. She didn't want Conner to see her until after they had left the wharf and were on their way to Jacksonville.

Juanita had engaged a stateroom for the round trip, using her own money. It was the first time. She was excited. She usually stayed in Conner's cabin, but never unless he had invited her to accompany him on shipboard. Their arrangement had never been discussed. She just tagged along. He'd arrive in Palatka, go to Monique's, sometimes spend a few days or sometimes only a few hours, depending on how the cards were running, tell Juanita to pack, that he had a particular player he wanted her to impress and that they were going to Charleston or Savannah or Sanford or wherever, and away she'd trot...right behind him.

It didn't matter if she was in the middle of designing a dress or hat or with a customer. When Conner said let's go, ..she went. At first she was just glad to be invited. She loved to get all dressed up in the beautiful gowns that Maeve had designed. The other women on shipboard stared at her enviously and would ask their husbands to find out from the gambler where his lady friend purchased them. Maeve's business flourished.

It wasn't that Juanita wanted to marry Conner. Somehow that really didn't matter to her - at least, that is what she told herself. She did, however, want his respect, want his admiration, and above all want his consideration, and she felt she had received none. Oh, she received his passion, his appreciation of her beauty, his dependency, but then he was also dependent on Maeve. It simply was not enough.

The single most important thing that Conner O'Farrell shared with Juanita was Harrison. He actually allowed her to be Harrison's friend. There was no jealously between the two of them, no envy, nothing but deep concern for each other and Conner. Juanita didn't understand their special relationship, nor had she ever witnessed it before. It was beautiful to her, and she felt privileged to be a partner.

There was pounding on the cabin door, not knocking, but pounding. "It's Conner!" She was excited. She heaved a sigh, and in as strong a voice as she could muster said, "Who is it, please?"

"And just who do you expect? The king of England? Who do you think it is?" he asked angrily.

"I'll not display any fear. I simply will not," but she was thrilled at the uncertainty of the situation.

Tying her wrapper around her, she opened the door a crack and said, "I thought it might be the steward bringing my tea, Conner. Would you like for me to order some for you?"

She could tell he was more than a little perturbed with her but had decided to not show it. In a controlled voice he said, "What, may I ask, precipitated this journey, Cherie?"

"This journey? I was not aware that I was to seek your approval, Conner. No doubt Maeve told you that I am on a buying trip in Charleston and Savannah for the shop."

"Yes, Maeve did say that you had decided to make such a trip, my dear," he said through gritted teeth.

She was delighting in their exchange, so proceeded with confidence. "Then she should have also told you that I made a large sale this morning, and because of it, we are now in a financial position to purchase some much needed notions and fabric."

"So she thinks that she can play her hand pat, does she? Well, we'll see about that. I'll just give the little bitch an opportunity to draw to a straight, or at least make her think she can."

"Cherie," he took her hand lovingly in his and looked into her surprised eyes. "What's he up to? He's up to something, I just know it. Conner O'Farrell doesn't give up this easily."

He tenderly pulled her to him and kissed the top of her yellow-white hair, loosening it, his long slender hands removing her soft wrapper. Before it fell to the cabin floor she had reached inside his shirt and begun massaging his muscled back, pulling him to her.

"Why do I always let him get to me? I just can't seem to help myself..."Conner"... She went limp.

CHAPTER III
DELIA ROSE

1883   Kissimmee City

Excitement prevailed. The wilderness town of Kissimmee had in two short years become Kissimmee City and was incorporated in '83. As promised the railroad was completed, and regular train traffic was heavy with the new Floridians taking up residence in the city, establishing businesses and taking the steamships into the interior for the first time in Florida's history. There was the *Floridelphia*, the *Colonist*, and the *Mamie Lown*, to mention only a few.

Disston's dredges had completed the deepening of the river and had finished digging the canal between the Caloosahatchee and the big lake, Lake Okeechobee. The sleepy villages in the valley emerged into bustling settlements. The sub-tropical wilderness that Disston had challenged was indeed tamed into a beautiful fertile land for the hungry settlers.

Conner had accepted the job that Disston had offered, to the amazement of Maeve, but not to Harrison and Juanita. They had noticed that his card games no longer seemed to fulfill him - he seemed distant - preoccupied. Harrison had joined him in Kissimmee and assisted him in coordinating the Disston enterprises in the state.

Juanita had not been encouraged by Conner to move with him and Harrison. She continued working with Maeve at Monique's and had assumed the position of buyer as well as designer. She had been very upset at first, but her frequent trips aboard the steamships to the cities of Charleston, Savannah and Jacksonville lessened her disappointment after a while. But her independence was not accepted by Conner. He expected her to be available when he summoned her to Kissimmee, and when she arrived, he made every effort to dominate her. Her resistance fueled his interest, and he found the new Cherie even more challenging.

It was a gala occasion when the first train arrived in Kissimmee, and Juanita was on board. Conner had wanted Maeve to accompany her, but she felt that she could not leave the shop, so Juanita went alone. She needed to be alone with him - she needed to tell him - but how? Would he accept the baby that she'd known about for three months but was afraid to even mention...not to him...not to Maeve. She had no one to share it with.

She'd been in the same situation before when she found out she was with child, R.J. Skinner's child, but he was dead, hanged, and her baby, her Angel was also dead. She tried to not think of that fateful, rainy night in Palatka when she fell from the high rope and lost the baby. That was the night she first saw Conner. Juanita shivered even though it was unseasonably hot. It was so very long ago, and she was no longer the inexperienced country girl. But how to tell him still eluded her.

She had been preparing herself for the entire trip, blocking out the noise of the train. "Maybe, just maybe, he'll take the news calmly, or joyfully," but then thought, "Or maybe he'll get drunk and go into one of his black moods, not speaking to me for days or not even knowing I'm around." She was preparing herself for any eventuality. Then leaning back in the coach seat, she decided that she was going to have a good time in spite of Conner O'Farrell. "If he wants to make an ass of himself, then so be it!" Having decided that, she felt better.

The train was packed with people from almost every state. Trying to take her mind off her problems, Juanita made light conversation with the ones sitting near her, the Makinsons from Maryland, the Brattons from Missouri, Mrs. Ira Bass from Georgia, whose husband had also accepted a position with Disston to work on the railroad. It was known as the Sugar Belt Railroad and was being built between Kissimmee on the northern shore of Lake Tohopekaliga and St. Cloud to the east.

They arrived at the little train station on Broadway, and it was bustling with dignitaries from the surrounding towns and from Tallahassee, Berta and Layke among them. The cheering crowd was led by a little band of Seminole Indians headed by Chief Tom Tiger and Billy Bowlegs III, dressed in their colorful ceremonial costumes, but Conner stood out among them with his white suit and Panama, and when Juanita saw him she got the same sensation that she always did. There was to be a large celebration at the Tropical Hotel, Conner had said, so she and Maeve designed and made the most beautiful dress she had ever seen, flowing white crepe de Chine with hundreds of pastel silk flowers bordering the low neckline, and many-tiered handkerchief skirt. Maeve had unthinkingly commented that it was pretty enough for a wedding gown, and later in the quiet of her room, Juanita cried lightly, giving into her sorrow, her lonliness and her fear of whether Conner would accept the baby.

The hotel was a sprawling, three-story building. A wooden boardwalk led to the train depot. Juanita waved to Conner and Harrison, and when she thought that they had seen her, she asked the porter to assist her with her baggage.

The crowd was thinning out, but she didn't see them anywhere - they seemed to have disappeared. By now she was angry, and not feeling well to begin with, the insufferable heat had added to her misery. "At least I don't get sick every blessed morning like before," she thought remembering how uncomfortable she'd been while carrying Angel.

She turned to the porter. "I'm sorry, but my friends seem to have vanished into thin air. Would you please see to my baggage? I'm staying at the Tropical Hotel just down Broadway." And with that she straightened her dark grey gabardine dress, picked up the train to keep it from becoming snagged on the wooden boardwalk and pranced herself right up to the hotel.

"Just who does he think he is? And, Harrison! I would have thought that he at least would have the manners to see to me, but no. Those two knew full well that I'd be on the train. Now why didn't they wait to attend me?"

The porter could see that the blond little lady was fuming. She was walking so fast that he was having trouble keeping up with her, and those big bags were so cumbersome that his bowed back felt like it was going to drag on the street, the only street in the entire country that was covered with grass. But Juanita paid no attention to that phenomenon, grass being grass. She had rather walk on it than sand, but why all the fuss about an old grass-covered street, she didn't know.

Juanita approached the desk and was about to ask if her reservation had been made, when she saw Conner out of the corner of her eye. He was leaning up against the wall, not paying a bit of attention to her, staring at... my goodness, it was Berta and Layke. Of all people! Why, she hadn't seen them since she left South Spring with the medicine show over five years ago. She knew that Layke had run for the senate and had won and that he and Berta spent most of their time in Tallahassee now. They were very popular, and there was always something in the newspaper about them.

"I can't believe this. I'm so glad I decided to wear this dress," she thought, mentally comparing hers with Berta's. "Mine is much more fashionable than that pale rose with that pretty little-girl, lace collar. Really, you'd think that a senator's wife would have better taste. Pretty...it's just a pretty dress like anyone would wear."

Juanita could hardly wait to get to them but decided to wait until Conner saw her. Then they could approach them together. She wanted to flaunt her new, sophisticated look and handsome boyfriend in front of Berta. Berta had been kind to Juanita, but now that she was a senator's wife, she no doubt would put on airs, Juanita reasoned.

"I simply will not call to him. Just what is the matter with him that he's staring at them like that, like he's in a trance? Dear me, I hope he hasn't started drinking again. Oh, for heavens sake, Conner..."

He turned her way then and slowly, without any animation at all, walked toward her. "A fine howdy do! Ride a blooming, hot, noisy train all this way, and he doesn't even act like he's glad to see me!" But then she got concerned. He looked drawn. "I hope he's not been sick." Then she thought, "Why do I let him turn the tables on me? He always manages to make me worry over him, when in truth, I should be angry that he didn't meet me at the station. Darn you, Conner!"

Harrison and Conner had known for weeks that Berta and Layke were going to attend the celebration in Kissimmee, and it was obvious to Harrison that Conner was concerned about it. He seldom ate a full meal and had lost weight, weight he couldn't afford to lose. But he hadn't resumed drinking, no more than a few brandies after his supper, and then only when they had guests. But he had become forgetful, his mind far away from his work, so Harrison had to cover for him more often than he should.

This was upsetting to Harrison, this obsession with Berta. If Conner had any sense at all, he'd know that Cherie was the one person who could tame him. Even Maeve recognized that. But he seemed to have this ridiculous notion that that pretty, blond, middle-aged woman was his to worry over. Harrison did not understand it, and he doubted that Conner did. Some people just loved to be miserable, and he figured that his friend was one of those.

Harrison had been in the hotel foyer watching Conner when Juanita came in huffing and puffing. He had been so concerned for Conner that he had forgotten all about her. "And I think Conner's losing his mind! I'm the one! I can't believe that I'd forget Cherie." He was about to approach her when he saw Conner leave his spot. "Good! Now maybe he'll be able to take his eyes off Mrs. Williams long enough to at least welcome Cherie. She looks tired. But then why shouldn't she?"

"Well, at least he had the good sense to kiss her, even if it was on the cheek. What's this? Does Mrs. Williams finally recognize him? And after all this time. I'd swear on a stack of Bibles that she does. I'm not believing this - the plot thickens, and now her husband is looking at the two of them."

"Good Lord! Are Conner and Cherie walking over to them? You'd think that he'd have better sense. Why are they laughing like they all know each other? I'd better get over closer so I can hear."

****

Berta had received several letters from Mary Garvin this past year. In one of them she had enclosed a newspaper clipping about Conner's new position with Hamilton Disston in Kissimmee. She had also told her that Juanita had not accompanied Conner because she had seen her several times on shipboard and at Monique's in Palatka. "Why should that excite and relieve me? This man I hardly know has possessed me. I'm just glad that Layke doesn't know what a fool he's married to." But she continued her fantasy - she was alone so much of the time now.

She had excellent house help and a nurse for the twins. Wes and SuSu were in school during the day, and she tried to fill her time with shopping and having the other ladies over of an afternoon for tea. But she would rather have been sitting on Stucky's porch in Old Town with Trudy and Luta and have an attentive husband warming her bed at night in South Spring. She appreciated his hard work and was so proud of him. He was one of the most respected senators in the state, and when he was home, he did make an effort to talk of his day's work, usually at the dinner table, and Berta knew that it was his way of trying to include her.

What really upset Berta was that she had believed that she would love their life in Tallahassee. As a young lady in Macon, she had found her parents' political functions exhilarating and was truly surprised when she discovered that there was nothing quite as boring as rehashed information about the various bills before the senate, that so engrossed Layke.

Their home on Calhoun Street, just down the street from Governor Bloxham's, was beautiful in comparison with South Spring, even with its new wing that they had to add the last year to accommodate their enlarged family. The huge live oaks, sweet gums and magnolias surrounded it along with palms of every discription, and the ornate iron fence across the front next to the wide street made a lovely setting she knew. But Berta, even though they had bought it, did not feel for it as she did for South Spring. She had enjoyed the decorating - it gave her something to do while Layke was so busy - but there was no *special* love - it felt so temporary. When they would return to South Spring after the session was over, everything changed. Oh, Layke still had his work and travel to do around his district and other political functions to attend throughout the state, but Berta and the children were able to resume their sleepy life on the river. She loved the little church in Old Town. She missed it so. The First Presbyterian Church they attended and The

Market Place, where they often had picnics after services on the park grounds, were lovely and she had become active in the women's circle, as should any respectable senator's wife. But there was something missing. When Berta wrote Trudy that she was homesick, Trudy at first thought that she said it just to make her feel better. She hadn't believed that she could miss anyone as much as she did Berta. But when the letters began arriving more frequently, Trudy realized that she was indeed homesick, so she and Luta and Emma tried to write more often.

Trudy hadn't mentioned it to the others, but she had detected another note in Berta's letters. It seemed to her that Layke was spending a great amount of time away from his lonely wife. She tried to not compare him with Reuben, but she couldn't seem to stop. Reuben would have sensed Berta's unhappiness and done something about it, but Layke was a driven man. She had always known that about him and knew that his intensity was one of the things that attracted Berta to him. She sighed. "Life just seems to get more complicated. I'll have a talk with both of them when they return next time." But she didn't. The time never seemed to be right, and when they were home at South Spring and Berta was with Young Reuben and his wife, Leonora, and Jonah, and had the rest of her family around her, she was her old self.

****

"I knew she'd be envious of me and Conner. I just knew it. I could feel her jealousy. Now, Berta Williams, Mrs. Senator, how does it feel to be on the other side? Huh?" Juanita was curled up on the high bed in her hotel room, her small hand stroking its satin coverlet, and she was feeling mighty proud of herself. When she and Conner had gone over to speak to Berta and Layke they seemed genuinely pleased as well as surprised to see her. And when she introduced Conner, she was amazed at Berta's shyness at meeting anyone that handsome and polished.

"I caught myself a gentleman, too, Miss high and mighty senator's wife. Grief! She was all tongue tied - couldn't even talk to him. And that husband of hers just kept looking at her then back at Conner." She laughed. "Why the two of them couldn't believe what a catch I'd made - little Juanita Jane Graves from La Belle. I showed 'em!"

The ball had been glorious. Juanita wore the most beautiful dress there - even Conner commented on it. Her queasiness had subsided enough for her to dine with the other Disston employees. She couldn't get over how dowdy their women were. She was by far the belle of the ball.

Then why wasn't she happy? Conner had been very attentive, dancing with her more than he ever had, and every man at their table had asked for a dance.

Then why wan't she content? Was it how he had kept staring at Berta? She did look...lovely, that was the word. Not beautiful, but Juanita had to admit that Berta's deep gold, silk gown, trimmed with purple velvet pansies on the bodice, with leg-o-mutton sleeves was very becoming. She especially liked the draping over the bustle. She must remember to tell Maeve about it. And her hair was very attractively arranged with the deep purple pansies woven in among the golden strands. "She probably had to have someone else do it for her," she thought. Juanita was always proud that she could arrange her own hair since she'd had it cut.

"Then why am I not happy?" she questioned. "Is it because Conner didn't come up here last night? It's been over a month since I've seen him, and he just squeezes my hand and kisses my cheek and turns and leaves. Is that a way to treat someone you invite to a ball? Now, is it?" She turned over with her head in her pillow and sobbed.

"Do you want me to have breakfast brought up, dear?" Layke asked the still sleepy Berta. "Why the hurry, sir? This is the vacation you've been promising me for months, isn't it?" she teased with her arms outstretched.

He went to her. "You were the most beautiful woman at the ball, my sweet. By far the most beautiful!"

When she didn't respond, he continued. "The gambler from New Orleans thought so, too."

Berta was taken aback. How did he know that Conner had been in New Orleans? You don't suppose that he's been reading my letters from Mary? Of course not! Layke wouldn't stoop to such tactics...or would he?

She responded hesitantly. "You mean Mr. O'Farrell? He is quite charming, isn't he, even if he has aligned himself with Juanita. Even with her new-found manners, she's still just a country girl."

Layke raised his brow as he said, "That doesn't sound like you, Berta. Yes, she is just a country girl, but she's trying to better herself. There was a time when you would have found that exemplary, my sweet." He kissed her forehead lightly and got up.

"Do you want to have your breakfast sent up, Berta?" He said it coldly.

The magic was gone. "Why did I have to say that about Juanita? Am

I jealous of her?"

She looked up quizzically. "No Layke, I'll get dressed and go down to the dining room." She thought a while and added, "That was an unkind thing to say about Juanita, Hon. I guess I'm just a little jealous about how beautiful she has become...and I'm feeling a little middle-aged...and..."

He reached for her. "Lady mine! Don't you ever think such a thing. You're the most exciting woman I've ever known. Berta...I know that I've been wrapped up in the Democratic Party more than I should be, but there is never a day that goes by that I don't know how lucky I am to have you by my side."

She blurted out, "Then why don't you say it? Why don't you tell me? I need to hear the words, Layke. I need to hear it." She was now crying.

"Oh, Honey, I didn't know..." Shuddering, she hungrily came to him.

"My God, woman, you are..."

Juanita finished buttoning her shoe. She put the button hook back in her small, black case and, stretching up, thought, "I'll be as big in the belly as the *Bertha Lee* in a few more months." She groaned. The *Bertha Lee* was an oversized steamboat that took fifty-three days to go from Ft. Myers in the dredged Caloosahatchee River up through the Kissimmee River to the Kissimmee docks.

Ed Douglas, who owned the Tropical Hotel, realized that steamboating was going to be big business in the area and went all the way to Peoria, Illinois, for her. He liked the idea of owning the largest boat on the river - too large. It was a sore point with him when people referred to a fat person as a *Bertha Lee*. But that was how Juanita felt that morning. "I'll have to make plans," she thought. "If Conner is going to be so distant, then I'll just not even tell him about the baby." She mulled it over in her mind. "Think I'll tell Harrison. Maybe he'll advise me." And with that thought in mind, she thought of food. "My, I could eat shoe polish. I really could."

She saw Conner immediately. How could she miss? He was by far the most attractive man in the dining room. Layke had gone to the desk for the morning paper, but there was none. Kissimmee had grown rapidly but still had to rely on outside papers for the natives. When he arrived in the dining room, he acknowleged Conner with a nod and a good morning.

"Have you ordered, my sweet?"

Berta shook her head, no. She thought, "I know that at my age I shouldn't be enjoying this, but I am. Layke's actually jealous. This isn't fair to him, really it isn't."

"Honey, I'm famished! You know I always am afterwards," and she winked.

He actually blushed. He took her hand and squeezed it. Berta looked up in time to see Conner witness the scene. "I am content, my love, my Layke. I am content," she realized. "I just needed that extra assurance, I guess."

She didn't see Juanita enter the room, hesitate, then with her head held high walk right up to Conner, stoop down to kiss him on his cheek, and say loudly, "Good morning, Honey. Have you ordered?"

Berta was only intent on a smiling Layke. "After breakfast would you like to stroll down Broadway, my sweet?"

"Whatever you say, Senator," and she kissed his finger tips.

The train was pulling out, but Juanita still lingered on the platform. Harrison said anxiously, "Cherie, you've got to tell him. He has a right to know. Well, at least tell Maeve. At least do that." But Juanita continued to shake her head, her large, navy blue hat with its red silk flowers bouncing with every movement.

"He doesn't deserve to know! Why, I came all the way over here to this nothing town that everyone is talking about, and he treats me like I've got the plague. Now you rightly know that, Harrison!" And she continued to sniffle as the train let out one last whistle.

"I know he has no excuse, but he has been very busy lately..."

"Don't you busy me, Talmai Harrison. I've been busy, too."

"Well, would you just look who's walking up the boardwalk. Would you just?" she said as she glared at Conner with lips pursed, her face all askew. She didn't say a word but turned in a huff, and she climbed up on the train step, turned around and, staring right at him with her two small fists planted on each hip, shouted as loud as she could, "Well, hello and goodbye, Mr. Conner O'Farrell...you about-to-be daddy!"

Everyone there who heard her and knew Conner began hitting him on the back and congratulating him, and he, taken completely off guard, just stood there grinning that mocking grin of his.

"If I live to be a hundred," Harrison said later to Maeve, "I'll never forget his expression...not ever."

"He's always loved children, Harrison. He's really a softy when it comes to anything or anyone helpless. It's one of the boyo's charms."

They heard a small cry, then a louder one. Harrison dashed out to the back where Conner was pacing and smoking, pacing and smoking, and yelled, "It's here, Irish! It's here, and it's a lusty one. Would you just listen to it yell?" He was hopping all around the table when Mrs. O'Leary yelled downstairs in a booming voice, "It's a girl, it is. And she's a beauty, Mr. O'Farrell. She's a beauty fer sure, sir."

All Maeve could think was, "I'll have to write Vincent tonight. Oh, he'll be so happy for the two of them. Maybe now he'll marry her, and it'll no doubt be up to me to see to her training. I must insist that she be baptised immediately. That I'll have to do."

Juanita held the small bundle close and Connor just stared at them. She pulled back the blanket and said hoarsely, "Delia Rose, meet you Da."

He stood, not saying a word, tears streaming down, and gently took her from Juanita.

"So, it's Delia Rose, is it now? Well, it's a pretty name for a pretty colleen. Indeed it is."

Harrison was in the doorway, crying.

CHAPTER IV
ARCADIA

"I must remember to write Berta about Callie and Thom," Kate said to Pierce. "She seems to have finally adjusted to being a senator's wife. I was truly worried about her." She filled the wash bowl that had been her grandmother's and had been brought over from Scotland many a year ago. How it had not been broken by one of the help she couldn't understand. They were getting more slovenly all the time. The only one who was worth her salt was Risa, and she was getting on in years. "I don't know what the world's coming to, I declare I don't," she said aloud.

"Mary, would you quit all this fussing, blow out the lamp and come to bed. We've got a big day ahead of us tomorrow. Why, the way you're carrying on about nothing would make a person think that you're nervous."

"Well, that's a fine howdy do, Pierce Garvin. Here, we're about to have our first grandchild, and you act like," she threw her hands up in the air and continued, "I don't know what, but you're something else, you are."

They were both nervous wrecks. Mary had been cooking all week knowing that her family was going to starve to death without her, and Risa and Harriett kept saying, "Miss Mary, wees can take care of de fambly jes fine...now you and Mr. Pierce go on down to 'Cadia an welcome dat baby."

They were nervous. Thom and Callie had been waiting almost four long years for this baby. Yes, they were nervous. "I'm at least glad that we can go by train," she continued, not paying a bit of attention to what Pierce said about coming to bed. "I declare, I think I'd not go if I had to go by buggy and boat again like we did for their wedding. That undoubtedly was the longest, hottest, most tiring trip I've ever had."

Pierce laughed. "You're just spoiled, Mary. Since we got the railroads you'd think that you and the girls didn't have a fine old time on the *Savannah* and the *Robert E. Lee* and all those others you could hardly wait to get on..."

"Pierce Garvin, how you do carry on! Why, I never said any such! You know how I love the steamers. Why there has never been a train ever made that can compare with one of 'em. It's just that it's faster by train, that's all."

****

Thom was at the station pacing up and down. ARCADIA, the sign said. He'd never get used to it. It'd been Tater Hill Bluff ever since he'd been trailing beeves all the way from Bullseye. ARCADIA...it was a pretty name. Most folks still called it Tater Hill, though. One thing he could say about the trains...they never were on time. He laughed when he thought it. His first born wasn't either. Doc Spooner had told them that was usually the case with the first one, but later Callie'd be able to spit 'em out. He laughed again.

He just wished everyone in town would quit reminding him of it. Every time he turned around, Jam or Slick or another of the cow hands would make a dumb remark like, "Hey, Thom, you gonna git him a horse fer his first birthday, huh, Thom?" Grief! They couldn't even let a fellow act like it was a helpless little baby, they couldn't. Already got him riding a horse!

He bet he'd have Callie's temper, 'cause that youngun could kick up a storm. He never saw anything like it. The first time he did it, near 'bout scared them to death, then they got to laughing so hard that Callie wet her drawers, and that really did scare them. This having a baby was a scary thing, it was.

He heard the whistle, then the train rambling down the track, and so did everyone else. They still weren't used to having a train come to town, so all who could ran to the platform. His Aunt Beulah and Uncle George, he could understand. But, what in thunderation did old man Jeeters need to be there for? When he saw Clay Willett get off, looking like he just stepped out of a magazine, he got a lump in his already taut throat. Every one in town knew that he still was unmarried and had been sweet on Callie for almost forever. Then he remembered that Mrs. Willett had not been well, so guess that was why he was there.

They had moved Callie into the hotel so she could be closer to Doc Spooner. Kate, Parker and Jay had all taken rooms near hers and Thom's, and they'd been there for an entire week. But the day that Mary and Pierce arrived, that baby decided to come. Thom laughingly said, "He's been waiting on his grandparents to get here. That's what!"

Doc Spooner lived just down the main street, and when George rapped on his door at about 2:00 a.m., he knew that Callie's time had come. "Beulah has that kitchen buzzing with half the women in Arcadia, Doc. She's got every tub she owns filled with boiling water, and they're ready for you and that baby."

When Horace Spooner examined Callie, he knew that they were in for trouble. She wasn't dilating enough...he could feel the head and it was a big one. He went out and stared at a hall full of kin. "This might prove to be a long one, folks. You might as well get some sleep."

"What's wrong, Horace?" Kate asked. She pulled him aside so Thom couldn't hear. "She's just not dilating enough, Kate, that's all. Her water broke, you said?"

"Yes, that's when Thom came a-knocking on our door."

"Well, it's her first one, and it usually takes a lot longer. Now don't you worry. Just see if you can get the others to go to their rooms, and I'll sit with her. If anything happens, I'll be sure to call you. And get Thom settled. He acts like he's gonna pop a gut, I declare he does."

"What ya mean I can't stay with her? Heck, it's my baby, too!"

"Now, Thom, Doc said since it's Callie's first that it'll be a long time coming, that's all, son."

And it was. Callie was in labor all the rest of that night, the next day and into the following night before Thomas Meade had to be taken. He was a strapping boy, weighing almost ten pounds, and Callie was completely exhausted. But Thom...well, he was hooting and hollering all over Arcadia. When Callie finally awakened enough to say hello to her husband and baby, Thom was so snockered that he just sat there grinning, every white tooth in his head gleamed at her.

"Isn't he pretty, Thom?" She laughed, "I mean handsome. Isn't he handsome?"

One Year Later

"Parker, you wait right there. Now don't you move 'cause I've got one more tray of cupcakes for you to carry," Mary said impatiently. "Mattie, are you ready? Here, I'll help you with that lemonade." Mattie had slowed down so much in the year since Meade's arrival, that Kate wasn't sure that she'd make it to his first birthday.

They had decided to help Callie and Thom out with Meade's first party. Marta and Maida and their two little girls and Willy Speare, Jernigan's and Sally's year-old boy and just the family who lived in Arcadia were invited. Callie still wasn't much in the kitchen, but there never could have been a more attentive mother.

Kate called from the buggy, and Thom was there to help her. He seemed a little out of sorts lately - even Parker had mentioned it the other evening. He said that he'd really been snapping at the hands, and Kate said it was probably because he hadn't been getting much sleep 'cause

Meade had had the croup. But he didn't think that was the problem. He didn't let on to Kate what he thought, though. Thom'd had plenty of sleep on the range and plenty of shine, too. Parker wasn't about to tell her that.

Beulah and George had already arrived. Their granddaughters, one-year-old Stella and Nettie, almost two, as rambunctious as two pups, were already running all over the place. Willie was Meade's age, about the same size, but also active. Callie sat holding Meade, trying to get him to get down and play with Willie, but he wasn't going to let go of his mother's skirt.

"Let him down, Callie," Thom said. Everyone looked at him when he said it. He seemed put out with her. "He'll get down when he's used to all this commotion, Honey," she said quietly.

"You're going to make him a sissy if you don't quit coddling him. He's not gonna break, you know."

Parker spoke up, "Here, I'll take him, and we men will go outside. How'd you like that, Meade? Tell Grandpa how you'd like that."

Thom walked out in the side yard with them. Parker was glad. He didn't like the way he was behaving, and he could tell that Callie didn't either. "He can't even say *mama*, Parker," Thom said softly. "All those other kids can say bye bye and mama, but he...well, he hardly ever even cries. Something's wrong with him. Callie knows it, too, but won't admit it."

"Thom, every youngun has his own way of growing up. He's as healthy as any kid I ever saw. Now, where do you get the idea that he's not...right?"

"I've known it for a long time. I saw Doc Spooner just last week and told him what I thought, and he said that sometimes when a baby takes a long time coming there's some damage...to the brain, you know..."

"Well, he acts the same as any other baby to me. That Horace Spooner doesn't know everything, Thom. He isn't God, for heavens sake!"

"Don't put that in your mouth, Meade," Thom yelled.

"I think you're out of line, Thom. It's none of my business, but I think you expect too much of him...he's only a year old."

Callie called to them. "Mama's bringing out the cake, so hurry up. Here, Thom, I'll take him. Come to your mama, Meade, and let's blow out the candle."

Parker looked at Thom's expression and actually got weak. "My God, he's jealous of his own son. What's wrong with him, anyway?"

****

1884 Palatka

Juanita had promised Maeve that she could keep Delia Rose in Palatka while she and Conner got settled in their new house at the end of Orange Street in downtown Kissimmee. Conner had designed it so she could have a small dress shop in the front of the house with living quarters upstairs and a large work area in the back. Conner had not seen the necessity of leaving Delia with Maeve, but Juanita, who had just weaned her, needed a rest, and Harrison and Mrs. Sullivan both said that they'd help Maeve with her.

She was a beautiful child and looked exactly like her father. There could be no doubt whose daughter she was, and Conner doted on her. Juanita need not have worried about his reaction to the baby. He took her to the office with him, to the park for her stroll and delighted at the passersby, who patted her and made over her. Her hair was as black and curly, her eyes as pale blue, and her skin as white as his. She had already won The-Most-Beautiful-Baby-In-Kissimmee Contest.

Harrison was as excited about her as her parents, but mostly about what a change her arrival had made in Conner. He no longer drank, was always on time at work, had become very demonstrative toward Juanita, showering her with gifts, flowers for no reason at all, and escorting her to every important function. In other words, he was a changed man, and Harrison was relieved. He had been so worried about his friend.

Maeve had come to Kissimmee for Delia on November the fourth, and she and Harrison took the train to Sanford, then the steamer *Marion* on to Palatka the following day. Mrs. Sullivan was there to meet them, and they took the horse-drawn trolley to Monique's on Water St. "She was so good, weren't you, Delia, my sweet?" Maeve kissed her forehead, but Delia just wanted to get down. "Here, Mrs. Sullivan. You'd better fix her some porridge before she starts to fuss. Now, Delia, don't touch that, dear," Maeve cautioned as Delia began pulling the tablecloth off.

"Harrison, would you be a dear and go to Lemon Street and ask Mr. Haughton to fill this order? He'll just put it on my bill. Then go to Mr. Mann's and get the meat. He knows exactly the cut of beef I like for the stew. I want it nice and tender so I can mash some up for Delia. I'm sure she can eat the broth with a little barley stirred in if the meats too tough, can't you, my sweet?"

The next day, the sixth, began as every other day at Monique's except for the racket Delia was making from the upstairs rooms. "Here, Delia Rose," Mrs. Sullivan cooed, "eat your porridge." Harrison couldn't help but laugh at the two of them. Delia was as stubborn as her father and mother, but Mrs. Sullivan was as determined as anyone he'd ever seen. She'd been trying to get Delia to eat for over an hour and wasn't about to give up.

Finally, Harrison said that he'd relieve her, that she was to get her dressed and that he'd take her to the park for a stroll, so Maeve's customers wouldn't think they were murdering someone up there. The minute he took Delia outside, she shut up. "Just as I thought, little girl, you're just like your parents. Like to have your own way, don't you?"

"She's finally settled down, Harrison," Maeve said. "I'm so tired! Think I'll write a little on my letter and then turn in. You've had a full day, too. There's the cot all set up for you in the back of the storeroom and some of Cherie's books that she didn't pack, if you want to read for a while. Good night."

Harrison heard the winds come up, but since there was no window knew that his room would still be insufferably hot. "Think I'll take this mattress out on the back walk to catch some of that river breeze." The small back yard, just large enough for the brick walk and the large river oak, was fenced in against any passersby. He remembered later that he was thinking what a good night's sleep he'd have if Delia didn't keep them all awake. It was not yet ten o'clock, and Maeve had been in bed for over an hour. She must have finished her letter to Vincent, he thought. Juanita had confided in him of her concern for Maeve and what a dunce she must be not to go to New Orleans and tell him of her love. Harrison decided to not tell her that he was a priest, a monsignor. That was Maeve's business and no one else's. They weren't hurting a single soul.

Harrison was awakened by the loud clanging of the fire engine and, realizing that it was close, went out behind the fence but could see nothing. He was groggy with sleep. He tucked his shirt tail inside his pants, pulled on his shoes and started walking down Water St. The wind was whipping up a gail when he saw the blaze. "My God, that's close! I'd better find out what's going on!"

People were all over the place, yelling and shouting orders to each other. The buildings he'd shopped in earlier already had flames shooting up through their roofs, and there was no water coming out of the fire hose. "What the hell's wrong with that pumper?" someone shouted. Harrison ran to one of the men and asked if he could help, and the man told him to get the people out of any close buildings, because the wind was going to burn down the whole town.

He ran as fast as he could back to Monique's. "Maeve...Maeve!" Up the stairs his long legs flew. Maeve got up coughing, "What in the world is going on? Is there a fire? Where is all the smoke coming from? Oh, on my dear mother's grave, what is it?"

The building was now filled with smoke, and she and Harrison quickly grabbed Delia up and ran. Down the stairs, out the back door, through the gate they ran, and began running toward Main Street away from the flames, that they could see were now spreading, engulfing the Water Street buildings. Harrison held Delia, who was yelling her head off, but when he turned around, he saw that Maeve was running away from them.

He yelled after her. "Maeve, don't go back there! My God, are you crazy?"

He tried to follow but was so out of breath, and the smoke was so thick, that he and Delia, who stopped crying the minute he finally stopped underneath the tall maple tree, never would have caught up with her.

"The fool woman!" he said outloud, crying uncontrollably. "The fool woman's going back for those dumb, stupid letters! That's what she's doing!"

When the sun rose on Saturday morning, the citizens of Palatka looked upon a scene of desolation. Even the beautiful Putnam House was burned, and Harrison, holding Delia protectively in his arms, stared at the ashes of what had been Monique's and Maeve O'Farrell. But all he could think of was Conner.

****

1889 Arcadia

Meade Garvin was going on six years old. He was sturdy, handsome, with Thom's all-color eyes set in Callie's heart-shaped face, dark brown, curly hair and had a ready smile for everyone. He was a favorite in Arcadia and would have been even if he hadn't been dumb; he had never uttered a word. Callie had accepted his affliction without giving it much of a thought, as had his grandparents. She loved him for himself. When he was four, she and Parker had taken him to see a doctor in Tampa and were told that there was nothing wrong with him physically, but he suggested that they take him to a doctor in New York City for another opinion. He gave them his name and address, but they decided not to go, that Callie would work with him at home. And she did, but without results. He could make grunting, laughing and squealing sounds and even cry, but no words came forth.

The past five years had been hard for her and hard for Thom. He simply could not accept Meade's condition. He knew that he was quick to learn. Miss Saunders, his first grade teacher, said so, and he could do his numbers as well as his classmates and seemed to have his uncle Jay's ability to draw and color. He could ride his pony, Buffey, and play ball and skip a flat rock on Old Piney Creek with his friends, of which there were plenty. He was as popular in school as any of the *normal* children. But his father could not or would not accept him, and his attitude was taking a toll on his and Callie's feelings for each other. She knew that he loved Meade. She had seen him look so lovingly at him when he thought she wasn't watching, but most of his time was spent raising his bird dogs when he wasn't on the range. A section of the barn had been set aside for them, and Thom spent many a night there. Callie had long ago stopped nagging him about not giving her and Meade the time of day and went about being a mother, daughter, friend, but rarely a wife. Whenever she got lonely at night, she'd roll over and stroke Thom's side of the bed, knowing that he was in the barn with his dogs and bottle of shine. The tears she allowed to form seldom welled out of her dark brown eyes anymore. She had cried them all out. Then, she would remember their wedding night and chuckle at how ignorant she had been, pull on her robe and tiptoe out to the barn, crawl up beside her Thom on the mound of hay and hug him to her, telling him how much she loved him, and once in a while he'd give in to his feelings. Kate and Parker knew that they should not interfere, but even Jay felt like saying something to Thom. Instead, they spent more time with Meade, Jay teaching him how to sketch and allowing him to help him with his stuffed animals' habitat, and Parker teaching him how to fish and trap. But Meade, sensitive and aware, wanted his father's love and acceptance, and it nearly broke all their hearts as they watched Thom shun his only child.

The one thing that really got to Callie was that Thom would not allow Meade to have one of his puppies or even go to the barn to play with them. That really got to her. "Now, why can't he have one, Thom? That just doesn't make any sense. He's gentle with animals - you know that - and it would give him some responsibility. That's good for a child. Now you rightly know that, Honey."

But no matter how often she brought the subject up, he always had an excuse for not allowing Meade to have one. "I make part of our living selling these dogs. Now you know that, Callie" or, "Every one of these puppies has been promised even before Dixie went into heat - now you know that, Callie." But she did not know it, or anything about it, because he never would discuss it with her. It was as if the dogs were his business, and Meade was her business, and the two of them didn't mix.

That is the only problem that she had discussed with her parents and with Mary and Pierce when they came down for a visit. Pierce had even had a talk with him about it, but Thom had told him the very same thing that he had told Callie. So, everyone just shut up about the entire subject, but were afraid to get Meade a puppy of his own.

They had had a beautiful fall, and winter had been mild, but when February came around, Old Man Winter decided to pay a visit. There were so many of the old people in Arcadia who had come down with bad bouts of influenza. Clay Willett's mother Cora was one of them, and she didn't survive. She had not been well for the past few years, so Clay had tried to visit often and was with his mother when she passed away.

His work as a features writer for the *Tampa Tribune* didn't allow him much time off, but when he could put together a few days, he always came home to Arcadia. He was worried about Callie and had made it a point to go to church, because he knew that she'd be there without Thom, and he wanted to support her by letting her know how fond he was of Meade. Everyone in town knew about Thom's feelings for his son.

Arcadia had planned a large celebration to honor Clay before Cora had become so ill. He had won a national award for his feature article *The Making Of A Senator,* and they were all so proud of him. What was more exciting was that he had used Layke Williams as his subject, and because so many of the Tater Hill folks knew Layke from his cowhunt days, it was even more meaningful to them. But when Cora died, they postponed the celebration. The bunting was stored in the Young Hotel until summer.

It was a Wednesday, and Cora's funeral was arranged for ten o'clock. Callie would never forget that day as long as she lived..nor would Thom. She awakened early. As always, she checked Meade's room, and he was still sleeping. Thom had made it to their bed and was sleeping soundly - she could smell the shine.

"I'll not disturb him but will have to get Meade up so's he can get dressed for the funeral. He always likes to see Clay...and so do I."

"I just wish that we could have had the celebration. Beulah said that Berta was going to accompany Layke. I bet she loved the article, especially the part about her. I know the folks in Old Town are proud of her. Why, without her support, Clay wrote, Layke's work wouldn't be as effective." She thought that she and Berta must be a little alike. She always tried to support Thom, even when he acted like he didn't want it.

She tiptoed around the kitchen trying to be mouse-quiet, but when Meade suddenly grabbed her around her legs, she let out a yelp, and Thom sat straight up in bed and yelled, "What's that?"

She and Meade laughed, and Callie said, "Go on back to sleep, Hon. It was just Meade trying to get a rise out of his mama."

Thom came into the kitchen rubbing his sleep-swollen eyes and said, "Aren't you going to the funeral? You're going to be late if you don't hurry."

"We've got plenty of time. You gonna come with us?" She said it just to be polite, knowing full well that he'd say no, that he would have something or other to do with the dogs. But he said, "Yes, I think I'll tag along." You could have knocked Callie over with a feather, she was so surprised.

"That's wonderful, isn't it, Meade? Your daddy is going with us." He ran to Thom and grabbed him around his legs, too, and Thom actually tousled his brown curls and for once stood still without backing off with some excuse or other.

"What's going on?" Callie wondered. Then, "Why am I so suspicious?"

The church was packed. Cora Willett had been a quiet pillar of the community. She had assisted at the school for as long as any of them could remember and had given piano lessons to most of the youngsters in Arcadia. And besides, her son Clay was one of the few real celebrities Arcadia could boast of - he and Jay Meade, that is. Oh, it had some well known cowmen and the likes, but that wasn't like being a writer or an artist.

This was the first time Thom had been in church for a long time, and everyone seemed genuinely pleased to see him. He seemed almost like his old self, Callie observed. "Maybe my visit to the barn earlier in the evening has some bearing on this change." She held his arm tight, possessively, and her action was not lost on the observers. Everyone liked Callie and Thom, and their problems, although not discussed in the open, were a concern to all of them.

It was a lovely service, everyone said. Clay looked so distinguished as he sat next to Ione and Gus Jeeters on the first row, his dark blue suit beautifully tailored. "I need to get Thom a new suit if he's going to start back to church," Callie thought. Clay stood at the church's door shaking hands and kissing the ladies' quivering cheeks and thanking all for coming to pay their last respects to Miss Cora. Callie, and everyone there, saw the tear tracks on his cheeks and were touched. He was a good son, and she had been a good mother.

"Raising a son by yourself isn't easy," Callie thought. "Grief! I should know."

Callie had just finished hugging Clay. She wanted to tell him how proud of him the whole town was but knew the time wasn't appropriate. Thom extended his hand to give his condolences, and Meade, looking up at Clay, smiled his sweet smile, extended his hand just as his father had, turned to Thom and said as big as you please, *"Go home, Daddy?"*

Callie turned around and looked at Thom, then down at Meade, and doggoned if he didn't repeat it, *"Go home, Daddy?"* Thom didn't say a word, just picked him up and ran all the way to their buggy with Callie right behind him calling their names.

"Willy," Meade said. He repeated, "Willy."
"What's he talking about, Callie?"
"I don't know, Hon. He wants us to follow him." Meade dragged them into the barn and pointed to Dixie and her five nursing puppies. He reached down and picked up the fattest one there and hugged it to him and repeated, "Willy. Mine."

****

Kissimmee city 1889

So much had changed since Juanita and Conner had come to Kissimmee. The Legislature had created Osceola County, named for the controversial Seminole Indian leader, and Kissimmee had been named the county seat. A new court house and jail were being built, and the town's first public school, a four-room structure on Church Street. Lake Tohopekaliga, called Toho for short, was a thriving port, and the trains ran daily, even if not on time.

The new waterway that Disston had promised eight years previously was a reality. The Caloosahatchee River was deepened, from its mouth in the Gulf to the flat-topped cypress at its end, and a three-mile canal had been dug from the river to Lake Okeechobee. North of the lake the Kissimmee was dredged out, connecting the small lakes all the way to the port on Lake Toho. Hundreds of steamships, some small and some large, floating palaces, brought people and goods into the interior. The river traffic was heavy. But all was not well with Juanita and Conner in Kissimmee City. She had had it with him! She was not of the fabric of the long-suffering woman - that was not Juanita Jane Graves. She loved him...oh, how she loved him! But she was not a fool, and she would not be trampled any longer. When Harrison returned from Palatka with Delia, Juanita had not been prepared for Conner's reaction to Maeve's death or to Delia. She had known that he would be devastated but had not expected this. It was as if Delia had been responsible for Maeve's death. Juanita could not believe his behavior. When she brought it to Harrison's attention, he at first was not able to give her an explanation. He mumbled something about Conner's over protection of Maeve and his mother, and ...did he say Berta? Juanita was very confused and believed that she had heard him incorrectly. But she had not.

The days were lonely and the nights almost unbearable. She would lie awake and listen for any noise, any noise at all coming from his darkened room. He seldom left it except to go to work or to buy another bottle. He was haggard, thin and unshaven, and if Harrison hadn't insisted, he would not have bathed. This was a man who had been fastidious about his appearance.

"Is he loving being miserable, Harrison? Is that what he's doing, trying to drag us all down into that black hole with him? Is that what he's doing?"

Juanita continued working in her shop, actually pouring herself into her work. She was a natural business woman, who loved caring for her patrons and took pride in every dress and hat she created. Maeve had given her that, and when Harrison finally told her that Vincent was a priest, she at last understood Maeve's love, and realized her strength. "I'll never be that strong, I know it. Almost five years is an eternity. How did Maeve stand it?"

Her work and Delia were her only pleasures now. It had taken Conner almost a year to get himself back together and to work, but he still rarely smiled, and the witty man she had loved was no more.

She could have put up with that. Harrison kept saying, "He just needs more time, Cherie," but time he'd had, and she hadn't seen much improvement. What really rankled her was his total disinterest in Delia.

"I honestly believe that he wishes Delia had been killed in that fire instead of Maeve, Harrison."

"Cherie, don't say such a thing."

"Why not? It's what I think. He's ruining that child with his aloofness. She doesn't understand why he's changed like that. She doesn't. And neither do I."

Juanita at last decided to take matters into her own hands. She took the steamship, *Bassinger*, down the Kissimmee to Ft. Basinger in search of her friend, Rose, who Juanita had met when she ran away with the Skinner brothers. Juanita had no idea that Rose would still be in Ft. Basinger, but she needed to find her, for she needed an accomplice. She had liked Rose from their very first meeting. She rationalized, there are some people that you just take a liking to and feel like you've known all your life. The fact that she was an excellent seamstress helped her fit into Juanita's plan. She thought she knew why Rose had left Alva so suddenly. She was positive that she was pregnant with Joe Bob Skinner's child, and when she was told by the people in Alva that Rose was taking care of her cousin's little boy, Seth Roberts, in Ft. Basinger, she was sure. Seth had been Rose's father's name.

When Juanita and Delia arrived, she found out that Rose and son Seth lived in Basinger across the river and not in Ft. Basinger. She still worked in Shipman's Boarding House. She knew that she had never married, because when she asked for Rose Shorter, everyone at the country store knew whom she meant. She didn't recognize Juanita at first, but Rose hadn't changed one iota. Juanita would have known her anywhere. She wore her hair the same with the light brown ringlets all around her round face and still had that sweet smile. "Juanita, is it really you? I can't believe it! I really can't!"

"It indeed is, Rose. And who is this handsome young man beside you?" She didn't have to ask. He looked just like Joe Bob, but with his mother's light hair. He even had his smile, which he used on Juanita and Delia.

Rose could tell that Juanita knew, and pulled her away from Mabel, who helped her with the cleaning, and whispered, "You're the only one who knows, Juanita. Everyone in Alva thinks he's my cousin's son...please don't tell. I think I'd just die if anyone knew, I really do."

"Oh, for heaven's sake, now why would I tell anyone? It's no one's blooming business, it isn't." She thought for a while, then added, "Conner and I aren't married, either, so Delia and Seth have a lot in common. Heck, he might as well be as dead as Joe Bob, 'cause he sure doesn't pay any attention to her, and not much more to me. Well, every now and then he'll pay me a visit - you know men..."

"But, if there's one thing I'll not allow, Rose, it's a man who'll walk all over me!" Juanita had conveniently forgotten the year after she had arrived in Palatka, when Conner tutored her in manners and dress. Her confidence hadn't returned until she realized her potential. Maeve had given her that. She had taught her so much, more than she cared to admit.

Juanita filled Rose in on most everything that had happened to her since she had last seen her, while Seth and Delia sat on the pier, their bare feet splashing in the river. Juanita and Rose talked and talked, and Rose decided to do something completely out of character. She decided that she and Seth would join Juanita and Delia in their venture.

"Harrison, have you seen Delia? If that child is over at Mr. Saunders' begging for candy again, I declare I don't know what I'll do to her. If we miss the 2:00 o'clock to Gainesville, we won't be able to leave 'til tomorrow, and I'll skin her alive. I declare I will."

"And where are Rose and Seth? They know that we have to be ready by now! Did you have Mac Peoples take the trunks? Harrison..."

She could see the light streaming from underneath Conner's door. "He's in there trying to get his majesty up, dressed and fed before we leave. Why am I thinking that when he's so pathetic...I can't think about it! I simply can't!"

She saw Harrison pass through Conner's door and close it quietly so as not to disturb him. He looked up when he saw Juanita and shook his head. He didn't dare tell her that the room was filled with charred letters from Vincent that Conner had been painstakingly pasting together for over four years. "What's it like in there? What's he like this morning? Oh, Harrison, I don't know if I can go through with it...I really don't."

"You have to. We can't save him, Cherie," he said so softly she had trouble understanding him.

"But why won't he try? I don't understand him...I never have. Why won't he try?"

"In his own time...in his own time. I left him a note so he'll know where we are."

He brushed away a tear, and when he passed by Conner's door again, he paused and said under his breath, *"Sorrow is a disease in which every patient must treat himself.* Voltaire, my friend, my dear friend..."

Juanita stood beside the door to the train station staring down the narrow gauge tracks. Seth and Delia had become antsy. "Delia, if you get dirty I'll have to give you a spanking. Now go sit down by your Aunt Rose...now...this instant, you hear?"

She heard the train...her heart raced a mile a minute. "I'll just not look back. If I see him, I'll never be able to leave. Oh, God, why are you doing this to me...is this my punishment...is this...?"

With her head held high, her small hand firmly holding Delia's, she nodded to Harrison, who got into the car for the colored people, and found a seat beside a middle-aged woman in a ridiculous hat.

"I'm Juanita Graves, and this is my daughter, Delia Rose." The woman beside Juanita commented on how beautiful Delia was and asked where they were going. "Oh, you're going to Monticello. Well, you'll like it, I'm sure. I have cousins living there, and they love it. Said it was a lovely town." Juanita replied, "If you ever decide to visit, please come see us at our shop, *Cherie's House of Fashion*. My associate," she nodded at Rose, "and I would be so happy to assist you in your selections. We're going to carry an entire line of children's fashions, too. Do you have children...?"

"I'll not look back...I'll not look back..."

VOLUME IV MONTICELLO

to be published in 1991

The continued romance of Old Florida
in the compelling series
THE FLORIDIANS

About the author:

Ann O'Connell Rust is a native Floridian, a "cracker". Her parents were pioneers in the Everglades in the early part of the century. Her father, Frank O'Connell, moved to Canal Point on Lake Okeechobee to work on Conner's Highway—the first hard road into the Glades. Conner was a friend of the West Palm Beach O'Connells, and young Frank wanted to be a part of Conner's thrust into the mysterious Glades. There he met Onida Knight, one of the beautiful Knight girls, whose father had homesteaded their land the previous year, and opened his own Knight's Grocery and Dry Goods Store in Canal Point. Luther Knight ultimately became a farmer/rancher and her father, a farmer, deputy sheriff and chief of police in Pahokee.

After schooling in Palm Beach County schools, Ann embarked on a very successful career in modeling—in Miami and New York City, where she met and married Allen, an FBI agent, and followed him to Puerto Rico, New Mexico, Washington, D.C., Mexico City and finally back to her love — Florida.

She has had an on-going love affair with romantic old Florida all of her adult life and four of their five children live in the state.

She is the owner of two modeling schools and talent agencies in Orange Park and Jacksonville and since her retirement has devoted all her energies to writing and sharing her love of this magnificent state. She and Allen spend their time between their home on the St. John's River and their ranch in Wyoming.

Are you unable to find *"The Floridians"* in your book stores?

Volume I Punta Rassa: Fiction, 1988, 275 pp., Softcover
Volume II Palatka: Fiction, 1989, 231 pp., Softcover
Volume III Kissimmee: Fiction, 1990, 208 pp, Soft cover and hardcover

Mail to: AMARO BOOKS
5673 Pine Avenue
Orange Park, Florida 32073

Please send check or money order (No cash or C.O.D.s)

I enclose $ _____ for books indicated.

Book Title: _____

Number of books: _____

Name: _____

Address: _____

City: _____

State: _____

Zip: _____

Please enclose $12.95 per book plus $1.50 for postage and handling of first book and .50 for each additional book. For hardcover (Kissimmee only) please enclose $17.50 per book plus $2.00 postage of first book and $1.00 for each additional book. Florida residents add 7% sales tax. Please allow 2-4 weeks for delivery.